PARAGNOSIS

BECA LEWIS

Published by:
Perception Publishing
https://perceptionpublishing.com

This book is a work of fiction. All characters in this book are fictional. However, as a writer, I have, of course, made some of the book's characters composites of people I have met or known.

Table of Contents

One

Hank Blaze stood beside the minister and stared at the wall. The minister was doing the same thing. Neither could believe what they were seeing. It was the Reverend's frantic call that had brought Hank to the chapel, and now he understood why.

Hank had been having a nice chat with Pete at the Diner while some of his men were finishing their breakfast before heading out to Emily's hill to start the new project she had hired them to do.

Hank's men loved it out on Emily's hill. In spite of it being the site where Dr. Joe's first four victims were found, it had turned into a jewel that the people of Doveland cherished.

Now that her art retreat had been functioning for almost two years, Emily was ready for expansion. Hank's company had already finished the little house on the property where she lived. They had also completed the dance barn and massive deck that jutted out from the hill.

Emily wanted to add a small building for writing, another for art, and one more for music. Once Hank's crew completed those buildings, she wanted to add a small residence hall. It would be where she could house visiting teachers. It would also house the few students who didn't live close enough to come out to the hill every day, or couldn't afford the tuition. Although Emily kept it as low as possible, sometimes that wasn't enough.

Almost everyone on the construction crew had a child, niece, or nephew who was part of Emily's world. That made them even more eager to do a good job. Hank was glad of the work for his men and equally glad that Emily didn't have to struggle to come up with the funds for the work.

As part of his pretense of being a good man, Dr. Joe had set up a trust for Emily's school. Emily had almost said "no" to the trust money but eventually had seen the wisdom of using Joe's money for good instead of turning it down. Besides, the trust was named after Edward's mother, May, so Emily chose to see the use of the funds as a celebration of May's life instead of Joe's.

Pete had just finished telling Hank how well the children's chef classes at the Diner were going when Hank's phone chimed. He was surprised. Typically, people usually sent him a text. *Who calls anymore, he thought.* He excused himself and stepped outside to answer the phone.

"Hank, this is Reverend Webster. I need your help."

Hank knew that Lloyd Webster had moved to town over the winter to take over for the retiring Unity minister, but he had only seen Lloyd a few times at town hall meetings. He'd never taken the time to meet him, so Hank was surprised to hear from him.

"Sure," Hank said. "What can I do for you?"

"Something happened at the Chapel. Can you meet me there?"

Hank had gone back into the Diner, taken a last sip of coffee, paid his bill, and told Pete about the call. Pete didn't know the minister much better than Hank, although he did know that Lloyd liked the burger named after Emily for his lunch. He came in about once a week. Pete didn't think Lloyd had moved with his family, or maybe he had a son. That was about all he knew.

Lloyd was one of the ministers that shared the chapel on Sunday morning. It was one of those things about the town that visitors would shake their heads over—multiple religions sharing the same space for their services.

The repair and maintenance of the Chapel fell to the town. However, members of the Stone Circle made sure there was always enough money in the town's hopper for anything that the Chapel needed, including a part-time maintenance person and grounds-keeper.

As Hank drove to the Chapel, he thought about the events he had been part of that had been held in the chapel. Joyous ones like Ava and Evan's wedding and Ben's christening; and sad ones like Melvin's funeral.

Dr. Joe's funeral had been held there too, but his feelings about that were neither joyous nor sad. It happened. Joe was gone. Amen to that.

Hank pulled into the side parking lot located in the back of the Chapel. It was newly paved, making it much easier to get into the church during the sometimes very snowy Pennsylvania winters.

Lloyd was waiting for him outside the back door of the chapel. As they shook hands, Hank detected a slight tremble. Was Lloyd sick? He looked like a reasonably healthy man in his mid-thirties. Lloyd ran his fingers back through his closely cropped hair and sighed.

"Didn't know what else to do. I don't think it's a matter for the police, but I don't know. I'm new here."

Since Hank didn't move, Lloyd sighed again and tapped his sneakered foot on the stone steps that led to the back door. "Guess the best thing to do is show you."

Hank followed Lloyd as they snaked through the tiny hall in the back of the chapel and emerged on the side of the front stage where the ministers stood for their services.

The decoration of the Chapel was neutral. Beautiful stained glass windows. Simple wooden pews and an arched ceiling that always lifted Hank's spirits when he walked in the door.

Not this time. Something was wrong. Sure, everything looked as it should with the early morning light streaming through the windows making colored patterns over all the pews on the east side of the building.

But the air smelled like dust and something else that Hank couldn't place. But it wasn't until he looked at the back wall that he saw why Lloyd had called him. The rear wall of the Chapel was in tatters. That was the best way he could describe it.

The closer he got to it the more Hank was confused. He and Lloyd stood looking at the wall and the crumbling plaster peeling off it and landing in a heap at its base.

"What happened?" Hank asked, staring at the wall. He had never seen anything like it before. There didn't appear to be any reason why the wall had started to peel away. There was no water damage or evidence of someone intentionally taking the wall down. It was almost as if the wall was tired.

A strange thought went through Hank's mind. He had the idea that perhaps the wall was revealing a secret. Hank filed the feeling away for future examination. He had lived around Sarah and her friends long enough to know that knowledge did not always come through "normal" channels.

"Nothing," Lloyd said, breaking through Hank's thoughts. "At least nothing that I know about. Yesterday it was fine. Today, it looks like this."

"I don't know how this could happen either," Hank responded. "Something is seriously wrong here."

"Or *right*," Leif said as he stood beside Hank. Hank knew enough not to start talking to the air while Lloyd was there, so he didn't stay anything. He would have to ask Leif later what he meant.

Lloyd turned around and looked behind him and then back at Hank. "That's funny. I thought someone else was here."

And I'll have to ask him about Lloyd too, Hank thought. Who is he? Is the wall like this because Lloyd came to town?

"I think it's a sign," Lloyd said, turning to the wall again.

"A sign of what?"

"I guess we'll find out."

"That we will," Hank agreed. "I'll bring a few men over and see what we can find."

Both men knew they were going to find more than a tattered wall. Something was going to come to light. In their own way, both men were confident that something important was going to be revealed.

The question they both wondered about was if what would come to light was dangerous, or a blessing. Maybe both.

Two

It was hard to pack his suitcase with Hannah and Ben bouncing on the bed beside him, but Edward didn't care. Technically, they were not supposed to be bothering the guests of the Bed and Breakfast, but he was more than a guest. At least that's what Ava and Evan kept assuring him.

It was still hard for Edward to imagine himself as a person who belonged. After running from his father his entire life and pretending to be someone else so his father couldn't find him, the fact that he could use his real name of Edward Miller was amazing. Edward still refused to use his father's last name. He was his mother's son, not his father's.

Even more astonishing was that his father, Dr. Joe Hellard, was dead and could never hurt him again. It was mind-boggling. And freeing. And yet, here he was still traveling. He was still doing what he had spent his entire life doing before he returned to Doveland last fall. There was a difference though. This time Edward was traveling as himself.

He was tracking his life backwards, visiting as many places as he could where he had made friends under a false identity. He wanted to see them all, tell them who he really was, and keep connected to them in the future, a luxury he never had before.

He had started a few weeks after his father died. Winter was on its way, so he went south first. He stayed away for a month, came back for Christmas, and left again, going west this time. For this next trip, he was going east. Edward thought it might be the last one he would take. After that, he wasn't sure what he would do.

As he traveled and met with old friends, he took pictures and notes thinking he might write a book someday. Or maybe just keep them for himself so he would never forget how lucky he had become. He had escaped a life of deception and fear. No matter what came next, it would always be better than what was in the past.

Some of his visits hadn't gone as well as he wished they had. It hadn't surprised him. He knew it would be hard for some of the people he had met to learn that the man they briefly knew and had then disappeared into thin air wasn't that man at all, but someone else.

Even when he tried explaining why he had hidden the truth from them, it didn't matter. To some people, it was too big of a lie, too much of a breach of confidence. It didn't matter. Edward had to do it. He had to find them and say what needed to be said. He had to make amends for the life he had lived before if he was ever going to figure out what he wanted to do with the rest of his life.

Most of Edward's life up until now had been about only one thing: Stay safe until he could bring the proof his mother had collected to people who could do something about it. Evidence of what his father had done.

Even with Hannah and Ben bouncing on the bed beside him spreading as much joy as possible, he could still feel the pain of losing both his mother and forty-eight years of his life to the man he had called father, a brilliant psychopathic monster.

His father had been the town doctor that everyone in Doveland had loved. That is until Edward came along and spoiled it all for them.

Finding out that he had a half-sister and therefore two nephews, had been almost enough to make up for all the pain his father had caused him. Almost, but not quite. It was a hole inside himself he was determined to heal before settling down for good.

Edward had prayed that the traveling and explaining would help heal that hole. He could tell that it was beginning to work. Even when people didn't accept him, it still helped close the gap between what he had pretended to be, and his true identity.

However, what was most healing was what he had found in the town he had run away from as a teenager. Doveland. It was more than he had ever hoped for, or dreamed about. It had turned into a place of refuge. A home. Even the people who knew the truth about his father, and who had suffered at his hands, didn't hold it against him. He didn't even need to ask for forgiveness for being his father's son. They knew he was his own man.

It hadn't happened all at once. At first, they were afraid of him. Not him really, but what he was bringing. They knew his return would bring back his father, Dr. Joe. They had hoped he would stay away forever, but in spite of the fear of what Edward's return meant, they accepted him anyway.

They knew that he had done them a favor. They understood the courage it took to be the son of Dr. Joe Hellard, admit it, and stand up to his father.

Even the people in town who still refused to admit that their beloved town doctor was also a serial killer accepted him. Even though they knew that he and his father were at two ends of the spectrum, that it was probably Edward's return that had caused his father's fatal heart attack. Even then, he was accepted.

It was hard for Edward to believe that these people could still think his father was a good man, but as Ava and her friends explained to him, that didn't matter. What mattered was that his father was no longer there to hurt anyone and that the town was united in its acceptance of Edward.

Doveland thrived on being good neighbors and kind to strangers. With all his travels, Edward had yet to find another town that could come close to matching the feeling of warmth that Doveland provided.

He suspected that it had become that way when Sarah and the Stone Circle had chosen it as their home. Learning who they were, and how he fit in, was something he wanted to spend more time on. But for now, Edward still had healing work to do. That meant he must remain split between two worlds, his past and his future.

He was staying and going at the same time. Ava and Evan were renting him a permanent room in the bunkhouse. Edward loved it. He had a place he could call home, and he had Ava and Evan's two children who constantly reminded him that joy was accessible to him if he opened up to it. He was working on it.

Hannah sat down on the bed and looked up at him. He looked down into her blue eyes which beamed back more wisdom anyone might expect in a child. He corrected himself because he knew that Hannah did not think of herself as a child, and sometimes she read his mind. If she heard him thinking she was a child, she would definitely give him a look of disapproval. He suspected she knew what he was thinking at that moment because she winked at him and laughed.

Hannah would be turning twelve in August and Ben had just turned two on April 15th. His birthday was why Edward was in town. It had been one of those celebrations so famous at the Anders' home. Because Lex's twelfth birthday was the next day, it had been a party for both of them. Lex's mother, Valerie, was grateful the two of them had a birthday together. It was a lot more fun to have the party at Ava's.

The Stone Circle and all their friends had brought food as they always did. Mandy had made a fantastic cake shaped like a unicorn, and of course, helped decorate the screened-in porch and deck. She turned it all into a fantasy wonderland.

Ava refused to do gender themed parties, or even age themed parties. She never gave a reason why, but Edward expected it was to keep all possibilities open. It was an intent that ran through the group. It was that intent that had allowed the possibility that Edward was a good man.

"You *are* a good man," Hannah said as she picked up the pile of socks and zipped them into his travel cube and then fit it into the suitcase for him. "Okay, yes, I heard you worrying, and I know I'm not supposed to listen, but some things I think you wanted me to know so you can be reassured."

Edward gave her a quick hug, knowing that Hannah was at the age that hugs were not always what she wanted, "I think you are probably right. And since you are reading my thoughts, you know that I will be back in time for your next life celebration."

Even though she already knew, Hannah asked, "Where are you heading this time?"

"East. Thought I would stop in and see Johnny at the University and head off from there."

"Cool. I can't wait to hear how Johnny is doing," Hannah said. She didn't want to tell Edward that she saw Johnny all the time. How often she practiced astral projections was something she kept mostly to herself.

Edward lifted the jumping Ben off the bed and swung him onto his back, picked up his suitcase and headed into the kitchen where he knew Ava had packed him a bag of goodies for his trip.

The car he had purchased for his return to Doveland was already packed with a tent, sleeping bag, and other survival stuff, just in case he decided to camp for a few days.

Evan clapped him on the back, Ava hugged him, and Ben grabbed his leg and wouldn't let go. "I'll be back in a month or two, Ben."

"Then you'll stay."

"Then I'll stay."

Edward bent down to give Hannah a quick kiss on the cheek before sliding into the car. Leaning out the window, he said, "See you soon!"

Watching him drive down to the road that led out of Doveland, Hannah thought to herself. "Yes, you will, Edward, sooner than you think."

Three

The last rays of the sun were slinking across the town square. Each beam was like a finger slowly drawing a line down the gazebo before retreating across the grass and down the street to the lake where the sun was sinking into its golden surface. For a brief moment, the fading light painted the gazebo a beautiful shade of pale pink.

It was the pink that drew her attention. She had turned the "open" sign over to say "closed" and was pulling the blinds down in the front window when she noticed that the man was still there.

Grace Strong had seen him earlier that day.

It had been a pretty day, the beginning of spring, but the air still had a nip to it. She had wondered how the man sitting on the park bench beside the gazebo was staying warm. An hour later, when she looked again, Grace realized that he was not someone she recognized from town, so she did what any good busy-body would do. Grace went out into the square to bring him a hot cup of coffee and one of Mandy's muffins.

She slid onto the far side of the bench and introduced herself as the owner of the coffee shop behind him, and thought she would do a bit of marketing by introducing him to her coffee and pastries. At first, he only stared at her while she held them out to him, smiling the most sincere smile she could muster.

Since he was staring at her, she stared back. A little staring contest never hurt anyone, and if that is what he wanted, she could stare with the best of them.

Grace had the thought that if the man took better care of himself, he might be reasonably good looking. But given that he looked as if he had been traveling without a mirror for weeks, and was covered in dust, she wasn't sure.

He had on a coat that was either tan or dirty, with tattered cuffs, and his shoes were scuffed and worn. She thought that one of them was missing a shoelace. His gray beard was scraggly, and Grace had an unkind thought as she imagined birds finding it a perfectly good nesting ground.

Grace waited, and eventually he reached out and took the coffee and muffin, giving her a slight nod of thanks as he did so. She waited some more, thinking he might say the words "thank you," or at least offer a reason why he was there.

Finally, since he wasn't talking, Grace decided that she could. Pulling her sweater tighter around her, she leaned back on the bench and let the sun's rays fall onto her face, and sighed.

"It's a beautiful spring afternoon, isn't it? I love this time of year. The birds are singing, and the trees have buds where their leaves will be. Of course, it's a mess for a while as the maple trees drop those red blossomy things and then their seeds. But still, even that is a joy. It's trees spreading new life."

When the stranger didn't even nod in return, she continued. "I moved to Doveland a few years ago. If you haven't been here before, I think you'll love it. I was following my friend, Sarah. It's the best thing I ever did. Well, it was the first best thing I ever did really. Then I opened my bookstore–coffeeshop that was wonderful. It's the one behind you, Your Second Home. I mean it too. You could treat it that way if you wanted to. But the best thing that ever happened to me is I got married."

Grace sighed. She was still married. Her sigh was because she rarely saw her husband, Eric. He and Sarah's husband Leif seemed to prefer the other dimension to their home in Doveland. Of course, she was only speculating. They never said so. *I'm just being peckish*, she thought.

Since it didn't appear she was going to get any useful information out of the man on the bench she decided to give him another chance for later. "Well, guess I best be getting back to the shop. Listen, come in and get warm if you like. More coffee and muffins on the house. We didn't name it Your Second Home for nothing. We mean it. And if you need a place to stay, I know someplace that you might like."

He handed her the empty bag and coffee cup, mumbled, "Thank you," and then went back to gazing out into the distance.

Grace didn't give up easily. She knelt down the best that she could directly in front of him, so she was eye level, and tried again. "Look," she said, "I know I appear to be nosy, which I am, I admit, and really, you don't have to say anything. I'll let you be. Just come in later and let me feed you."

The old man lowered his dark gray eyes that almost matched his gray beard and the strand of gray hair peeking out from his dirty fisherman's cap, and said, "Much appreciated. I'll think about it," and then turned sideways on the bench so that Grace was no longer in front of him."

Grace pushed herself up using the bench as a handhold and tried not to groan as her knees protested the position she had put them in. She lightly touched the man's shoulder and then headed back to the store.

Your Second Home got busy after that, and she had

forgotten about him. Besides, she was sure that he must have moved on by then.

She didn't know if he was homeless. They didn't have a homeless population in town. If someone passed through needing something, someone always noticed and then offered food, or a place to stay.

If that wasn't enough, Craig and his friends had set up a small shelter that helped them out until they got on their feet or moved on. That is where she wanted to send the man on the bench, and she intended to call someone later if he was still there.

But she forgot. And now it was dark, and she could still see the old man sitting there. There was no way she was going to let him spend the night in the cold. If he wouldn't move, at least she could bring him blankets, more food, a hot drink, and water.

It took only a few minutes to pull it all together, and using a flashlight she made her way to the bench, thinking that she should have remembered to put on a coat.

This time she didn't bother trying to get him to talk. She tucked the blankets around him, handed him the coffee, and placed the water bottle on the bench, along with a sandwich and an apple.

Before leaving, she asked him once again if she could be of more help, or help him to the shelter for the night. He shook his head no and mumbled another thank you.

Grace sighed, said good night, and hurried back to her shop. She locked everything up, glanced outside one more time to see him take a sip of coffee, and then headed upstairs to her apartment.

In the morning, she would get help for him whether he liked it or not, she thought.

It would be many, many months before she would allow herself to believe that what happened to him wasn't her fault. What if she had done more? Maybe she could have stopped it from happening.

Four

The door creaked slightly as Mandy Minks opened the back door of Your Second Home and slipped quietly inside. She would have to find the can of WD40 and oil the hinges. Grace was a sound sleeper, but Mandy didn't want to wake her with a squeaky door. Grace would be down soon enough once the coffee aroma made its way upstairs.

Mandy had come in even earlier than her usual time, so early that it was still dark outside. But she wanted to get started on her baking before the shop opened. Mandy loved the solitude of the morning. Just her and the ingredients of what she was baking. Together they would make something perfect for others to enjoy.

Unless she was trying a new recipe, there was very little creative thinking involved. Instead, it kept her mind busy enough that she could let herself daydream, or catch ideas, as she called it. Sometimes she went for a walk to catch ideas, but on a chilly morning like today, baking served the same purpose.

Besides, she had a full day of designing to do, and even though Grace didn't mind that Mandy wasn't always there to wait on tables, she never wanted to leave them in the lurch without baked goods.

Of course, Sam had always said that he would be happy to step in and provide the baked goods for the bookstore-coffee shop, at least some of the days, but Mandy wasn't quite ready to give up her baking duties in spite of her own thriving design business, Your Second Home Design.

Over the winter Hank had renovated Valerie's home. He had divided it in half so that Mandy had a design studio in the back of the house. Valerie kept the second floor, and they shared the kitchen. Or more accurately, Valerie let Mandy share the kitchen.

It was a dream come true for Mandy. It worked for Valerie too. Valerie was able to stay in their big home after her husband Harold had died. The house was in a perfect location, right across the street from the coffee shop and facing the square. It was easy for her clients to find, and Mandy loved being part of the tiny downtown community.

Mandy had only been in her new space a month, but already she had filled it with projects both big and small. Sometimes Lex, Valerie's boy, came in and watched her work. He told Mandy in confidence that he couldn't decide if he wanted to be a Chef or a designer like her. Mandy had assured him that at twelve he should continue to explore his options. There was no reason to decide now what he would do with his life.

No matter what he chose though, Mandy was sure it would be in a field that allowed him to be creative and share his unique vision. But, it wasn't Lex that was on her mind today. It was Tom.

Tom was bored, and he was making her crazy. He either had to come up with something to do himself, or she would have to find something for him. While she was crazy busy, Tom wandered around the house, lost. No longer interested in traveling, and no longer a key player in the Good Ole Dudes group, he needed a project. She had thought about asking him to work with her. She wasn't as good at business as he was. But was it a good idea? Would it ruin their relationship?

While the muffins and scones baked, Mandy made sure the coffee was ready to go, and that everything was in order in the room. She loved the place that she and Grace had made together. There were just enough books to be inviting, but not so many it felt like a bookstore.

It was a coffee shop with books. Anyone could take a book off the shelf and read it. If you wanted to take it home, you had to buy it.

At first, she and Grace were worried that books would be ruined, but decided they were willing to absorb the cost of replacing the books as needed. It wasn't something they did too often. Most of the time people were respectful, or if they got a coffee stain on the book, they purchased it without any prompting.

Mandy unlocked the front door and turned the sign over to "open." She always stayed through the first of the morning rush to help Grace out.

Sooner or later they would need to hire someone on a more permanent basis. They had used a few friends of their cook, Alex, but most of them were not that interested and moved on within a month or two of working.

One problem with a town as small as Doveland, there wasn't a large workforce. However, Hank said he was hiring a few new members for his construction crew. Maybe one or two would have a daughter who would like some part-time work. If so, it was a great way to meet new people.

That's how she and Grace knew everyone in town. Everyone who lived there either ate at the coffee shop or were talked about at the coffee shop.

"Those muffins smell delicious," Grace said, opening the door that led to her apartment above the shop.

"I see you timed it perfectly once again, Grace," Mandy replied handing her a cup of coffee in her favorite mug along with a still warm cranberry muffin.

"You don't live this long without learning the perfect time to show up," Grace answered, right before taking a huge bite of the muffin. "This is delicious. Did you do something different today?"

"Added a touch of grated ginger. Wondered how it would turn out."

Mandy reached over and tweaked a corner off of Grace's muffin, and Grace pretended to slap her hand away. They always shared food. More than friends, they were partners in each other's business, and even though it was rarely said out loud, thought of each other as mother and daughter.

When the first customer opened the outside door, Grace caught a glimpse of the park bench.

"Wait, is he still there? Oh no, it was cold last night. This is terrible!"

"Who are you talking about?"

"Grace pointed to what looked like a pile of blankets on the bench.

"That man. I tried to get him to come in yesterday, but he wouldn't. Took blankets and food to him thinking he would move on before it got too late. But it looks as if he is still there.

"While I take care of the customer who just came in, would you check on that man on the bench? He wouldn't say anything to me yesterday. Maybe you can get him to come into the store to get warm, or at least find out how we can help him."

Mandy poured a cup of coffee into a take-out cup, grabbed a fresh muffin, and headed across the grass. It was still cold.

It would warm up later, but at the moment she could see her breath.

The man didn't move even though she tried to make noise as she walked up so that she wouldn't startle him.

"Sir, Grace sent me with some more coffee to warm you up," she said as she rounded the bench to talk to him.

His head was on his chest, and his hands hung limply by his sides. The blanket had started to drop away from his chest, so Mandy put the coffee and muffin on the bench and gently lifted the blanket to place it around his shoulder.

He still didn't move, and Mandy froze.

Looking out the window, Grace froze too. She knew it. She should have done more. As she ran out the door with her cell phone to her ear, she started crying.

As she reached Mandy, they hugged each other, tears running down their faces. "No one should die alone," Grace sobbed.

Eric and Leif stood off to the side. Invisible this time. The man on the bench didn't die alone. They had been there. And even though the man had not seen them, he had felt a warm presence as he took his last breath.

His final thought was that he had done his best. But it might not have been enough.

Five

This is not the kind of thing that happens in my town, Police Chief Dan Williams thought as he watched the paramedics lift the old man into the waiting ambulance. They had procedures in place to make sure it didn't happen. And yet it did. An old man had died in the town square.

It was still early morning, so Dan had asked the ambulance not to sound its siren. There was no need to wake the town. Once he had checked the man on the bench, it was evident that there was nothing they could do for him. There was no need to rush. The old man already had run out of time.

When Grace had called the police station, Dan was already there. He hadn't been able to sleep. After lying awake for a few hours, he decided to go to work early and get some paperwork done before the day began. It was a small police station, just him and a few part-time deputies. There was no need for more.

That meant he was the one who answered the phone when Grace called the station. Actually, it was always him who answered the phone because when he wasn't at the station, he had the calls forwarded directly to his cell phone.

His wife didn't particularly like this decision because sometimes he was awakened by someone who only needed assurance that the noise they heard was an owl in the woods.

He understood how she felt. But for him, it was part of the duty of being a police officer. And it was a privilege. He loved the town of Doveland and was grateful beyond measure that he and his wife had stumbled across it a few years before when they were looking for a good place to raise their children.

It was one of the best decisions he had ever made, and he was grateful for it most days. Even today. Because it meant he could help. He wouldn't take the death lightly as he knew some of his colleagues would do. "Just an old man," they would say, implying that it didn't matter. But to Dan it did.

This death wasn't an emergency, but it was disturbing. Who was the man and how did he die? The ambulance would take the old man to Dr. Craig Lester's clinic. There was no place else to take him. Since there was no sign of foul play, Craig could perform the autopsy.

It was up to Dan to find out who the man was and then let his next of kin know. Informing the family was not something he was looking forward to, but once again Dan was glad that he was doing it instead of someone who didn't care. The family would know that someone took good care of their loved one. But first, he needed a name.

Because there was no crime, there was no need for crime scene tape, so a small group of people who lived and worked around the town square had gathered by the bench to watch the old man being taken away. Valerie and Lex had joined Grace and Mandy, along with the manager of the grocery store who had been getting the store ready when he glanced outside and saw the gathering of people

Valerie had thought about asking Lex to stay inside but decided against it. He would have come anyway if only to support everyone else, and these were the kinds of things she wanted him to know how to handle. Besides, compared to what they had gone through the year before, this was nothing.

Still, what is it about April, she wondered. Two years before in April, Jay Kalan, Hannah's past-dad, had come to town. That had ended with both Jay's and Grant's death. Last April, bodies were found on Emily's hill which led to the discovery of more bodies and a master criminal who had been living within Doveland for years. And now this.

Seeing Dan standing by himself looking official in spite of the dejected look on his face, she walked over to stand beside him.

"What is it about April anyway?" Dan mumbled.

"That's what I was thinking. At least this doesn't look like it was intentional. Perhaps a sickness, old age or maybe he died of the cold?"

"We won't know until Craig does the autopsy. I did a brief search of his pockets and didn't find any identification. No wallet, nothing. I'll be heading over to Craig's clinic to find out more, but right now he looks as if he was homeless and lost.

"Grace said she tried to talk to him and help yesterday, but he only mumbled thank you and wouldn't say any more than that. At least he accepted the blanket and some food."

"However, she doesn't appear to be taking it well," he said while lifting his chin in Grace's direction.

Valerie glanced over at her friends. Mandy had her arm around Grace's shoulder, and Grace was crying silent tears. As she expected, Lex had gone to stand next to Grace offering his quiet support.

"Is there anything that I can do, Dan?"

"Try to stem the flow of gossip?"

Valerie paused before answering him, "Maybe it should be the other way around. Get the gossip going to see if anyone knows him. We could ask through social media too. We'll need a picture to use. I mean if that's okay with you."

Dan turned to look at Valerie. He had to admire her strength. In the last few years, she had gone to hell and back. In spite of that, her kids were doing well, she was in a healthy relationship with Dr. Craig, and she had found a new half-brother in Edward. Not many people could have come through the last few years of trauma and still look as if they believed in the goodness of life.

She was right. They needed help.

"Great idea, Valerie. But I don't want to take a picture of him the way he looks now. That doesn't feel right. We need a sketch of his face instead. However, I don't know anyone who can do this. Do you?"

Valerie glanced over at Mandy and wondered if she knew the secret Tom was keeping. Well, perhaps this would be a good time to bring it out into the open.

"As a matter of fact, I do," she said. "I'll take care of that part if it's okay with you. Although we'll run the picture by you before we start posting it. And we'll let you know what we plan to say. I know we don't want to tell his next of kin over social media that he has died. We'll have to say something else. I'll work on it and bring it to you."

Dan nodded his assent and then watched Valerie join her friends. When he had moved to Doveland that group of people hadn't arrived yet. The town had been lovely but also a bit lonely.

Now that they had come and opened diners, and coffee shops, and supported the town in such a big way, the loneliness had vanished.

They had also brought upheaval, though. Dan wasn't complaining. What they had uncovered needed to be uncovered.

But it had been a hard few years to get through. Now, this.

However, he didn't think this was something that would bring Sam Long back into the role of FBI consultant. He knew that Sam was enjoying running a catering company much more than he ever enjoyed being in the FBI.

Coming to Doveland to track Grant Hinkey had also transformed Sam. He had fallen in love with Mira Michaels and moved to Doveland to be with her. It was good Sam was here though. Dan thought that he might need some guidance on this case.

Perhaps Sam's friend, Hank Blaze, could help too. Dan had heard that Hank had a past that only his closest friends knew about. Sam trusted him though, and that was enough for Dan. Sometimes it takes someone who has lived with evil to understand its subtleties. He was grateful that it didn't have to be him.

Six

The talk at the Diner and Your Second Home was all about the man on the bench. Because it was Grace who had found him, it was her coffee shop that had gathered the most people curious to know what had happened. If people thought they would get more information being at the coffee shop, they were wrong. Grace and Mandy weren't talking. They did everything they could to avoid the questions.

Finally, after what seemed like the hundredth person had asked them what they knew, Mandy did something that surprised even herself.

She stood on a chair and rapped a knife against a water glass.

"Excuse me for interrupting, but I thought I would answer all your questions at one time. No, neither Grace, nor I, nor anyone else at the moment knows who he was. We are getting a sketch of him, and then we'll start sharing it on social media to see if we can find his family. This is the way we are helping Dan out.

"But that is all we know. If you find out more on your own, or if you met the man on the bench or know when he came to town, please tell Dan. "He is doing all he can, and I am sure he will appreciate your help. But I doubt that he needs our conjecture about things none of us know. Let's all only share facts. Thank you!"

As Mandy stepped off the chair with a helping hand from Grace, there was a moment of silence. Then someone clapped. And the rest of the room joined in. Mandy's face had turned a bright red by then, but she did a slight bow to acknowledge the room. They were her friends and clients after all. But as soon as everyone stopped looking, she took herself back into the kitchen to get away from it all.

It felt like years had passed since that morning when she was happily baking muffins in the quiet of the kitchen. *Poor man,* Mandy thought, *outside all alone while I was warm and safe in here. I wish I would have known.*

In the kitchen, away from prying eyes, Mandy called Tom to tell him what had happened. Amazingly, he already knew. Valerie had called him. When she asked why Valerie had called, Tom had been evasive and said he had to rush off. He'd talk to her later.

Now who's being secretive? Mandy thought. Last year she had been the one keeping secrets. She had been afraid to tell Tom that she wanted a design space that was all hers, and a place where clients could come and talk.

In retrospect, she had no idea why telling him had worried her. Perhaps it was because she had to admit that she wanted a life of her own. It included Tom, but she didn't want to be a stay at home anything. Including a mom.

That was the next thing she still hadn't brought herself to say to him. She had spent the last few months during her private time thinking about it. Just because she loved playing with children didn't mean she wanted any. Did Tom? She was still worried about that. What if he did? Would she change her mind? Would it ruin their relationship?

Now she was worried about the phone call. Was Tom evasive because of a secret he was hiding that would make her sad or angry? It was all her fault for being so private. She needed to talk to him about children. But before that happened, she wanted to find out what he was hiding. Why did Valerie know? Why hasn't either of them told her what was going on?

There was always the chance that it was something good. That's what she was going to cling to. Tom had a good secret. And somehow Valerie knew about Tom's secret? Simple. Except, Mandy thought, that was easy to say, not so easy to believe.

****

Hank was sitting at his regular seat at the counter at the Diner. He was halfway through the breakfast he had every day before he started hearing people talking about the man on the bench. The next time Barbara came around to pour his coffee, he asked, "What's everyone talking about? What man on the bench?"

She shrugged and said she didn't know. She and Pete had come down from their apartment above the Diner just as the crowd was dispersing. All she knew was that an old man had died on the park bench, and no one knew who he was.

Once it was apparent to Hank that there wasn't much that he was going to find out about the man on the bench, his thoughts went back to what he and Lloyd had found at the Chapel. In all his years of doing construction, he had never seen anything like it.

The wall had crumbled for no apparent reason. Hank had brought over one of his men, and they cleaned up the mess and taped up sheeting in front of the remaining wall.

It didn't look as if there was any structural damage. That

meant he had time to get a work permit and go to the town council for the funds needed to repair it. He had already started the process, and they assured him it would all be in place in a few days.

What might hold up getting the work done was his work schedule. He already had two crews out working, and neither one of them would be free soon.

He could pull a few men off of each job, but he would need another foreman to help him out. He had been putting off finding one for too long. When Hank moved to Doveland, he had no idea that his construction crews would be in such demand.

He was grateful for the work even though he had never intended to be a large company. Now the Chapel job was pushing him towards hiring more crew and to getting that new foreman in place.

One of his men had talked about a brother who lived in Pittsburgh, working as a foreman on a big construction crew, and who was interested in moving to a small town. Doveland would be great. Their family could be together.

Hank had put him off, but with the wall happening he thought that perhaps now was the time. Checking his phone, he found the number the brother had given him and placed the call. When Hank got his voice mail, he left a message asking Elliot to call him back.

One way Hank would be able to tell if he wanted even to meet the guy was how quickly he called him back. Hank had a few tricks up his sleeve that he always used when hiring someone. This was one of them. Response time.

If that went well, he would send him a simple questionnaire to fill out. That was also about response time and completing a task. In the meantime, he would run a background check. A problem in the background check didn't always mean Hank wasn't interested. After all, if someone ran his real background, no one would ever have hired him. Hank was all about giving people a second chance. After all, he had had more than one.

Next would be referrals. After calling all of them, if Hank was still interested, they would schedule a time to meet. If that went well, a few days working on a regular job with the rest of his crew would give him an idea of how well the new guy worked with others.

After that, he would start work on a probation status for a month. If all worked well after that, and his current crew gave him a thumbs up, he would hire the guy.

Within five minutes of leaving a message, Elliot called back. Hank had not told him anything in the message, just asked for a return call. Elliot had passed the first test. Hank explained that he was looking for a new crew member and that Elliot's brother had recommended him.

Elliot said that he was more than interested. His brother had told him over and over again how much he loved Doveland, and working on Hank's crew. Hank sent Elliot the questionnaire and they were off into Hank's hiring process.

Hank's first impression of Elliot was good. If all went well, he might be able to start on the chapel in the next week. Something was tugging at him about the wall. He had no idea why, but he was anxious to get to it.

There was absolutely no evidence of it, but for some reason, it felt as if the man who died the night before and the crumbling wall were tied together somehow.

Not for the first time, Hank marveled at how much he had changed after meeting his niece, Ava, and her friends. Somehow they always knew things other people didn't know. Hannah had told them there was a word for it. Paragnosis. It meant, *knowledge that cannot be obtained by normal means.*

Hank wondered if it was something that could be learned and if perhaps he was already learning it.

Seven

On his way further east to see friends from his past, Edward had stopped to visit Johnny at Penn State for a few days.

Johnny had come home briefly for spring break but was not coming home between sessions. He planned to stay for the first summer session and then go home when it was over.

Everyone missed him, which is why Edward thought a brief visit would be in order. But for some reason, that was three days ago, and still, Edward didn't feel like moving on.

Maybe it was because he enjoyed seeing his nephew in his new college setting, or perhaps it was because he was enjoying the astonishing fact that he had a nephew to visit. Edward had never dreamed that he had a sibling. But once he had found his half-sister Valerie and her two boys, a whole new world had opened up to him.

When Edward had arrived at his dorm, Johnny was overjoyed. He wanted to show Edward everything about the town and the campus. One of the first places Johnny took Edward was to see the ducks that lived on the campus grounds.

It was a favorite tourist spot even though it was only a few ducks in a tiny pool of water. Edward and Johnny had laughed about it remembering all the ducks that lived at the lake in

Doveland. This seemed so puny in comparison. What was it that made it so popular? Johnny wondered if it was because it was hidden behind buildings and was only a block from the main street. It was a secret hidden in plain sight.

Edward thought that it was more than that. Somehow sitting on the benches watching the ducks felt like a safe place to talk, and that's what they had done. At first, they had skirted around the issue of Harold, Johnny's father, and the fact that Edward had known him when Harold was a teenager.

It was Harold who had been given the task of burying the women that died on Emily's hill. Dr. Joe had taken Harold under his wing and taught him things, but not the right things. It gave Johnny some comfort to hear Edward tell how manipulative Dr. Joe had been. How he had pulled Harold in, as he did with everyone, with the promise of love and protection.

Edward reminded Johnny that Harold had left town. He had found the courage to get away from Joe. Harold had gone off to college and then stayed away. To Edward that meant Harold had a sense that what Joe was offering was not what he wanted to become.

"Then why did he come back to Doveland?" Johnny wanted to know. "Didn't he know that Joe was still there and probably still doing terrible things?"

Edward said he could only guess that perhaps Harold thought that with a wife and a child he could ignore Joe and have a good life.

"Or perhaps he felt guilty, and part of him wanted someone to find out what he had done?" Johnny asked.

"We don't know, Johnny, but your dad underestimated my father."

"I guess we both know what it's like to have fathers we don't admire, or in my case, both hate and love."

"We do," was Edward's answer.

They sat in silence for a while after that, both of them contemplating what life had brought them so far. They watched families bring their children by to watch the ducks, and they both wondered if what the families showed to the world was what was really going on with them.

These were the kind of questions that occupied Johnny's thinking. He wanted to be able to see past the surface of things and find the truth. He knew that his studies in school were helping. It gave him a new window into worlds that he had never known, and for that he was grateful.

But, he wanted more than that. He wanted to know what wasn't visible. What the senses weren't telling him, or were lying to him about, or showing him only what he believed. He thought back to Doveland and the people that lived there and who had become friends of his family.

They knew things other people didn't know. Hannah had even visited him at school. She had appeared one day when he was sitting quietly outside under a tree, taking a break from classes. She had scared the crap out of him.

Hannah had done that before in Doveland, but it never occurred to him that she could go anywhere. She had apologized for scaring him. She just wanted to say hi and check on how he was doing.

He had stared at her. At first, he wondered how he could talk to her without people thinking that he was crazy, and then he had the idea to pretend to talk on his phone. That worked.

They had a pleasant conversation. She filled him in on what was happening at home, and he sent messages back to his brother Lex and his mom.

That kind of ability was something Johnny wanted to know

more about. When he had mentioned astral projection or remote viewing to a professor, he was told that it wasn't possible. And yet, Johnny had experienced it. He hadn't done it. But he wondered if he could learn how.

Hannah had said she heard him wishing he was home, so she had visited. She was right. He had wished he was home. But how did she know?

And then there were Leif and Eric, and even Suzanne and her Forest Circle. They traveled between dimensions, or at least they said they did. But he had seen them blink in and out, more than once, so he believed them.

In class, he learned about perception and how each person's brain filtered out what the mind thought wasn't needed. It made that decision based on what the person said they believed. It wasn't a bad thing. It was how people survived in the midst of infinite possibilities and unlimited knowledge. Johnny wondered if people went "crazy" because they had too many channels open, too much information that they couldn't handle.

So how to shut those channels when they needed to be closed, and how to open them to see what others couldn't see was the question. Johnny was burning with the desire to know, and afraid at the same time.

All these thoughts had gone through Johnny's mind while sitting with Edward while watching the ducks.

Edward knew something was going on with Johnny, but he didn't want to disturb his thoughts. They had walked and talked a bit more, and then Johnny went off to class. It was on his way back to the hotel that Edward had decided to stay longer.

He had been traveling for a few months and seen most of his old friends, and made amends where he could, but it was Johnny who probably needed him most. Or perhaps he needed Johnny the most. The past was over. It was time for the future.

When Edward told Johnny that he would stay longer, the look of gratitude that Johnny sent him was enough to bring tears to Edward's eyes. Johnny hadn't seen, he had rushed off, but Edward thought that perhaps an apartment in town wouldn't be a bad idea. He could come and go. Maybe Valerie and Lex could use it too.

And that's why while waiting for Johnny to join him for lunch, he was looking at apartments on his phone and didn't see the man sit down in the booth across from him until he heard his name.

"You're Edward, right? Sorry, Johnny asked me if I would join you for lunch. I'm a professor of his, Joshua. Joshua Baines, Josh, please."

As Edward reached up to shake Josh's hand, he felt a flash of something. It passed. But having lived in fear of his father for so long, Edward paid attention to it. Was it fear that he had felt, or something else?

Eight

Craig could see why Dan wanted a drawing instead of a photo of the man's face to share around town and on social media. Showing a dead man's face didn't feel right at all. Craig had cleaned him up, so he didn't look homeless anymore, but still, there was nothing he could do about the fact that he was dead.

That was the part that was bothering Craig. He knew it was also bothering everyone else involved in finding out who this man was. How could this happen in their little town? Craig knew that Grace was suffering the most. She felt as if she could have done more. But what? What could she have done differently? Everyone told her that. So far it wasn't helping her much.

The autopsy hadn't revealed anything surprising. The old man on the bench had died of old age. His body had merely shut down. Leif had visited and confirmed what the autopsy had shown. Nothing terrible had happened to the man on the bench except that he had died alone and unknown.

They had searched every inch of the man's clothes. He had no wallet and no identification. He did have five one dollar bills and some change in his pocket, but of course, there was no way to tell where he had gotten the money.

He had been wearing a very old pair of Carhartt coveralls, and an even older lined plaid jacket with rips around the cuffs. His long sleeved t-shirt looked as if it hadn't been washed in weeks. Although his shoes were in reasonably good condition, they didn't quite fit him, and blisters had rubbed on his heels, which had not yet entirely healed. Which made Craig think that perhaps he had gotten the shoes fairly recently. Perhaps from a shelter? It would have been enough time to have rubbed blisters and then begun the healing process.

None of which seemed like it would be of much help in finding out who the man was, and why he chose to come to their town. There was no public transportation to Doveland. Did he walk there? If he did, from where? Or did someone drop him off? Was it someone who lived in Doveland, or someone passing through?

One thing they needed to do was give him a name. Calling him the man on the bench was not good enough. And Craig didn't like the name, John Doe. He was trying out various names when Valerie knocked on his office door with Tom in tow.

After getting up to hug Valerie, he motioned to Tom and Valerie to sit down in the two chairs he had placed in front of his desk. As she sat, Valerie noticed his pad of paper with names scribbled on them and asked him what he was doing.

"Coming up with a temporary name for our dead guy."

"You could call him DG for dead guy," Tom laughed and then caught himself. "Oh, probably not funny."

"I don't know," Valerie said, "I kind of like it. It describes him, without turning him into just another John Doe."

"Seriously?" Craig asked. "You guys aren't pulling my leg are you?"

When they both shook their head no, Craig agreed. "DG it is."

So, you guys are here to sketch him?"

"Not me," Valerie answered. "I'm not that good. Tom's going to do it."

Craig turned to his friend in surprise. "You're drawing it? When did you learn to draw?"

Tom blushed and looked at Valerie for support. She shook her head at him.

"Well, it happened by accident. Valerie knew that I've been looking for something to do, so she asked me if I wanted to help out at the school a few days a week. Mostly running errands for teachers, doing odd jobs."

"Oh, you've been doing more than that, Tom."

"Not really. But thanks. Anyway, I was spending a lot of time in the art room helping out when the art teacher asked me if I wanted to do what the kids were doing. At first, I did it because it helped the kids, seeing an adult learning along with them. But then I started liking it."

Craig looked at his friend and shook his head. "How come none of us knew about this?"

"I asked Valerie to keep it to herself. I didn't want to make it into a big deal. I kept meaning to tell Mandy about it, but since she is such an artist in her way, I was rather embarrassed. The longer I waited to tell her, the harder it got."

"So you got good enough to draw this DG's face by taking art classes with the kids in school? How long have you been doing this anyway?"

"Um. Well. Since last fall. And no, I ended up taking private art lessons."

Craig clapped his hand to his forehead. "Tom. You are pretty good at keeping secrets. If I have one, you'll be the person I'd tell. But now I'd say you are in a bit of trouble keeping this from Mandy all this time.

"The rest of us, well, I would guess that more people know about it than you think, given the abilities shared by a few of our friends. For sure Mira knows."

Tom turned pale. "Of course she knows. What was I thinking? And she hasn't told."

"And Hannah must know too," Craig added.

Tom turned to Valerie. "I'm an idiot, aren't I? I have a sister who I met because she remote viewed me, and Leif and Eric who pop in anywhere. Then there's Hannah who knows all. Good grief, probably everyone knows but Mandy."

"Yes, you are an idiot, but a lovable one," Valerie said. "And I doubt everyone knows. But those that do have kept it a secret for you. It's yours to tell, Tom. But I suggest you do it soon because she will find out that you did this drawing today.

"Why not take it home with you, and tell her you did it. Confess the whole thing. Tell her how it happened. She'll understand."

Tom nodded praying that Mandy would. He had no idea what he had been thinking. He had learned a long time ago that secrets were not a good idea.

Of course, the guy he was sketching had been keeping a secret of some kind, and look what happened. If they don't figure it out, he'll have taken it to the grave with him.

The three of them moved to the room where Craig had DG lying peacefully under a sheet.

While Tom worked on the sketch, Valerie asked, "What happens to him if no one claims him?"

"The coroner can hold him for about a month, and then if Dan can't locate a family, he'll be cremated or buried in a pauper's grave."

"If we don't find family, I think Doveland can do better than that," Valerie said. "Are these his clothes? You didn't find anything in them?"

Valerie picked up his flannel jacket holding it at arm's length. The smell was terrible. As she stared at the jacket, she thought about Hannah and how she hid lady bugs appliques in her mom's and Mandy's clothes. If you didn't know they were there, you wouldn't see them. *Poor man, he would have loved one of Hannah's ladybugs,* Valerie thought.

As she returned the coat to the pile, she noticed a small rip in the seam and what looked like a piece of lint stuck in it. Out of habit, she picked at the lint to throw it away and instead pulled out a tiny slip of paper with writing on it.

Squinting, she tried to make out the words. They were faded and smeared, but she thought it said, Lisa Lane.

She doubted the man had stuffed a stray piece of paper in his jacket seam. It had to mean something. Who was Lisa Lane?

Nine

"I don't know, Ben," Hannah was saying. Ben sat staring at her not saying a word. After all, at two years old he wasn't expected to say much. But Hannah knew differently. They had been speaking to each other since Ben was a few weeks old.

It had taken him that amount of time to figure out that the voice in his head was someone else. Up until then the world had all moved as one, so Hannah talking to him was just part of the universe flowing as one entity.

It had both disappointed him and excited him to realize that there were people outside of himself that weren't a projection of his imagination. When he was a few weeks old, he had smiled at his mother Ava realizing that she was outside of his head. His dad Evan came next, and then there was Hannah. Who wouldn't want her as a sister? She heard him talk. Everyone else heard babbles.

Maybe it was because Hannah still remembered her past lifetime that made her so smart. She said there were more lifetimes, but the one that had just passed was quite enough for her to remember.

Besides, this lifetime and that one were connected, so it was vital for her to remember what had happened. She even had her past-dad Jay with her for a while in this lifetime. Jay hadn't liked remembering both of the lifetimes that much though. Hannah had no problem with it. Perhaps it was because she and her mother had died from a house fire when Hannah was only eight years old and so she hadn't had time to regret things.

Hannah had come back almost immediately as Ava's daughter. But Hannah had been adopted for the first eight years of her life because Ava had been so young when Hannah was born.

Ava's friend Mandy knew who had adopted Hannah though, so when Hannah's adoptive dad died, and his wife didn't want her, Mandy took Hannah away. Mandy had kept Hannah safe until Ava found them both and brought them, and Ava's mother's adoptive father Eric, back to Doveland with her.

After Ava and Evan married, Ben had been born and Hannah couldn't have been happier. It was with Ben that Hannah shared all her secrets. Now that he was two, he was even more fun. She loved teaching him things that she knew how to do. But right now she was expecting him to understand something he wasn't old enough to understand.

What did she mean when she said, a man died on a bench? What man, what bench? Died? What did that mean?

Hannah heard him ask all those questions, but she wasn't really looking for answers from him. She was talking to figure things out. She knew that sooner or later someone in their big circle of friends and family would call a meeting. Everyone would gather, and she would hear more about what was going on. But she was getting impatient. She wanted to know more now.

The old man on the bench was looking for someone. Who? Did it have anything to do with what Suzanne had told the group the last time she visited?

Suzanne was part of the Forest Circle, and they rarely saw her anymore. Leif and Eric had taken her place as the liaison between the Earth realm, and the other dimension where the Forest Circle now lived. But Leif had promised to start telling them about where he and Eric went, which meant that there was a chance she could learn how to travel with them.

She didn't want to leave this life though. However, she needed someone to figure out how to travel between the two realms and take their body both places. Leif and Eric didn't do that. They didn't have a body anymore in the Earth realm. They appeared kind of like a wispy spirit. Maybe what people called ghosts?

When they visited from the other dimension people in this one had to learn how to see them. Hannah thought they had bodies where the Forest Circle lived, but she wasn't sure. There was so much to learn.

However, Suzanne said they had to wait for another person to complete the Stone Circle before there was even a possibility of other people traveling between the realms. All they knew about the person was it was a man.

"It couldn't be the dead guy could it?" Hannah asked Ben. She was making a list of all the men who had come into town since last fall when Suzanne had told them not to go looking for him. He would find them.

"Let's hope not. Well maybe it would be okay, maybe when we find out why he was here, that would solve the problem.

"But there are other new guys. What about the new minister, Lloyd? Or Hank is getting a new guy to help on his construction crew. I think his name is Elliot. Or maybe his brother Eli?

"Oh wait. Johnny said that he met an interesting professor at school. Of course, he doesn't live here, at least not yet. Maybe it's that guy. Josh? I think that's his name."

By then Ben had toddled off looking for something more fun to do than listen to Hannah talk about who was coming to town.

Hannah looked down at her list. She needed more information. She could listen in on people's thinking but had promised her mom not to do that unless it was an emergency or she had been given permission. She could project herself places and find out what was going on, but once again, she had promised not to do that unless she was sure she had been invited, or once again, if it was an emergency.

She had kinda broken her promise when she visited Johnny, but in a way, he had invited her. She was stretching the truth she knew, but still, he had been happy to see her. That's when he had told her about the writing professor that he liked. He was going to introduce him to Edward because Johnny thought he would love to hear Edward's story.

Well, who wouldn't, Hannah thought. *But how much of it should be told?* She wasn't worried about that. Edward was a smart man. He would do the right thing.

One thing Ava and Evan had done since last fall was to turn the house into a Bed and Breakfast. They were only accepting a few people at a time, especially now since they had two young children, but the people that stayed were always interesting.

On Edward's travels, he would tell people about Doveland and the Bed and Breakfast, and some of them had come to visit. They always had wonderful stories to tell, and Hannah's awareness of human nature and the world they lived in was expanding rapidly.

Without thinking too much about it, Hannah knew that she would need to expand what she knew if Suzanne was going to let her be one of the dimension travelers. Reading as many books as she could definitely helped. Being among all the people in Doveland who were able to do some of the things she could do also helped.

The fact that Leif and Eric visited her and let her talk over what she was learning played a big part in her growth. Although she was only eleven, almost twelve, in this lifetime, Hannah always added an extra eight years onto her age since she remembered her past life.

To Hannah, that meant she was nineteen going on twenty. An adult. Yes, still in a child's body, but that was one of her strengths. She was constantly underestimated.

Although Ben had lost interest in Hannah's speculations, he was still thinking about what she had told him.

Ben never saw Hannah as a child. To him, she was the wisest person in the world. He would follow her anywhere, even if that meant she took him wherever Leif and Eric kept disappearing to.

He hoped it wouldn't be too scary, and that he could return to see his mom and dad. But still. He would go if she asked him to.

Ten

Elliot reminded Hank of someone he used to have on his crew years before. He wasn't sure that was a good thing.

He and Elliot were at Emily's hill where Hank was attempting to introduce Elliot to the men working there. Up until now, Elliot had passed all the hurdles he had put in front of him with flying colors.

Elliot had returned the paperwork promptly. He had excellent references, and people who had worked with him in the past seemed to genuinely like and admire him.

Now Hank could see why Elliot had garnered so much admiration. At least on a personal scale. Hank had yet to see how Elliot worked in a crew, but he sure knew how to be part of one. Elliot was doing something that Hank and his team called fromelizing. It had been a new word for Hank until a few years before when one of his crew members had complained about one of his work buddies. Said he was fromelizing. It turns out it was a word in the urban dictionary that describes when a coworker is left alone because his tool buddy is too busy chatting and socializing.

Hank watched Elliot stay and chat with each man in the crew, clap him on the back and then turn to the next man.

Fromelizing was precisely what Elliot was doing, leaving Hank to wait for him to catch up. Hank shook his head and decided not to waste time waiting. Instead, he went to talk to Emily who was sitting on her porch swing watching.

"New guy?"

"Yeah. Don't know how he'll work out. If he works as good as he socializes, he could be a nice addition to the crew."

"I know better than to ask, Hank, but I'm going to do it anyway. Do you know when you'll have this finished?"

Hank understood why she was asking. Her immaculate setting on the hill was strewn with machines and construction materials.

"As long as I have been in this construction game," Hank said, "it always amazes me what a mess construction is until it's done. Yes, unless something happens that we haven't anticipated, you will be ready for your summer session.

I know Shawn is going to teach music, and you're teaching dance, but do you have your art and writing teachers yet?"

"I have a lead on a few possibilities. Worse case, I'll use the art and writing teachers the kids have in school. But I'm hoping to expose them to other styles and ideas, so a new person would be great."

By then Elliot had made his way up to the porch and stood looking at the two of them with his hat in his hands. Emily stood to shake his hand and introduce herself.

"This is a beautiful place, Miss Emily," he said.

Emily laughed. "I only ask my students to call me Miss Emily, but I have to admit I like the name. Still, you can call me Emily."

Hank stepped off the porch and motioned for Elliot to join him. A few steps away from the porch, Elliot stopped and turned back. "I saw an old bus sitting behind your garage. Are you doing something with that?"

"I hope to. I want to have it fixed up to pick up kids from town and bring them out here this summer. I guess I need to find someone soon to get that done."

Elliot tapped the toe of his boot on the step trying to decide if he was going to say anything. Finally, he thought, *what can I lose?*

"Me and my brother could do it for you. We've restored vans and small buses before. Can't do much for the engine, but we can make the inside and outside look real pretty.

"That's if it's okay with Hank. I won't do it on work time. I have pictures, Hank. I can show them to you both and see what you think."

Hank liked that Elliot had picked up on the fact that he was protective of Emily. She was family to him as much as Ava was his niece.

"Let's see how you work out on the crew, Elliot. If you do, show me the pictures, and we'll decide. I'll need an estimate from you for what you will charge."

Elliot smiled at the two of them and headed up to the crew working on the art building.

"What do you think?" Emily asked.

Hank's curt "We'll see," made her smile. She loved Hank for being so protective. She had never had that before, and it felt like a gift. To top all that off, he was responsible for building her beautiful space.

She had some feelers out on the internet for teachers for the summer session, but so far no one had inspired her. The problem was the arts camp would be open in July, only a few months away. So besides having the construction done and the bus ready, she needed teachers.

This year, she was still only going to run the camp during

July. It was a trial run to see how it would go for having it open all summer for kids, and spring and fall for adult retreats.

Some people had asked her if she would ever open full time, but she didn't think so. She liked the quiet of the place when no one was there but her. She also wanted to bring in different guest teachers for different sessions. Living in a small town like Doveland, the kids, and their parents, wouldn't have as much experience with various forms of art unless she brought it to them.

It thrilled her to the core to think about how she could make a difference through the arts that she loved. Emily knew that the Stone and Forest Circles had gifts that she might never acquire, but she had gifts and abilities to teach too. She could teach new ways to view the world. Ways to learn how to see what wasn't visible unless you knew how to look for it.

Standing on her hill looking down into the village she knew that if she had her binoculars, she would be able to see the roof of Dr. Joe's house. No one knew what to do with that house.

Edward wanted to tear it down, fill in the bunker, and turn the whole thing into a park. Not everyone thought that was a great idea, but Edward and Valerie were the next of kin and had final say.

Joe's house was the one thing he never put into a trust or his will. Emily thought there were probably multiple reasons why not. But for whatever reason, he had neglected to state his wishes, the house would soon be out of probate, and a choice would need to be made.

As long as it didn't bring the sense of evil back to Doveland, Emily didn't care what happened to it. She never wanted to experience someone like Dr. Joe again.

Eleven

Edward and Josh hit it off right away, just as Johnny knew they would. Something about the two of them felt the same to Johnny. He had no idea why. He barely knew his teacher and Edward had come into town about the same time Johnny had gone off to university so in many ways Edward was still a stranger to him.

Of course, they had some family gatherings together, so he was learning about Edward. But it still felt strange to know his mother was the daughter of Dr. Joe. That made Edward his uncle. An uncle who had watched Johnny's father grow up and who knew him when he had done those terrible things at Joe's request.

Hannah was always telling Johnny that lives circle around each other in each lifetime, and that if he were listening and watching he would see it for himself.

But still, he wondered if knowing that made it any easier to deal with all the events that had happened to him in the last few years.

That was another thing Hannah had said. Things don't happen to you. They happen. It's how you view them that makes them feel bad or good.

Johnny thought the jury was still out on that, but it worked for Hannah, and as young as she was, she sure knew a lot. One thing she had told him was to write about what had happened, and because of that advice, he caught the eye of his teacher, Joshua Baines.

In Mr. Baines' English class the assignment had been to write a short piece about the strangest thing that had happened in his life. That was a hard piece to write. Not because there hadn't been many strange things, but because there had been so many of them.

However, since he was still interested in heritage and bloodlines and choices about becoming yourself, he wrote about his mother finding a half-brother, and both of them being the children of the town's beloved doctor who turned out to be a monster. Which made him the grandchild of that monster?

Johnny could have written more how he felt about that, but the piece was not about feelings. So he kept those to himself until Mr. Baines asked him to stay after class. Walking up to the desk at the front, Johnny found himself trembling in fear wondering what he had done wrong.

The first thing Mr. Baines had done was have him sit beside the desk so they could talk, and then he asked him to stop calling him Mr. Barnes. Josh would do.

Johnny was still afraid. He had learned that monsters came in many sizes and shapes. They weren't the scary creatures in children's books. They were regular people living ordinary lives.

But all Joshua wanted to know was if it was possible to meet Edward. He was writing an article about children of psychopaths, and he would love to interview Edward. And that's how that happened.

When Edward came to town, Johnny had them meet, and now they were turning out to be good friends.

Was this what Hannah meant? Were Edward and Josh supposed to meet? Did they know each other from before? Were they part of this Karass that he belonged to?

And then there was always the question, which Johnny sometimes asked himself: What was before? Before what? He was learning that all things happened at the same time, so how was there a before?

Too many questions, Johnny said to himself. *One thing at a time.* And this one thing was meeting Edward and Joshua again for lunch. Johnny thought that Edward kept suggesting lunch as a way to make sure that Johnny was eating well.

Whatever the reason, Johnny was looking forward to the lunch at the Indian place this time. Edward was trying out almost every restaurant in town. This one was the next on the list. Doveland didn't have such a vast variety. Edward was taking advantage of the many choices while he had them.

Yes, Johnny thought, my life is better because Edward came into it. That was the one thing he was going to focus on at the moment, and the fact that he was going to have a real lunch again today. He would enjoy these simple pleasures because Johnny had a feeling life was going to get more complicated very soon.

****

After lunch with Johnny and Edward, Josh headed up the Centennial Walkway towards the campus. The walkway was a brick sidewalk flanked by The Tavern and other smaller buildings.

Each brick had the name of a person or two inscribed on it. People who wanted to remember a friend or family member had bought the bricks.

It had been a great way to raise funds for the walkway's restoration, and it made the walkway a favorite place to visit. Every day people of all ages could be seen searching the walkway looking for the brick bearing the name of a loved one.

Eventually, someone would yell, "It's over here," and friends and family would rush over to snap a picture of the location in case they forgot where it was the next time they visited.

The sidewalk ended on College Avenue where lived a five hundred pound bronze statue of a pig named Centennia and her two piglets named Ed and Hope. They had been installed in 1996 to commemorate the hundred year celebration of the official incorporation of the State College borough.

Although the pigs would never take over in popularity for picture taking from the Penn State Lion statue found on the campus, it was still a place where people stopped to take photos of riding on Centennia's back.

"Why a pig?" Josh had asked the first time he had seen them. It turned out it was because of a picture taken in 1894 of a pig rummaging around for food near the corner of College Avenue and Allen Street.

Passing the pig statue, Josh crossed the street weaving between the cars waiting at the stop light and headed up to campus. He had a student to meet.

Josh could have been mistaken for a student. Although he was in his mid-thirties, he gave the impression of being at least ten years younger. When he went out to get a beer or two with friends, his ID got checked every time. It didn't bother him. Josh figured that when he got older, he might enjoy the fact that he looked younger than he was.

As his long legs ate up the distance, he barely paid attention to where he was going. He was thinking about Edward and Johnny. When he had read Johnny's short essay, something had caught his attention. It wasn't the writing itself. It was the story about Johnny's mother Valerie finding her half-brother that drove him to ask to meet Edward, a man who had hidden from his father his whole life.

It was the opposite of what Josh's grandfather had done. His grandfather knew he had a sister, but didn't know where she had gone. Josh thought that his grandfather had been searching for his sister his whole life. As far as Joshua knew, he had never found her.

Josh wanted to meet a man who had found a previously unknown sister. Perhaps it would bring him good luck. Because now he was not only searching for his grandfather's sister, he was searching for his grandfather.

The bells of Old Main rang out reminding him he had only fifteen minutes to get to his appointment with an incoming student. He and Edward had made plans to meet again.

There was something there, he just knew it. But right now, a student was waiting.

Twelve

Mandy stared at the picture that Tom had drawn of the old man on the bench, thinking about what had happened after Tom had brought it to her. She was waiting for him at her design offices in Valerie's house, ready to distribute it to all the social networks that she could find.

As he had pulled the picture out of his portfolio to show it to her, he had done his best to hide the fact that his hands were trembling, and she had wondered why.

Mandy had taken one look at the picture and told Tom that it was an excellent likeness.

"Really, you like it?" he had asked, sitting down with a plop. They were in the little waiting room she used for clients. It wasn't a room off by itself. Instead, her office was one big room, sectioned off in different ways. The only room that had walls from floor to ceiling was the bathroom.

She loved the space she had designed. In spite of the openness of the layout, it was quiet and serene and exciting at the same time. She had little nooks where she met with clients, or put together sample ideas.

She had an even tinier niche where she drew and worked on projects by herself. Everything about her office was precisely what she wanted. Each day when she saw the sign Your Second Home Design on the door, she felt like pinching herself or doing a happy dance.

When Tom had plopped onto the purple plush couch in the waiting room with a smile on his face, she had been confused. "What are you smiling about?"

"You like the picture!"

"Yes, I do. It will be perfect for making posters and putting up on social media. So, thanks for getting it done," Mandy had said, "But I still don't know why you are smiling like that."

Tom reached up and pulled Mandy down to sit beside him. Keeping both of her hands in his, he said, "Because I was the one who drew it."

Mandy was not proud of her reaction. She had laughed and said, "Sure you did."

Tom answered with a little less joy in his voice, "Sure. I did."

Mandy had gotten up, turned off the ringers on all her phones and turned the sign on the door to say "closed."

"Okay. Tell me about it."

And he did. They had talked for the rest of the afternoon. It started with why he had been keeping the secret of his drawing from her. But they eventually wound around to all the other little things they had neglected to tell each other. Finally, Mandy had taken a deep breath and told him the worst secret that she had been keeping.

She whispered, "I don't want any children."

"That's it? That's your deep dark secret?" he had said and then replied. "Mandy, I don't want any children either. We can do lots of wonderful things for the children we know, and the children of the world, but I like our life this way. I have no desire at all to have my own children."

The two of them had laughed, kissed, and promised each

other not to keep secrets anymore. Then arm in arm they had headed over to the Diner to get a piece of pizza from Pete and Barbara's new pizza oven.

Mandy thought that perhaps the old man on the bench would be happy to know that he had brought the two of them closer together. If they found his family, she would be sure to share the story.

So far, all the outreach hadn't done much good. Dan was planning to spend a day visiting as many small towns around Doveland as he could to show the picture around, just in case someone had seen him that wasn't on social media. Perhaps they would catch a break.

Mandy took one last look at the picture Tom had drawn and promised the man she saw there that she would do everything she could to find out who he was. She knew in her heart that someone was looking for him, and would be heartbroken to find out that he had died, but grateful that people cared enough to not give up on him.

She had never given up on anyone, and she wasn't going to start now.

****

Hannah was right. Her mom planned a party. Not quite the one Hannah expected, but it was a gathering.

At school, Hannah and Lex had learned about Maypole dances, and Ava thought it would be fun to have a version of it at their house. May Day was on a Wednesday however, so they decided to have it Sunday afternoon after church and pretend it was May 1st.

It had only been a few weeks since Ben and Lex's birthday party, but everyone said they were always ready for another celebration. As Valerie said when asked if she and Lex could come, "Every day is the perfect day to celebrate with friends."

Hank invited the new minister to the party, thinking that he might like to get to know the group of people better who technically were paying for the restoration of the wall in the chapel. Lloyd said that he would love to come and asked if he could bring his wife and son along.

"Of course," Hank said.

What Lloyd didn't know, and could never have expected, was that there was another reason for his invitation.

Leif and Eric had shared with the Stone Circle what Suzanne had told them. There would be no possibility of anyone traveling to the Forest Circle's dimension until the last person who belonged to the Stone Circle arrived.

Not everyone wanted to travel to the other dimension. As Mira said, "I'm just getting a handle on this one." But Sarah Morgan did. If her husband Leif was going to live in both places, she wanted to do that too.

The other person who couldn't wait to travel between dimensions was Hannah. Suzanne had said that anyone could learn and Hannah couldn't wait to go. She didn't care if people would say she was too young. She knew she wasn't.

So while all the children and some of the adults took turns holding colored ribbons attached to the Maypole ducking over and under each other to weave a beautiful design on the poles, others were watching Lloyd.

"Is he the one?" They asked each other. Finally, Leif and Eric arrived in their midst and told them to stop it. They couldn't figure it out that way. What needed to happen would without their forcing it. They just had to pay attention.

"Do you know who it is, Leif?" Craig asked.

Craig hadn't told anyone yet, but he was thinking that

traveling between dimensions might ease his heart, still hurting after the betrayal of his friend Dr. Joe. Joe hadn't betrayed just him. He had betrayed everyone. So Craig was embarrassed at how much it had hurt him and never spoke of the pain that he felt. He could have. His friends already knew and did their best to ease it for him.

"I don't, Craig. I have to watch and wait the same as you do. I wouldn't worry about this right now. I think you all will have another mystery to solve first."

With that enigmatic statement, he and Eric faded away, but not before air kissing their wives who giggled like school girls.

"I swear when he does that he is laughing at us," Evan said.

Sarah laughed. "I assure you, that's exactly what he is doing. But he's right. There is nothing that we can do to make this all happen. So let's have some fun while we can. Anyone up for a Maypole dance with me?"

"Me!" yelled Hannah.

With that, they all rushed out to grab a ribbon. This time it was Lloyd who watched from the side. *They have a secret they're not sharing,* he thought. *I hope someday I'll find out what it is.*

What Lloyd couldn't hear was Leif's answer to him. "I assure you, Lloyd, you will sooner than you think."

But he did feel an assurance that something was coming, and there was nothing he could do to stop it.

Thirteen

Monday morning after the May Day party, Hank met his crew at the Diner and bought breakfast for every one there. Including the people who weren't part of his crew. The people of Doveland knew that Hank did that sometimes and loved it if they happened to be there when it happened.

If they knew Hank's schedule, they could have figured it out. Hank almost always paid for breakfast when they were starting a new job. Hank would have the whole crew meet him at the Diner where he would hand out work assignments.

Even if the job only required a few men, Hank held the breakfast anyway. That was the case this time. He only needed two men for the Chapel job. The rest of the crew would be heading out to Emily's hill because finishing it was a priority.

Hank had decided to use Elliot and his brother Eli to help him with the Chapel. The Stanton brothers. When Hank had asked them why the names Elliot and Eli, they said their mother liked the sound of it. If she yelled "Ell," both of them would come running. Perhaps in that way she had trained them to watch out for each other since if one got in trouble, the other did too.

Maybe that was why they worked well together, Hank thought.

He planned to have Elliot, the older brother, act as foreman. The job didn't require one, but it was just one more item on the list of things Elliot had to pass before he would be hired on permanently. Elliot's fromelizing had calmed down a bit, mostly because he now knew everyone on the crew better than Hank knew them himself.

Although his whole crew was eating at the Diner, Hank was careful to keep breakfast calm and contained. Pete didn't need a bunch of rowdy guys in his Diner scaring off his other customers, free breakfast or not.

With a full diner, Alex and Pete were busy cooking while Barbara tried to keep up with the orders. She knew most of their orders by heart, which made it easier, but she was still struggling because their latest part-time hire had failed to show up—again.

As she poured and rushed around trying to do everything at once, Barbara decided that this was the last morning she was going to work like a crazy woman. It was time to hire full-time help. Maybe hire two more people. That way perhaps one of them could also work at Grace's Your Second Home if there wasn't enough work at the Diner. It was going on her agenda to talk about it at the next woman's council meeting.

Seeing her struggle to keep the coffee cups filled, Elliot quickly finished his breakfast and got up and offered to help. She handed him the carafe and headed back to the kitchen to pick up orders. Thirty minutes later, Hank had finished handing out work assignments, everyone was on the way to their job, and the Diner had returned to a normal flow.

Barbara turned to Elliot, who was still keeping coffee mugs filled and had also retrieved orders from the kitchen, and told him he was a godsend.

"Thank you, ma'am. It was my pleasure." Wiping his hands off on a napkin, he reached out to shake her hand and to introduce himself. Instead, he got what Pete called the famous Barbara hug.

"Not ma'am. Barbara, please. And I know you're Elliot. Hank has told us about you, but I believe he forgot to mention that you know how to get up and help when needed."

"Me and my brother, we helped our mom out a lot. She was a single mom, so we did our best, and sometimes I went and helped her out when she was waitressing."

"Well, tell her that she raised a good boy."

As Elliot glanced over at his brother searching for how to respond, Barbara said, "Oh. You said, was. I'm sorry."

"It's okay. It's been a few years. And I got Eli."

"Well, you're welcome here anytime, young man," Barbara said.

"Let's go you two Ell's," Hank called from the door. "We have a chapel wall to fix. It's not going to fix itself." Mumbling to himself he added, "Although it seems to have got broken all by itself."

Even though Hank was acting as if this job was just like every other one, he didn't think it was. If Melvin were still around, he would be telling Hank to be careful. "Don't go tearing down that wall boy as if it wasn't telling you something," he would have said.

Heading to his truck, Hank thought Melvin would be right. He would take his time taking the wall down. It was a job that would only take a few days anyway. No point in rushing it.

Hannah would be telling him to listen to the wall first, too. Between Melvin, that old coot, and Hannah he was learning there was much more going on than what appeared on the surface.

As Hank closed the door to his truck, he glanced over at the park bench where the man they had started calling DG had died. He was sure that somehow those two things were connected. No clue how though. It was just a feeling. But he was learning that feelings counted much more than he ever thought. And this was a big feeling.

Fourteen

On the way over to Sarah's house, Grace tried to formulate her thoughts. What did she want from Sarah? But she could barely put one foot in front of another, let alone think.

The weather matched her mood. The sun had barely risen, and it was overcast and drizzling. Not enough for an umbrella, but enough to dampen her raincoat to match her mood.

She had been in a massive funk since the morning they found DG. Nothing anyone said to her had helped.

Everyone told her over and over again that it wasn't her fault, but she had a hard timing believing it. She thought that she could have overridden his decision to stay outside in the cold. She could have had him arrested so that he slept in the jail instead. Maybe a medical team could have helped him, instead of dying in the cold on a bench in a park. Alone.

Well, not alone. Leif and Eric told her that they had been there. But there was nothing they could have done for him.

Trying to comfort Grace they told her that at the last minute DG looked as if he saw them there, and then smiled and reached out his hand for someone. They said he had died happy.

Sure, was all that Grace could think. *Happy about what?* She remembered how unkempt he had been and worried that he must not have felt loved to be looking so ragged.

While Grace was in her down-in-the-dumps-mood, she knew that everyone that came into Your Second Home tiptoed around her. They were afraid they would make it worse if they tried to comfort her.

When she had woken up that morning, she realized that it couldn't go on this way. Almost two weeks of moping had not helped anyone. So in a moment of clarity that she needed help, Grace texted Sarah and asked if she could come over. Within seconds she got her answer: "Of course."

Grace didn't waste any time. She knew if she hesitated she would not go. Within seconds of sending the text an overwhelming feeling of lethargy had come over her. She just wanted to lay down and go back to sleep. Mandy would already be getting the coffee shop ready and would be fine for the next few hours.

The feeling of not wanting to do anything was so strong it scared Grace enough to throw on a pair of leggings and a sweatshirt and drag herself downstairs to the shop. Still pushing herself, she stopped to tell Mandy where she was going and to grab a few fresh muffins to bring to Sarah's. She knew that if she delayed, her determination might flag.

Mandy tried to hide her expression of relief that Grace was going to Sarah's, but it was evident that she was happy to see Grace choose to get some help. However, instead of making a big deal of it, Mandy added a few cookies to the bag, gave Grace a quick kiss on the cheek, and walked her out the front door.

It was a not so subtle gesture telling her to get going. Grace found herself grateful for the extra impetus. She needed every ounce of fortitude she had to walk the few blocks to Sarah's house.

Sarah had a sweet little white picket fence around the front of her house, with a squeaky gate. She wanted a squeaky gate. That's how Sarah knew someone was arriving. This morning though, she was watching for Grace, knowing that it was going to be a hard walk for her. But when Grace got there, she would have conquered the first hurdle to overcoming the depression she had fallen into.

Sarah waited until Grace made it all the way up onto the porch, looking as if she was dragging a thousand pound weight, before Sarah opened the door. Putting her arms around her friend, she ushered her inside and helped her sit on her favorite chair.

They had bought it together one day when she and Grace had been out visiting garage sales. Grace had spotted the purple plush chair and talked Sarah into purchasing it for her new home. Sarah knew it was because she wanted to come over and sit in it, and that seemed like a fine reason for buying it. It had been well used, but after having it restored, it was beautiful. Like an old friend wearing a new dress.

"Muffins for us?" Sarah asked lifting the white bag out of Grace's lap while depositing a cup of coffee on the table beside her. Grace simply lifted her deep brown eyes and nodded yes. Sarah looked at her normally overly energetic friend sitting like a lump in the chair, gray hair sticking out where it shouldn't, and missing her ever-present glasses on a chain, and wondered how it had gotten that bad.

But she didn't say anything. She brought back a muffin on a plate for Grace and placed her own coffee and muffin on the coffee table that sat between them.

"Take a sip, Grace," she commanded, using a voice that almost no one ever heard. "And now a bite of muffin."

After Grace had done both and looked a tiny bit better, Sarah said, "So you're here because you finally decided that being in that mood, allowing that depression, is not working." Not waiting for Grace's response, she continued. "So, my friend, what is this really about? And don't tell me it is all about DG's death."

Grace had heard this tone of voice from Sarah once before. It was six months after their husbands, Leif and Eric, had moved to the Forest dimension. Then, the two of them had been moping around wishing things were different, until one day Sarah said, "That's enough."

Grace recognized that was what she was saying again. "That's enough," and Grace knew that it was, but she wasn't sure how to stop it. At that time she knew her mood was because she had been missing the physical presence of Eric. Now, she wasn't so sure what had pulled her into this funk.

So instead of answering she merely looked at Sarah, and said, "Help."

"So you don't know what this is about?"

Grace shook her head no.

"Okay, then let's start with the facts. Yes, that poor man died outside of your store. But, and this is important, he chose to be there. He was old. No one killed him. You couldn't have done anything more than what you already did. And, Grace, you know it.

"Next, since I met you we have overcome every adversity. You and Mandy have two thriving businesses. Ones that you never thought you would have. You have a boat-load of friends. In fact, I don't think there is anyone in Doveland who doesn't know you and loves to come into your coffee house and see your smiling face.

"Yes, you don't have Eric in your house. On the other hand, you don't have Eric in your house, and you still have Eric."

Sarah paused and let that last part sink in, and then she winked at Grace and Grace burst out laughing. No socks to pick up, no meals to make, and still Eric's love and presence. I have it all, thought Grace.

"Here's my prescription for you my dear friend,' Sarah said.

"Get involved with finding out who your friend was. He came to you after all. You found him. You took care of him. Now take care of finding out why he was there. It's a mystery, not a tragedy, and you know how you love mysteries.

"And now, get off your lazy butt and help me out in the garden. It is in desperate need of weeding."

Sarah knew that fresh air, and flowers, and hands in the earth would restore Grace faster than anything else, and she was correct. Within an hour of working together planting seeds, weeding, and getting ready for summer blooms Grace was restored almost to her true self.

Sarah was right about something else too. Grace would be part of solving a bigger mystery than just the man on the bench.

Fifteen

Hank and the Stanton brothers headed over to the Chapel, but not before stopping at Your Second Home for a cup of coffee to go and a few of Mandy's pastries. They all had eaten a good breakfast, but Hank was not above going overboard the first day of a job to ensure his teams' full attention.

Lloyd was waiting for them at the back door of the Chapel looking stressed but trying to hide it. Knowing Lloyd would be there, Hank had brought him a cup of coffee and a pastry too. Seeing it, Lloyd visibly relaxed. Nothing strange could be going on if there was coffee and pastry involved, could it?

"What's up, Lloyd?" Hank asked while handing him the coffee. You look a bit distressed.

"I don't know. It's the wall. It keeps doing strange things. Oh, never mind. Just come in, and I'll show you."

Eli and Elliot followed Hank in. They hadn't yet laid down the floor coverings so they wouldn't track in dirt, but then, they hadn't started doing anything to the wall yet.

The brothers had looked at each other when Lloyd said that the wall was doing strange things. "What can a wall do anyway?" Eli had asked Elliot when he thought Lloyd was out of earshot. Elliot had just shrugged.

They found Lloyd and Hank, coffees in hand, standing side by side looking at the back wall of the chapel. Hank's plastic sheeting was still covering the wall, but it hadn't stopped it from another form of crumbling.

The only way Hank could describe it to himself was that it looked like a big animal had been chewing on the plaster edges. And since there were no big animals in the wall, he had to agree with Lloyd. It was strange.

Elliot took one look and said, "Hey, looks like this wall is asking to be torn down and getting impatient about it. Wonder what's behind it?"

Hank turned to look at him and realized that was precisely what it looked like. The wall was losing patience. Years ago he would never have assigned a quality like impatience to a wall, but that was before he met Ava and her friends.

"Okay then," Hank said. "Let's do what it wants."

Lloyd said he would be in the back office completing some tasks left over from the Sunday service. He asked them to let him know if they found anything interesting.

Elliot and Elli returned to their trucks and brought back the floor coverings, sledgehammers, and crowbars. Everything that came off the wall would be thrown in the dumpster that was being delivered that morning.

"I'm not sure we should sledgehammer this thing," Elliot said once everything was in place. "What if there is something behind the wall and we break it? Let's pull it down as carefully as possible."

Hank stood back and let Elliot and his brother do the work. He liked how Elliot took charge. Not aggressively, but thoughtfully. The two of them worked quickly but safely. At one point Elliot paused and peeked behind the wall, but not seeing anything to worry about, motioned for Eli to go forward.

Although Hank had done some rewiring work on the chapel a few years before, it was apparent that more needed to be done. He was looking over the wiring when he heard Eli say, "I found something."

Hank and Elliot stopped what they were doing and walked over to where Eli was kneeling on the floor and pulling at something stuck behind the part of the wall. It took the three of them to finally pull off the last piece of plaster and free the metal box that was thoroughly wedged between the studs and the outside wall of the chapel.

Hank texted Lloyd that they had found something. While they waited, they cleaned off the box the best that they could. A small rusted lock held it together. Hank was clipping off the lock as Lloyd arrived.

"Do you suppose this is what this crumbling wall was all about?" Lloyd asked.

"Well, I have some friends I can ask, but my guess is that. yes. it is," Hank replied.

Hank carefully lifted the lid to reveal what looked like letters and pictures. He gently picked up one of the letters and realized he couldn't read anything on it. The writing was too faded.

"It seems wrong to be pawing through this box. I would rather we did it later if you don't mind," Hank said. "A few years ago we went through Melvin's things, while he was still alive, and sorted it all for him. "This feels like the same kind of thing. It's important to someone. Maybe we can do this over at Ava's with the same group of people. Do you mind, Lloyd?"

"Not, at all. I trust that you'll keep me in the loop, but I think that Ava and her friends are a safe place to take this box. Really, at the moment I am most interested in getting the wall fixed before the next service. I think there is a group that comes in on Wednesday nights. Do you think that at least you could have it cleaned up by then?"

"Absolutely," Hank said as he closed the box back up. "I plan to have the whole thing done by your next Sunday service. I'll need to get my electrician in here to fix those wires, and Elliot and Eli can get the rest done."

Hank stayed for another thirty minutes making sure the Stanton brothers had everything they needed for the moment and then headed over to Ava's. He had already texted Ava about the box, and by the time he got there, he knew that she would have contacted everyone else.

There was no way he could have gone through the box without them all together. He couldn't imagine the grief he would get if he opened it without them. Besides, if anyone was going to figure out what made the box so important that the wall had to call attention to it, it would be the Doveland Karass.

Sixteen

Hank was right. Ava had texted everyone to come over, but as much as Hank wanted it to happen immediately, he had to wait until they could get there. Since it wasn't an emergency, not everyone could leave their store, or work, and rush over.

Which for Barbara and Grace highlighted the fact that they needed help. They wanted to be able to leave at a moment's notice if necessary. They both needed someone they could trust to take over when they were gone.

Pete and Barbara had Alex to do the cooking, but he couldn't wait on the tables at the same time, unless the Diner was empty, which was a very rare occasion.

Mandy, and now Sam, provided the pastries for the coffee shop, but no one but Grace was there to wait tables after Mandy left in the morning. Grace and Barbara knew that they needed help, not only so they could get away when they needed to, but because they were tired.

Neither one of them had planned on working full time, but that was what was happening. Barbara had made a list of all the young people in town who might be interested in working in either place. The idea was that perhaps between their two businesses they could find more than one person who would be willing to fill in wherever and whenever they were needed.

On the list were some of the boys from the group that Pete and Hank were working with, even the ones working construction. Barbara also added Dan's children and Lloyd's son, Jake. She knew that some of Hank's crew had children. Barbara added them to the list too. She would make a case for their need for help at the first opportunity.

Sam and Mira were having much the same discussion. Their catering business had grown enough that they could use assistance. Although they could have closed down for the afternoon when Ava texted, it would have caused them to run behind in preparation for their next job.

They had a few of the kids who were taking Pete's Junior Chef Classes come in on the weekends and help. It was part of the curriculum, but they needed people who could handle work during the week. Besides, they spent most of the time with the kids teaching them, something they were delighted to do, but it didn't help their need for getting things done.

Mira was also busy working on a cookbook. They were continually testing recipes, and once they had confirmation from their clients and friends that the recipe was perfect, she added it to the book.

They were not the only ones providing recipes for the book. So far, both Pete and Mandy had supplied their favorites. It was turning out to be a cookbook from Doveland, which both Sam and Mira liked.

Valerie also couldn't come right away. She was in the middle of the school day. But she promised to be there after school, and she would bring Hannah and Lex with her.

Craig had patients, and he would be late unless someone canceled. His practice had settled into just the right amount of work, and rest time. He had finally found an assistant that took much of the paperwork off his hands for which he was eternally grateful.

Emily was teaching dance classes, and Shawn was teaching his music students. Neither of them would be there because they taught lessons into the early evening.

After Ava finished texting and getting responses, she walked out into the garden to talk to Evan. There were no guests this week, so they were using the time to update and prepare. They liked the ebb and flow of guests. Neither of them wanted a full bunkhouse all the time.

She settled herself on a deck chair and held out a glass of water to Evan as an invitation to join her. After telling him about Hank's request to gather people because he had something to show them, she said, "I think our group is settling into their own lives. It's a good thing, right?"

"I think it is. No new murders, no evil man trying to destroy the Stone circle. Yes, it seems like a good thing. We're not the new people in town anymore."

"Still, we do have to figure out who DG is, don't we? And Hank said he found something in the church walls. So that's a little mystery too," Ava said.

Evan laughed. "So this is all a bit too calm for you, and you're looking for something more sinister or scary?"

"No. At least I don't think so." Ava paused. "Well, maybe."

"Perhaps you miss the element of excitement that danger brings?

Ava shook her head. "If so, I don't like that. Do we need danger to have an exciting life?"

"I don't know if we have a choice, Ava. Perhaps we are all in a slow spell, but I doubt it's going to stay that way. It feels more like a pause between things."

Ava sighed and reached out to hold her husband's hand. She

knew he was right. She hoped the pause lasted a long time.

****

Suzanne stood in the yard watching the two of them, choosing to be invisible for this visit as she had since the death of the man on the bench. Ava and Evan were right. They were in a pause, but she knew the break was almost over.

What she and the other members of the Forest Circle had feared would happen had begun. There was a renewed interest in the Earth Realm now that the Stone Circle was almost complete.

If it were possible for her to stop it, she would. She and the rest of the Forest Circle were doing their best to downplay the worry among the inhabitants of her realm about more people from the Earth Realm moving into their dimension. Worry that what had happened before would happen again.

To decrease the tension as much as possible, Suzanne had asked Leif and Eric to make fewer trips. But she had also asked them not to tell Sarah and Grace about why. Instead, they explained that events were going on in the Forest Circle dimension that needed to be attended to, and since things were quiet in Doveland, it seemed like a good time to take care of them.

What events? Sarah and Grace had asked but didn't receive an answer. In itself that was worrisome. Leif and Eric always did their best to answer their questions, even the ones where they didn't quite understand the answer. However, there was one question they had asked when Eric first left, that Suzanne said was almost time to answer.

Sarah and Grace had wanted to know what to call the realm where Suzanne and the rest of the Forest Circle lived. They didn't get an answer then, but Suzanne knew that it was nearing the time for them to know the name. In truth, she wouldn't tell them anything new. She would remind them of what they already knew but had been made to forget.

She hoped that they would make the connections to what was currently happening in Doveland soon. Otherwise, they would be like the pigs in the straw house. The wolf would be calling soon, and he would be able to blow their house down with ease.

She would do her best to delay the inevitable until they had built their house of stone. But they were running out of time.

Seventeen

Once the plaster was off the walls and thrown into the dumpster, there wasn't anything else for Elliot and Eli to do until the electrician finished with the rewiring, so they decided to head out to Emily's hill and work on the bus.

Emily was in town teaching dance classes, but most of the rest of Hank's crew was there working on her new buildings, so they knew that they wouldn't be alone.

After hearing that they would be willing to make her bus look new, Hank had taken it into town to the mechanics, and now that it was running perfectly, it was ready for its makeover. Elliot and Eli had already run their plans by Emily and had gotten a thumbs up. She wanted to have it done by summer, which they assured her would happen.

First, they had to take out anything that they couldn't restore. After that, the brothers would begin with the interior and work their way out. At first, they worked in silence, used to working as a team since they were young because they were often alone together. When their mother was alive, she was always working to keep them sheltered and fed.

They had no idea who their father was. She never told them, and they had no desire to know. As far as they were concerned, he was dead. They blamed his absence on their mother working herself into exhaustion until she was too weak to fight off what was supposed to be a simple case of the flu.

They had lied about their age when social services came to call. Eli never knew how Elliot made his birth certificate say he was eighteen when he was actually only sixteen. But he didn't care. It meant they got to stay together.

They moved to another small town where no one knew them. Eli went back to school, and Elliot worked any job he could find while doing his best to study on his own.

They found a run-down one room apartment, which worked well enough. They put two mattresses on the floor and felt grateful for the roof over their head. Even though he was underage, Eli managed to talk the manager into letting him help after school at the same garage where Elliot had found work.

It helped pay the rent and was instrumental in keeping them well fed. Often the guys at the garage said they brought too much food in their lunch box, and gave the extra to the brothers claiming they would have to throw it away if no one ate it.

Everyone knew that they packed extra, but let the pretense stand. Eli and Elliot's mother would have approved of the kindness, and their wisdom in accepting it, as long as they passed it on.

By the time Eli graduated from high school, and Elliot had gotten his high school diploma online, the brothers had moved into construction. Although they loved the guys at the garage, it was evident that they weren't mechanics.

They had heard a construction company was hiring and with the great references as to their work ethic they were hired on as trainees. It didn't take long for the brothers to realize that they had found a place where they could excel.

Eli had stumbled into the work with Hank when one of

the men on the crew had heard about the job in Doveland and asked Eli if he wanted to travel with him to check it out. The brothers didn't hesitate.

The brothers knew that small offers were often the opening to something important, so when Eli called Elliot and said he found a town and crew he loved, Elliot gave him his blessing to stay. They knew sooner or later they would work together again.

Although apart for a few years, they both used the time to learn how to be alone, so now that they were together again, they were stronger than ever.

The bus was the first project they were doing on their own without outside help. At the garage, the two of them had learned how to restore cars, and they were happy to put what they learned to the test. If they got stuck, they knew they could call on the men at the garage to tell them what to do next.

The quote they had given Emily was way underpriced. They were doing two things. Passing on kindness and showing their desire to be accepted as people that could be trusted. If all went well, they could do more restorations. They weren't worried about people thinking they would always do it for such a low fee. Everyone understood this was a trial run for them.

Once they got into the rhythm of the work, Eli started asking his brother about the box they had found in the wall. "Why would someone leave that there? How old do you think it is? What do you think is in it? Why did Hank take it to his friends? Who are those friends anyway?"

Elliot knew that they didn't have answers to any of his questions, but he was curious, too. As they worked, they bantered about answers they thought might be right. Both of the brothers were romantics, and they made up stories about the letters. Perhaps they were written to someone hoping they would be found someday and be reunited.

They concluded that scenario couldn't be right, because why bury them in a wall? Too hard to find.

Besides, whomever the letters were written to must have died, given that the box had to have been placed there around eighty years ago. They had heard that the chapel was built in the early 1940's. The wall that they had torn down looked like the original wall.

That realization sent them down the pathway of thinking it was a construction worker just like them that had done it. Still fantasizing, they made up a story that since it was a construction worker, and they were construction workers, perhaps they were related. Maybe a long lost relative.

Wishing for a relative, even a long lost one, wasn't new to the brothers. Their mother had never told them about her family. They always got the impression she had run away. Maybe her family didn't like their father. Well, they agreed with that one. They didn't like him either. Whoever he was.

By dinner time the brothers had taken everything out of the bus that needed to be trashed and put it into the construction site's dumpster. They had also run out of ideas for the letters.

They hadn't even started on Eli's question about Hank's friends. But they both harbored a wish that they would become someone that Hank would confide in.

The one question they had left, they left unspoken. Why were they the ones that were there when the box was found? And that question kept a spark burning inside both of them that perhaps, just perhaps, something in that box was meant for them.

Eighteen

After dropping the box off at Ava's, Hank checked on his work crew at Emily's. Since all was going well, and he had a few hours before everyone was meeting at Ava's, he decided to see if Dan had any news on DG.

Hank thought about dropping by the tiny police station behind the town hall but thought better of it. Besides, knowing Dan, he would be out and about the town, assuring people that all was well.

Just as Sam, as ex-FBI, was a strange friend for Hank as an ex-criminal to have, so was Dan. But as they both had told him, with a different upbringing he probably would have ended up in one of their professions. But since he didn't, he brought insight into the minds of people working the dark side of life, which was helpful for them.

When Hank called, Dan was doing what Hank thought he would be doing. Taking care of the small things of town life. He had just finished coaxing a cat out from underneath the porch of one of the elderly residents of Doveland. The cat had been frightened by a dog off its leash. Dan had given the dog's owner a strong warning about the town's leash laws. The next time he would give the owner a ticket.

The owner of the dog had been a ten-year-old boy who felt both honored for being trusted to do right next time and chastised for not paying attention. When Dan reminded him that it was for the dog's protection too, the boy had shaken Dan's hand and told him he would take better care from now on.

Dan was chuckling at the encounter when Hank found him. He was delighted to be interrupted for a meeting with Hank. They decided to meet at the ice cream place out by the lake. It had opened a few weeks early because the weather had warmed up quickly, and the first ice cream of the season sounded good to both of them.

Besides, how bad can things be if the police chief was seen licking an ice cream cone?

Hank told Dan about the box found in the wall, and that they were going to open it and go through the contents together later that day. They both wondered why someone would bury a box in the wall of a chapel, and they came to much the same conclusion that the Stanton brothers did. It was probably either a construction worker or perhaps someone who was watching over the building. That could include a minister, or someone in the town council, who knew the right time to bury it behind the plaster wall.

Talk turned to the search for DG's relatives. Dan had a DNA panel run on him, paid for by Grace, who was determined to find out who he was.

DG wasn't in the system, and so far there were no other matches for him. The two days that Dan had spent traveling to small towns around Doveland to see if anyone recognized him were fruitless. The thing that bothered Dan the most was although DG looked ragged when they found him, he didn't think he had been homeless for long, maybe six months or so.

Until then he had been well fed and well taken care of. Something had caused him to leave home. Among the many unanswered questions was if he headed to Doveland on purpose or stumbled upon it. If Dan had to guess, he would say it was intentional. And maybe picking up on some of the empathic skills of the Stone Circle, Dan said he believed DG knew he was dying and chose to do it in plain sight, hoping someone would figure out what he was doing there, and finish it for him.

Hank nodded in agreement as Dan laid out what he was thinking. Surprisingly it made sense. Something drove a man to leave home and come looking for something. The fact that they had found something at the same time seemed like too big of a coincidence to him. Besides, Hank didn't believe in coincidences. Things didn't happen randomly. There was an order to everything.

However, if DG was about eighty, and the box was buried in the wall when the church was built around 1940, it would have had to happen when DG was a young boy. How would he have known about a box in a wall?

****

When Hank told him that he was going to take the box to Ava's, Lloyd had a moment of anger. Who did Hank think he was? The box belonged to the church after all. Lloyd thought he hid the flash of anger well and he prayed that no one noticed. It was both shameful and dangerous.

Thankfully, his rational mind had kicked in almost immediately, and he pulled the anger back and put it where it belonged. Deep inside. The trouble was, Lloyd thought, keeping it meant it could betray him at any time, and that was something he couldn't afford.

So he tried talking to himself to make it go away or at least stay away until it didn't matter anymore. He reminded himself that the church didn't belong to him any more than it did to Hank. It belonged to the town.

However, as Lloyd knew, it was Ava's friends and family, which included Hank, who were taking care of it, and in that sense, they had more rights than he did. Even though Lloyd was new in town, he knew who the people were that were supporting the town's restoration, and when he wasn't angry he was very grateful.

Lloyd had returned to the church's office to do some quiet work, and to calm himself down. But the office didn't belong to him either. He shared it with other ministers and the rabbi who used it for their services. This community sharing of both the church structure and the essence of a church was what drew him to Doveland in the first place.

At least that is what he had told everyone. There was a bit more to it than that. And that extra bit was what had sparked his anger. However, anger was not going to help him. Patience and support would. Lloyd would trust that Hank would share the results of what they found.

It was very doubtful that anyone would figure out that something in that box was going to point back to him. Besides, he wasn't even sure if there was anything for him in it.

He wasn't expecting to find a box. There was no reason that what he was looking for would be in there. But it might be, and that's what worried him. In the meantime, he would have to trust that if it was there, it would provide the answers that he needed.

Nineteen

Josh scanned the group of students sitting in front of him, wondering if any of them would show enough talent or interest in learning that it would pull him out of his doldrums.

It was hard to tell. The boy slumped in his seat might actually be brimming over with excitement about learning how to write well, or he could be what he looked like, bored, and only taking the class because he had to. The alert young lady in the front row could be pretending, hoping that her attractiveness might earn her a good grade.

There was one bright light though. Josh saw Johnny sitting to the far right of the classroom. *Now that is a kid who has something going for him,* Josh thought.

Josh wasn't sure what it was, but it meant that he would have someone paying attention every day and that could be enough to make teaching the class a pleasure again. However, Josh knew he shouldn't blame the students for the fact that he was not as engaged as he usually was in teaching.

He loved his job, and accepting the position at Penn State was one of the best things he had done for himself in a long while. He had moved to State College to be closer to his grandparents, who had done so much for him that he wanted to repay them somehow. Josh's parents had passed away when he was a teenager. He had made his way on his own for the most part after that, but his mother's parents had made sure he had what he needed. When he told them that he wanted to go to college, but wasn't sure how he could, they helped him pay for his college education. During school holidays, whenever he could, he would come to visit them at their home in State College.

As he got older, he visited them less and less. But they still supported him with little gifts and constant cards of encouragement. Finally, after years of school, he got a teaching job at a little college and with girlfriends and a teaching schedule his visits dwindled to almost nothing.

A few years ago, when Josh discovered that his grandmother wasn't well, and his grandfather was having trouble keeping up with her care, he quit his job and moved into their small home to help. When a teaching position opened up at Penn State, he took it without hesitation. By then he had decided to make State College his home.

Between Josh and his grandfather, they made his grandmother as comfortable as possible, and she repaid them by staying around two years longer than anyone thought she would. Finally, he and his grandfather told her that it was okay for her to go. She had become dependent on others for her care, and as she said, she wasn't having fun anymore.

Once she believed them that they would be okay, she passed away peacefully in her sleep. For the first month after her passing, Joshua and his grandfather roamed the house and gardens barely speaking to each other. Not because they were angry with each other, but because they were afraid to speak. Finally, one morning over breakfast which consisted of coffee and a piece of toast, Josh broke down and told his grandfather how much he missed his grandmother. That broke the barrier. Between them, they shared memories and tears and laughed when they recalled how much fun she had been.

Josh thought that all was well. He enjoyed living with his grandfather. Josh had lost interest in dating and found renewed interest in teaching and writing. He even had begun to write a book about his grandmother's life, plumbing his grandfather's memories since he and his grandmother had known each other since they were children.

To Josh, everything was going well. They had both settled into a life without her, and Josh had even learned to cook. He was halfway through writing his book when his grandfather disappeared.

Joshua tried to think back on what could have happened. Were there warning signs? Did he go by himself or with someone else? Did he go on purpose? His grandfather had not exhibited any symptoms of mental disease. He was still sharp as a tack, remembering the tiniest details of life with his wife and reminding Josh when he forgot something that he was supposed to do.

So, Josh was reasonably sure he had gone on purpose and for a good reason.

It had taken Josh a full day to realize that his grandfather had left. That morning his grandfather had hugged Josh as he headed off to work, and told him he loved him. That wasn't unusual. He often did that. If there was something that gave him away, Josh didn't catch it then, or all the times he had replayed the scene in his mind.

When he got home from teaching, his grandfather wasn't there, but that wasn't unusual. He often went off for walks, or a friend would pick him up, and they would go downtown and have coffee together. That night, Joshua had stopped at the market to buy supplies for his grandfather's favorite dinner of steak and roasted potatoes. Later he was going to see if he wanted to go to the movies together.

When his grandfather hadn't come home for dinner, he started getting worried. He called his cell phone, the one he had pressured him into carrying, but it went to voicemail. Josh had installed an app, Find Friends, on his grandfather's phone but when he searched for his grandfather's location, it showed that he was home.

With a little searching in his grandfather's room, asking his forgiveness as he did so, he found the phone in his grandfather's top drawer of his dresser. His wallet was gone, and one of his jackets.

It was hard to explain to anyone the shock of it. It had knocked Josh right off his feet. Sitting on the floor of his grandfather's room he tried to make sense of it. Why had he gone? Where had he gone? Why hadn't he told him? Was it something he had done?

After calling all of his friends, Josh eventually went to the police station and gave them a picture of his grandfather and asked them to start searching. Although they waited until the next day, they eventually took the time to do a thorough search. But there was no sign of his grandfather anywhere.

Months went by, and each month brought a fresh pain.

One night, to comfort himself, Joshua pulled out a picture album from his grandmother's childhood. He had looked at it countless times with her as she pointed out different people that she had known, and of course pictures of her and his grandfather when they were little kids. Already holding hands.

As he flipped through the pages, he found a completely blank page. He knew there had been pictures there because the rest of the page had faded around four square areas. Who took them out? Was it his grandfather? And if so, why?

Josh thought that if he could only remember what pictures had been on that page, it would give him a clue where his grandfather went.

He missed him so much. All he wanted to do was find him and bring him home. He didn't think that was asking too much of the universe. Six months without him was long enough.

Twenty

The box lay in the center of the table. It was still unopened waiting for everyone to arrive. It had been sitting there all day tempting her.

Every time Ava passed it, she had to fight off the urge to open it and peek inside. Instead, she dusted it and put the rusted and deeply pitted tin box on top of a placemat. She was proud of herself for not looking, and she thought the placemat gave it a feeling of importance.

Finally, Ava, Evan, Hank, Sarah, Grace, Tom, Mira, Sam, and Mandy were seated waiting for the big reveal. Hannah stood behind her mom and Ben played in the living room. Nothing was going to keep Hannah from being part of the opening of the box.

Out of the group, they were missing Craig, Valerie, and Emily. They had begged off, saying that they would catch up with them the next day.

It's just an old box from the church, Emily had said to herself. She didn't say it out loud because she knew the importance her friends were putting on finding it. However, it certainly wasn't the same as finding four dead bodies buried at her hill, as she had the spring before.

Nobody wanted to acknowledge that they were hoping that Leif and Eric would show up. But Leif and Eric had told the group a few weeks before that they couldn't come to visit for a while. The group missed them but understood they had pressing work to do in the dimension where they lived.

Finally, Hank stood and asked if everyone was ready. "Shall I wave a magic wand or something?" he asked jokingly. When everyone waved off his comment, he opened the box and took out the contents one by one and placed them on the table.

There were two letters, a few pictures, and what looked like a deed of some kind.

"I was hoping that these would be readable," Hank said.

Sarah picked up one of the letters and tried to read the writing on the front, but couldn't make out what it said, and there was no return address. The envelope was so brittle that she was afraid to pull out the letter. She tried another letter and had the same problem. She placed them both back on the table and picked up one of the pictures.

It too was faded. But a couple could be seen standing together. The background looked as if it might have been taken by the lake, but it was so hard to make out that Sarah wasn't sure. What looked like a deed appeared even more brittle than the letters, so she left it on the table too afraid to touch it.

"Well, that's a letdown," Hannah said, expressing how everyone else felt.

"It is," Sarah agreed. "The question is, do we think this is important enough to hire an archivist to try and make sense of what we have here? I think if we touch them anymore we might make it worse."

"Absolutely," Ava said. "This piece of paper that looks like a property deed of some kind might be relevant to the town, and of course the letters and the pictures are going to be important to their relatives. That is assuming we can at least read the address and find the family of whoever sent them, or who they were written to."

"Do you think that the person who wrote it hid them, or the person who received them hid them? Or maybe someone else altogether who was trying to keep them apart?" Mira asked.

Tom smiled at his sister's romantic musings. "Well, it is a mystery. And we all love mysteries. Especially the kind where there are no dead bodies, and we don't have to find the murderer."

Everyone laughed and shuddered at the same time, thinking back to the past few years when that was the case.

"I agree," Hank said. "I think we should find out what this box is about. Does anyone know who we can call to do this? I'd be happy to pay for whatever it takes to find the answers."

As everyone nodded agreement to finding out more, Sam spoke up. "I don't know anyone personally, but I am guessing I could find one by going to my old team at the FBI and calling in a favor."

When everyone nodded approval, Sam pulled out his phone and got a yes from his friend. He'd take the box to him the next day.

"Still, it's disappointing," Grace said as she and Ava slipped each document into a separate plastic bag and sealed it so that Sam could take it with him. "I was hoping to have something that would take my mind off of not finding out who DG is."

"Really, Grace? Would it have worked? You need another mystery to take your mind off the one we have? Perhaps this box and DG are related. Did you think of that?" Sarah asked.

Grace looked at her and said, "Wait, so you think they are?"

"Well, I didn't until I said it, but now I am wondering. What's the likelihood that these two mysteries show up at the same time?"

Grace nodded in agreement. "Well, then we might as well add it the mystery of who is the person you are all waiting to add to the Stone Circle so that Suzanne will let you dimension travel.

"That might be stretching it a bit far," Sam said. "Aren't you two just looking for something to do.? Perhaps you're bored. Is the town too quiet?"

"You're right, Sam," Grace said while looping her arm through Sam's. "I am bored. Let's go into the kitchen and see what we can find that's good to eat."

Sarah stayed behind wishing that Leif was there so that she could ask him if they were making connections where there weren't any, just because they were bored.

The idea that she was bored gave her a shock. Perhaps it was time to do something different. Maybe it would be a good idea to take a trip to see Johnny and Edward and the townhouse that Edward had rented.

Her text to Edward was answered within seconds.

"Yes, come. And maybe bring Mandy if she can take the day off? I need design help."

Sarah showed the text to Mandy who agreed it was a great idea. A road trip. A short one for sure, but it would get them out of town, and help them wait out the time until the contents of the box were deciphered. Maybe bring both Edward and Johnny back to town for Mother's Day.

When Mira asked if she could come too, another text confirmed that there was plenty of room as long as they didn't mind sharing a bedroom.

"Let's hope this little road trip doesn't end up like the one we tried to take to see Valerie's husband, Frank," Mira muttered.

The three women shuddered remembering Dr. Joe's trying to

get into their minds to control the car and kill them all.

This trip would be nothing like that. It was a pleasure trip with nothing at stake other than a getaway to visit a friend.

Suzanne sighed as she listened to the group make plans. Although she had been there from the beginning of the conversation, she still wasn't allowing herself to be seen. She was being extremely cautious about letting anyone know that she was visiting the Earth Realm.

Suzanne was worried. Suzanne knew that a ruler of the dimension where she lived was not happy about the Stone Circle. Even though he didn't know who they were, he didn't like interference in his plans to be the only ruler of his realm.

The Forest Circle had slipped into his realm before he was aware that they were a danger. He tolerated them, but he would never want another circle coming and going in what he considered his territory, especially when they were there to thwart his plans.

How far he would go to stop them, Suzanne wasn't sure. But she did know that it was vital that the Stone Circle be completed so that all their power was in place. Until then, she wasn't going to let anyone dimension travel.

Sarah's road trip was a good idea. It would take them one step closer to solving all the mysteries in front of them.

Twenty-One

Hannah wasn't worried about not being able to go on the road trip to see Johnny. She had become quite good at both remote viewing and astral projection because she spent a lot of time practicing them. She used them both, but for different reasons.

If she wanted someone to see her, she astral projected. That's what she used when she visited Johnny, which she was doing much more than her parents would be happy about. But Johnny seemed to like it, which is all that mattered to her.

However, if she just wanted to see what was going on, but not be seen, she remote viewed. Hannah liked the part about not being seen, so she often practiced remote viewing when she was supposed to be sleeping. When she read about something, instead of looking up pictures of it on the internet, she remote viewed it.

Most of the time, no one ever saw her. But once in a while, she ran across someone else who was also remote viewing the same location. It was a rare occurrence, and usually it caused them both to withdraw immediately. Hannah was not ready to meet someone in that way. At least not yet.

However, she loved the story of how Mira and Tom found

each other, so she knew that it could be a good thing. She had heard how Mira was randomly remote viewing and found her brother, Tom, and his friends entirely by accident. Evan was in the room and was able to see her, which led to them all to meeting in Sandpoint, Idaho, where Leif and Sarah had lived at the time.

That was where they were all given their stones, which were supposed to mean something, but not one of them knew what. Hannah had a suspicion that it had something to do with completing the circle.

Evan didn't practice his skills much. In fact, he rarely mentioned them. Hannah thought that perhaps it was like learning anything. If you didn't keep up any skill you once had, it would eventually fade away. For Evan, his family had taken over his life, and as far as Hannah could tell, he was happy about that.

She was happy about that too since he was now her father. She was grateful for all the circumstances that brought her mother and Evan together. Evan was the kind of father every girl wished for, and not many had. He might not be practicing his skills, but he understood that Hannah was someone special and he did everything he could to help her practice her abilities, and learn new ones.

Both of them had discussed the fact that she needed a teacher. Not a regular teacher like at school, or even Emily who taught her dance, but a teacher that could help her practice all the things she knew how to do now, and show her new ones. The ones she knew now were all mental skills, which she was grateful for, but she also wanted to learn how to do things that no one else in the Stone Circle could do. Or if they could, they weren't telling her.

Hannah suspected that Suzanne knew much more than she

told them. She thought that Suzanne and maybe the rest of the Forest Circle knew how to work with nature, and do things like control the weather or do physical things like throw fireballs like the Avengers did in the movies. She knew that they were make-believe in the Earth Realm, but what if they weren't where Suzanne lived?

Hannah had many questions that she wanted to ask Suzanne, but every time she saw her, Suzanne was hiding or thought she was hiding. Because, obviously Suzanne didn't know that Hannah could still see her when no one else could. And Hannah was not going to give her secret away just yet.

Hannah knew there must be a good reason that Suzanne was staying invisible. Since Hannah trusted that Suzanne knew what she was doing, Hannah wasn't going to betray her.

But sooner or later Hannah would have to tell her. And it had to be before Suzanne noticed Hannah watching her. Suzanne would not be happy about it, and that might ruin Hannah's chances to go to the other realm with her.

Hannah wondered about Suzanne. Hardly anyone spoke about her. Probably because they barely knew her. Ava's mother, Abbie, had brought Ava to Suzanne when Abbie knew she was dying, so Ava probably knew her best, but she never talked about their time together.

Hannah thought it was strange that Suzanne had remained such a mystery because she and her husband Jerry were Tom and Mira's parents. All of them had only seen Jerry once in the distance when they met in Sandpoint. Jerry never seemed to travel between dimensions, so he was even more of a stranger to them.

Suzanne and Jerry had given Mira and Tom to different families for adoption, knowing that they would find their way back to each other once they had grown up. They had sacrificed their chance to be a family to protect them.

They had let their children go to keep them safe. In the Earth Realm, Suzanne and Jerry were also skilled at remote viewing and astral projection, like Hannah. However, unlike Hannah who was protected within the Stone Circle, Suzanne and Jerry had been alone and were being hunted by people that wanted to kill them so they couldn't use their gifts.

Suzanne's parents, Earl and Arial Weiland, and her brother Gillian were the other members of the Forest Circle. Gillian had stayed in the Earth Realm to help the Stone Circle for awhile but had eventually gone to join his parents and sister in the Forest Circle.

Hannah was beside herself with curiosity about the other realm. She wanted to travel there more than she had ever wanted anything before. It was why she was so diligent at practicing her skills. She knew it gave her more of a chance to be allowed to go when they were ready. That could be any day.

They had to find the other person to complete the circle, or he had to find them. With all her skills, Hannah had no idea who he was, only that he was near.

Twenty-Two

Mandy said she wanted to drive, and Sarah—who didn't like driving all that much—and Mira happily agreed.

For the first hour of the trip, they listened to music that Mira had on her phone. She had picked the Traveling Wilburys thinking that it was perfect for a road trip. Sarah agreed. She was a huge fan of Roy Orbison.

They sang along and laughed together, and when it was over, Mira looked over at Mandy and asked, "Do you ever think about the fact that if you and Tom ever got around to getting married, we would officially be sisters?"

"Well. Where did that come from? How long have you been thinking about this?"

"A while. I always wanted a sister, and then you came along and felt like one right away. And then you started dating my brother, and, I don't know, I kind of wish it was official. Besides wouldn't it be lovely to have another wedding? It's been a few years since Ava and Evan got married. I think we are due for a wedding! And you could design such a beautiful one. The perfect wedding. Sam and I could make a wedding cookbook, and use your wedding as the pictures.

"This is a fantastic idea!" Mira gushed on, happy with herself for coming up with the idea.

"Holy cow, Mira. What has come over you? Of course, we are sisters. We don't need a wedding to prove it. Besides what about you and Sam? What's up with that? Are you two ever going to get married?"

Mira looked out the window and took a big breath before answering. "Sam keeps asking me when, and I keep holding back. I have been single for so long that I'm not sure what kind of wife I'll be."

"Don't make me pull off the road, Mira. What do you mean what kind of wife you will be? What are you thinking? Do you think that getting married means you have new roles? The two of you have been living together. Do you have husband and wife roles now? Of course not. What's this nonsense about changing because you are married?

"And just so you know, yes, your brother keeps asking me about when do I want to get married, and I keep stalling too. Even though I have no intention of taking up a wife role, I also worry about being single for so long. What will it feel like to be not single?"

Mira started laughing. "Listen to us. Single? We aren't single. We've been living with these men for a few years. That's not single. Neither one of us thinks there is anyone else for us. At least I don't, and I don't think you do either.

"I think we are stalling because we are afraid we won't get it right. What do you think, Sarah?"

In the back seat, Sarah smiled at the two of them. She knew that sooner or later Mira and Mandy would have this conversation. Sarah thought back on her years of being married to Leif before answering.

"Of course, there are practical reasons for being married when you know you have found the perfect person. You have legal rights. That counts for quite a bit. But then there is also the sweetest sound when you say, my husband. I wouldn't trade saying that for anything."

Mira and Mandy looked at each other and burst out laughing. "What will the boys think happened on the trip when we call them and tell them we're ready?" Mira asked.

"They'll say that Sarah must have done something to both of us," Mandy answered. Looking in the rearview mirror, she added, "And they'd be right. Thank you, Sarah."

Sarah smiled at them both and then sat back to enjoy their chatter as they planned their weddings. The first decision was to have the weddings together. No point in gathering everyone twice. The second decision was where to have it. That didn't take long. The Chapel had become the place they celebrated. The reception would be at Ava and Evan's.

"One thing," Sarah added from the back seat. "You might want to have this wedding before people start traveling between dimensions."

Mira didn't need to ask why. She picked up her phone and called the woman who managed the dates for weddings at the Chapel and asked her what the soonest open time was.

The woman said that a couple had changed their mind, and now June 8th was open. If Mira wanted that date, she could have it. Mira said yes, and asked her to keep it a secret until they had a chance to tell everyone in the family. Mira knew how fast gossip spread. Sam and Tom could hear about it before they got a chance to call them.

"Okay, we're on for a month from now. June 8th. We can do it, can't we, Mandy?"

"With all the help we'll get, I believe we can. However, did you realize that is the same date as Ava and Evan's wedding?"

"Do you think they'll mind sharing it with us?"

"Mind? I think Ava will think it is the best idea we ever had."

The rest of the trip was filled with ideas and planning. Mira kept notes as Mandy drove, and Sarah wrote down things that needed to be done. Mira and Sam often catered weddings, so of course, they would cater their own. They would ask Pete and Barbara to oversee the serving at the wedding though.

Neither woman called their future husbands yet. Sarah knew that they were waiting to talk to them privately. But Ava was called, and as Mandy predicted, she squealed over the idea that they would share a wedding date, and she promised to keep it a secret until they told Tom and Sam.

"We have one big problem though, Sarah," Mandy said. "It would be wonderful to have Leif marry us the way he married Evan and Ava, but since not everyone will be able to see him, that doesn't seem like a good idea. Imagine what they would think if they saw us up there talking to nobody."

Mira started giggling at the thought and then looking at Mandy she knew where she was going.

"So Sarah, could you do it? Would you marry us, please?" Mira asked as Mandy nodded agreement.

Sarah could barely speak as the gratitude for what they asked welled up inside of her.

"I couldn't be happier or more proud," was her answer.

By the time they pulled into the parking lot of Edward's new townhouse, all three of them were vibrating with excitement.

Edward opened the door to three women who were the most radiant women he had ever seen.

"Good God, ladies. That must have been some trip!"

"Oh, it was!" Mandy answered, "Wait until we tell you about it, but first we both have to make a phone call."

As he watched the two women head to separate rooms,

Edward turned to Sarah and said, "So they decided to say yes?"

"Edward," Sarah answered, "All those years of running from your father and studying people have made you a very wise man.

"I am not sure I told you before how grateful we are that you came back, and now for taking such a huge interest in Johnny. We are all so much better off because you are here."

Overcome with emotion, Edward reached out to hug Sarah, and whispered, "Thank you." Those words said it all for both of them.

Twenty-Three

When Mira and Mandy told Edward the news, he reacted as if he hadn't guessed. Then he asked if he could help throw the two men a party. Maybe a guys' weekend together?

"In fact," he said, "Maybe we could have it here."

"What?" Mira said, "A guys' sleepover?"

"Sure, why not. It would give us all a chance to talk."

When Mira and Mandy stared at Edward at the idea that guys would talk, Sarah started laughing. "Obviously you two haven't noticed a fundamental fact of life," she said.

"Let me give you the news. Men talk. More than women. Think about it. When you see a western movie, who is sitting around on the porch, talking. Women? I think not.

"Have you ever watched a construction crew, or a road crew, or anywhere that men are working together? Have you seen the clumps of men gathered together? What do you think they are doing? Talking.

"Now, what they talk about is another thing, and that may be why you haven't noticed this fact of life. They talk about their toys, guns, hunting, fishing, food, fixing things, politics, motors, and women.

"That is, of course, a generalization, but listen to them

sometime. Men talk at bars, on porches, at jobs, at work sites, but maybe not so much at home.

"I think the reason it takes a while to notice this is because women are busy. They are working, running homes, raising children. No time to spend hours talking. They grab time when they can, but it's not an everyday occurrence."

Seeing Mandy and Mira's face as the realization of what Sarah had said started dawning on them. They both turned to Edward, and Mandy asked, "This is true?"

Edward laughed and said, "This is true."

Shaking their heads at the revelation, Mira and Mandy plopped down on the couch together. Mira finally found her voice, "Okay. We'll check with the guys and see if they want to drive here to have your guy sleepover. Might be nice, Johnny could come too."

"And a new guy I met," Edward added. "I think he'll fit right in with everyone. He's one of Johnny's teachers. We've had coffee a few times. He helped me find this place."

The three women looked at each other, all of them thinking that here was another new man. Was this the man that would complete the stone circle?

After everyone settled into their rooms, Sarah decided to go for a walk. Mira wanted to hang out on the balcony, enjoy the view that took in Beaver Stadium where Penn State football was played, and read a book.

Mandy and Edward were already busy measuring rooms and talking colors and furniture styles. Mandy was in design heaven, and Edward was enjoying every moment of her attention.

He hadn't thought of it before because the purchase had moved so quickly, but this was the first time he had ever bought something where he could live forever if he wanted to, although that hadn't been his intention. His intention was to have a place for him, and the rest of Johnny's friends and family, to stay when they came to visit. Watching Mandy measure and listening to her ideas brought tears to his eyes. This was his home. His. He wasn't running anymore.

Sarah noticed his face change as he watched Mandy and smiled at him. He had changed so much from the first time he had come to town as Dr. Joe's son. Edward had done it even though he wasn't at all sure if anyone would accept him, and he knew that his father would try to kill him once he knew his son was back in town.

No longer tense, always looking around to see if there was any danger, Edward was relaxed and happy. He had found a half-sister in Valerie, and nephews in Johnny and Lex. For Edward, this was a dream come true. A dream he had never dared to imagine.

The chance to do something wonderful for the men in Doveland who had saved him and brought him into their circle, was so exciting that he had to remind himself to pay attention. Mandy was here now, designing for him. Only him. The way he wanted his life and home to be.

Impulsively he hugged Mandy stopping her words in mid-stream. "Thank you," he said, his voice clogged with emotion. Mandy understood how he felt. She had been like him just a few years before. She turned to hug him back, kissed him on his cheek and said, "This is my honor, Edward, now come on, we have work to do." Pulling him by the hand, Mandy dragged him into the kitchen to discuss wall color.

The last thing Sarah heard before she went out the door was a discussion of what kind of sink Edward should get for the kitchen. Mandy was doing a great job of convincing him that what he wanted was a large farmer's sink.

Sarah wondered if Edward understood that he might as

well say yes to whatever Mandy suggested because she would be right. She suspected that Edward knew that already.

They had already made a dinner date with Johnny, so Sarah knew where to meet them in a few hours. Actually, only Edward had made the date with Johnny. The three women were keeping their visit a secret. They wanted to see Johnny's face when he showed up for dinner and found them there.

After looking on her phone for a trail that would take her into town, Sarah set off following the GPS instructions. She knew it would take a few hours because she planned to dawdle and enjoy herself.

The sky was a robin egg blue, with a few fluffy clouds making their way across the sky. Birds were singing spring songs and flitting from tree to tree. She had on a light jacket because there was still a chill in the air, but with the sun shining she knew she would warm up soon.

She planned to make her first stop the Penn State Arboretum. She had heard fantastic things about it, and sitting in a garden sounded like a perfect place to collect her thoughts and listen for guidance.

She had a question to ask, and since there didn't appear to be anyone around who could answer it for her, she would have to find it within herself. Sarah was hoping that a quiet garden, one she had never seen before, would open up new ideas and channels of listening.

In the meantime, the feel of walking on her own, fanny pack around her waist, filled her with contentment. At the moment, life was perfect, and that was what she planned to revel in for the next few hours.

Twenty-Four

The three women got their wish. Johnny was as surprised as they wanted him to be. They met for dinner at The Tavern near the three bronze pigs. While waiting for him, they played with the pigs.

Mira had to contain herself because she thought that even though the pigs already had names, she was going to call the mama pig, Sarah and she and Mandy would be the baby pigs. At least for the time being. *Maybe it will catch on*, she thought.

To confirm her intention to share the pigs' new names, she had Edward take a picture of the three of them sitting on their personal pig. All three of them laughed hard enough they had to hold on to the pigs' ears to keep from falling off.

After playing with the pig sculpture, they waited in the restaurant for Johnny. When he walked in the door, they popped up and yelled, "Surprise!"

As soon as he got over the shock of seeing them, Johnny hugged each one separately over and over again, and couldn't stop saying, "I can't believe you came to see me!"

It was only after the hugs were over and the hostess had come to seat them, that Johnny realized he had forgotten to introduce his teacher.

When the women yelled surprise, Josh was as astonished as Johnny. But he knew that they weren't there for him, so he faded back and watched the interaction with growing delight. He had no idea who the women were but suspected that they were friends of Johnny's mother and were all from Johnny's hometown.

If they are all this friendly, maybe I should visit, he thought to himself. He hung back and waited, knowing that Johnny would eventually remember he was there. Edward had caught his eye when they walked in, and was also hanging back watching the hugs. Edward winked at Josh, and the two of them waited to see what would happen.

It was Sarah who took control. She had watched Josh come in with Johnny and then step back while the rest of them exchanged hugs.

When the hostess came to seat them, Sarah reached out to Josh and said, "You're Johnny's teacher, aren't you? I'm Sarah, and this is Mira and Mandy."

"Oh dang it!" Johnny said, "I was so excited to see all of you I forgot to introduce. I'm sorry, Josh. I mean Mr. Baines."

Josh laughed and shook Sarah's hand, and said, "It's Josh when we are not in the classroom, Johnny. And I can completely understand how you could forget me when you have these three lovely ladies fawning all over you."

Johnny blushed beet red, grateful for the chance to follow the hostess to their seat.

The meal was a complete success. As Edward had predicted, Josh fit right in. Johnny apologized for not letting them know he had invited his teacher, but then he had thought it would be just Edward and he knew the two of them were friends.

"Well, now we are all friends, Johnny," Mandy said.

"How long are you staying?" Josh asked.

"Just tonight," Mandy answered. "We all are playing a form of hooky and need to get back. But, maybe we could convince the three of you to come to visit over the weekend.

"It's Mother's Day, Johnny. This time you could surprise her. Edward and I could do some more planning on his home, and Josh, you could meet the rowdy and strange group we have."

"If they are all like the five of you, I'm in," Josh answered.

"If you mean, are we all fabulous, friendly, and gifted?" Mira said, "Then yes."

"And humble," Mandy added.

"Definitely humble," Edward replied. "No matter what they tell you, you will never know how amazing they are."

Johnny looked at Edward, and nodded in agreement, thinking about all the town of Doveland had done for them both.

The three women blushed and looked back to their food.

"Well, there appears to be more than meets the eye here, so now I am even more intrigued. So, sure. Why not?"

"Oh, cool!" Johnny said. "Wait until I introduce you to everyone at home! He can stay with you at the bunkhouse, can't he, Uncle Edward?"

"That's a great idea. We just need to make sure Ava hasn't rented out the place for the weekend."

"She hasn't," Sarah said. "She said she's looking forward to meeting Josh, and she promises to keep Johnny's arrival a secret."

When no one questioned how Sarah already knew the answer to the question when no phone calls had been made, and they had just decided to visit, Josh spoke up.

"Am I supposed to understand how you did that?" Josh asked.

"No. And even when you do know how she did that, you might still not understand it," Edward answered, as all three women smiled at him.

Johnny watched, wondering if he was doing the right thing, introducing his teacher to the Karass community. But Sarah hadn't stopped him and seemed to be supporting the decision, so he figured that it must be okay.

However, it worried him a little bit. What would Josh think of him once he got a taste of what they could do?

Johnny also knew they were looking for the final person to complete the Stone Circle. Did they think Josh might be that person and that's why they wanted him to visit? Did they know that he knew they were looking to complete the Stone Circle?

It was Hannah who kept him informed. He didn't know why she felt as if he should know, but he was grateful that she did. He had started to become a little bit more comfortable with her appearing to him as a projection.

Maybe it was because now she "asked" him somehow in his mind if it was okay, before showing up. He always said yes out loud, but she told him that wasn't necessary. Just say so by thinking about it.

Johnny wasn't all that happy about the fact that she could appear in his mind, but she had promised that she didn't go deep or listen to his thoughts. That would be more like a phone call when what she was doing was a quick text.

That analogy kind of made sense to him. Besides, Hannah was spending time teaching him how to keep his mind closed. Not answer the phone, or open the door, so to speak. She also used the analogy of covering the camera of your computer when not using it. "Do the same thing in your mind," she had said.

"Why?" Johnny had asked. "You promised not to come in without permission."

"That's true," Hannah said, "But other people are always trying to get inside your thinking. Color your perception. Make you see the world their way. Confuse you. Distract you. You have to learn not to let them in, whether they mean harm or just don't know better."

"Do a lot of people do this?" Johnny had asked.

"The world does this," Hannah had answered.

For a twelve-year-old, Hannah is amazingly smart, Johnny thought. He was grateful that she had chosen him as her friend, and was teaching him things his school could never teach him.

Watching Josh talking to his friends, Johnny had a feeling that everything was falling into place somehow. What that meant, he wasn't sure. Maybe Hannah would know. He'd see her for real in a few days and ask her then.

Twenty-Five

Mandy and Mira's phone calls had sent Tom and Sam into a tailspin. They had both hoped that someday the women would say yes, but in many ways, they had each resigned themselves to the fact that they were in love with independent, self-sufficient women. The fact that they were loved back was enough, they had told themselves.

But the phone calls had disproved that theory.

Tom had hung up the phone and surprised himself by collapsing on the couch crying in relief. Even though Mandy had assured him over and over again that he was her one and only, watching her become more and more sure of herself and bloom out into the world had scared him. Tom wanted her to succeed more than he wanted anything for himself, which is why he had kept his worries to himself. At least most of the time. It was why he had hidden his drawing, afraid that his doing something new would separate them.

Perhaps it was because right after he and his twin sister were born and he had been separated from both his parents and sister, that separation anxiety sometimes popped up and disturbed his happiness. In fact, looking back he realized that he had exhibited separation anxiety all his life.

He was the child that cried when his adoptive mother left the room. He was the boy that went home after school to make sure the two people that adopted him were still there.

He was the young man who had to be convinced that going away to college would be a good thing. His adoptive parents promised him that they would be there when he came home to visit, and they always were. Until they weren't, dying in a car accident after he finished school.

Until his sister Mira had found him, he had been alone. By choice, he knew. But he was afraid of getting too attached and then losing again.

Yes, he had his group of friends doing good in the world, but in many ways, it was how he kept loneliness at bay. It was why when he followed Mira to Sarah and Leif, he had been angry and confused.

Now years later, with friends who would never leave him, and a-soon-to-be wife that he had let himself love in spite of all his fears, it was almost more than he could take.

The fact that Mandy cried on the phone with him when she told him yes, confirmed for him that she too was healing the piece of herself that in the past had led her down roads of unhappiness. She had been even more unlucky. Wonderful parents never adopted her. She had lived her young life in foster homes, abused and unhappy.

As soon as she could escape, she did, right into the dangerous world of being an escort for unethical men. She was losing hope that there would be any other life for her, until one day she made friends with a sixteen-year-old runaway named Ava.

When Ava became pregnant by the man who owned Mandy, Mandy was the one who watched over the child when Ava gave her up for adoption. Unknown to Ava, the child was adopted by the father and his wife. When the man died, and his wife didn't want the little girl, Mandy took her in. It was Mandy who found the little girl's grandfather, Eric.

Eric had rescued and adopted Ava's mother, Abbie, when her older brother had left her in the clinic where Eric worked. With no father or mother, Hank thought that Abbie would be better off with Eric.

In that, he had been correct. Eric loved and cherished Abbie. When Abbie died, he was devastated. Ava went to live with Abbie's friend Suzanne, and Eric and Ava lost touch.

When Mandy found Eric and brought him Ava's child, the two of them kept her safe until Ava came looking for her daughter, Hannah.

We have all found each other through a long roundabout circle, but worth every moment of the journey, Tom thought.

As he silently cried on the couch, Tom waited for the next phone call, probably from Sam. Instead, it was a knock on the door. Not a knock. A pounding. Opening the door, Tom found a joyous Sam dancing on the threshold. Sam, who was always calm and collected, burst into the room almost knocking Tom over in the process.

They hugged each other and almost threw each other around the room in their exuberant joy. It was then that Tom realized he was receiving even more than he thought. He had a brother. It was unbelievable. Beyond what Tom ever thought possible for himself.

Although he and Sam were friends, it was at that moment that Tom realized he knew next to nothing about Sam's past. Sam had always been the man that brought the cavalry.

Disguised as a chef, he had saved the Karass circle from Grant, who wanted to destroy them because of their gifts. Sam always found out the things that they needed to know.

Sam was the one that captured the evil men and kept them away from Doveland.

Sam had saved them over and over again, and now they were brothers.

The realization was so intense that Tom started crying again. Sam took one look at him and picked him up and spun him around.

"Happiness! I know what you mean," Sam said.

Putting Tom down, they faced each other with tears streaming down their cheeks and high fived each other.

A few beers later they were still high fiving each other. Sitting on Tom's back deck that he built specifically for a going away party for Johnny, they stared off at the beauty surrounding them.

"We've come a long way, haven't we, Tom?" Sam said.

"And I bet that we have a long way to go. But we get to travel with friends," Tom said.

"And brothers," Sam said, as they clicked the bottles together.

Suzanne smiled to herself as she watched the two men. She had indulged herself and allowed herself the visit. Suzanne needed to see happiness in action.

Where she and the Forest Circle lived, things were getting worse. The need for members of the Stone Circle to join them was becoming more than a friendly visit. It was becoming a necessity.

But there was nothing she or anyone else could do to speed up the process. Everything was moving into place, one piece at a time.

With one last glance at the two happy men, Suzanne faded away thinking how delighted Leif and Eric would be to find out that there would be two more weddings.

All of them would do their best to make sure the weddings were peaceful and as beautiful as the people involved wanted them to be.

They would do everything they could not to let the danger from their realm seep into this dimension.

Twenty-Six

Emily watched the Stanton brothers work on the van. They had shown her the plans, and she couldn't be happier with what they were doing. Every row of seats was going to be a different color. She could already imagine people choosing the color they wanted to sit on based on how they wanted to feel that day. Even the driver would have a different colored seat.

Emily had no idea how they were going to manage colored seats, but the Stanton brothers said they had it under control. It was something she would never have thought to ask for. They had come up with the design all on their own. When everything inside was finished, they would take the van into town to get it spray painted. After that, they would have the logo she had designed applied on the sides.

After everyone started calling her art retreat, Emily's Hill, Emily decided to stick with that name and the logo included a stylized version of the hill. She also had a sign designed that said, Melvin's Bus. That would be the finishing touch. If she ended up having other buses, she wanted to be sure that they named the first one after Melvin.

Just thinking about Melvin brought tears to her eyes. Everyone missed him, but she knew that she, Hank, and

Hannah missed him the most. He had adopted the three of them as his family, providing them with all the warmth and wisdom she could ever hope to get from a grandfather.

As she looked out over her hill, she knew Melvin would approve. The additional buildings looked just as she had imagined them. Shawn's music building was finished enough for him to start getting it ready for the students he would have this summer.

Shawn had hired Lex to help him with design ideas. Emily was grateful for Shawn taking Lex under his wing this way. Valerie had talked about her son to Shawn and suggested that he might be a mentor to Lex. She knew that Lex's world was going to look different than most men's, and he would need a guide. Emily thought about how wise Valerie was, getting Lex to help and not keeping him away from a supportive community.

Sam and Mira had Lex as part of their crew too. He helped serve at parties when it was appropriate and sometimes helped make food. Pete and Barbara's courses for young chefs were going well, and so far Lex still claimed that a chef was what he wanted to be when he grew up.

Emily knew plans changed. Hers certainly had. She was going to give up her dream of an art retreat until her mother left her money and told her that it was to build her dream. Now, she would be able to encourage art, in all its forms, in every child.

Emily had ended up asking Violet, a woman who taught art in the middle school, if she was available to teach art this summer for her. Emily would have preferred someone new so the children would have a fresh outlook, but this was better than nothing. Besides, Violet said she had lots of new ways to teach since she wasn't as restricted at Emily's Hill as she was inside the school system.

That meant Emily only had to find a writing teacher. She

could always get one from the regular school the same way she got Violet, but she wanted to find someone new. Emily had written to a few people to ask if they were free for a few weeks in the summer, but so far no one was open, or they didn't like that it was for such a short time and so far out of the city.

Still wondering what she was going to do, Emily walked down the hill a bit, past the buildings to the rock that had been her favorite spot before any of the buildings existed.

It was the perfect place to dream, plan, and trust that everything would work out. Despite considerable bumps in the road to what Emily had now, it had all worked out, much better than she could have ever expected. She would have to trust that the right person would show up, in the right time, and would be even more than she hoped for, just as everything else had turned out to be.

****

Thirty minutes later, Emily watched Hank's truck make its way up the long driveway. Hank stopped to talk to the Stanton brothers before making his way down to her rock. They had sat together on the rock many times over the past few years. Sometimes just taking in the view, other times talking over the evil that had been Dr. Joe, Edward and Valerie's father.

It had proved to them both that everyone had a choice to make about who they would become. Edward and Valerie, and even Johnny and Lex, had confirmed that the power of goodness could overcome a heritage or bloodline. Hank too had proved that he wasn't his father or the troubled and dangerous boy he had once been.

"Those two are hard workers," Hank said as he took a seat beside Emily. "A full day's work at the Chapel and they still came here to work on your van. I'm impressed. I think I'll have them teach restoration to the kids who come to The Barn."

"That is such a wonderful program that you and Melvin began."

They both fell silent thinking about Melvin until Emily asked Hank if he had heard anything about the papers in the box. Even though she hadn't been there when they opened the box, the more she heard about what was in it, the more curious she had become.

"No news yet. Sam did get the papers to a friend he used to work with at the FBI. She seemed to think that it would be possible to pull some information off of them, hopefully enough to find out if the deed means anything, and get the letters to the right family."

"It is likely that the family is someone here in Doveland, isn't it? Otherwise, why hide them in Doveland's church? But then why hide them period. Perhaps whoever it was wasn't supposed to have the deed and letters so they hid them until they could get them later, and then something happened that meant they couldn't," Emily said.

"Ah, another romantic, I see," Hank said. "But you are probably right. At least part of it. Sarah seems to think that the box is related to DG. I hope so. We still have no idea who he is, and now that so much time has gone by, I'm afraid he'll be forgotten."

Emily reached over and took Hank's hand. "I promise we won't forget him. We found my aunt, didn't we? And she was missing for over forty years. We can definitely find someone who has only been missing for a few months."

Hank patted Emily's hand. As far as he was concerned, she was the daughter he never had. She was right. He had been found too. Found by his niece and given a chance at this life.

They would all do the same thing for DG and his family. And for the people the papers in the box impacted. They would find them. Hopefully, it would bring them the same peace that Hank had found.

Twenty-Seven

The three women arrived back in Doveland just in time for lunch. They had hugged Edward goodbye, thanked him for his hospitality, told them that they would see him, Johnny, and Josh in a few days, and then drove as quickly as possible back home to share the news of the upcoming weddings.

By the time they got to Your Second Home, Mandy and Mira were almost exploding with anticipation. They practically ran into the store to find Grace and anyone else they could to hug.

Sarah laughed at the two of them as they twirled Grace around the room. Grace did her best to look dignified while spinning in circles. Finally coming to a stop, they explained why they were so happy. Grace said she could have guessed it by herself. What else would they be so excited about?

Luckily Grace had just hired a young man and woman to work at the shop on a temporary basis. It was a test to see if they liked it enough to stay. It was perfect timing that they were both working that day because Mandy was going to drag Grace next door to the Diner for lunch, customers or not. Grace was delighted. It gave her a chance to see how well the new help did on their own.

At the Diner, Mandy and Mira swept Barbara up into their joy and Pete gave them each a hug saying he thought it was the best idea they ever had. Finally, when they were calm enough to eat, Pete brought them all their favorite lunch before they even had to look at the menu.

"What if I had wanted something different this time, Pete?" Sarah asked as he put her favorite sandwich in front of her along with her new favorite drink, diet Dr. Pepper.

"I would have known," Pete answered.

Sarah looked up into Pete's kind face and wise eyes and said, "I believe you, Pete."

As Grace and Sarah listened to Mandy and Mira tell Barbara about their wedding plans, Sarah and Grace looked at each other in understanding. A big wedding was something neither one of them had ever experienced.

Both of them had chosen to marry quietly.

Leif and Sarah were married long before they had met all the people they now called their friends. It had been a simple wedding with just the two of them, and it had been more than enough.

Grace and Eric had married only a few years before, having met late in life. They had snuck away on a Saturday with Hannah in the back seat and headed off to their private wedding. Hannah had come along because she had figured out what they were doing and demanded to be part of the ceremony. Of course they pretended to capitulate to her demands, but in reality, they were delighted to have her with them.

Grace leaned in and asked Sarah, "Is there a reason for such a rushed wedding?"

But before Sarah even had time to answer, Grace understood. "Oh. The Stone Circle and dimension traveling. You thought this needed to happen before the circle was complete, didn't you? Are you still planning to learn how to become a dimension traveler?"

"Yes to all that. Especially yes to learning how. At first it started as a whim to see if it was possible. I wanted to be with Leif, and he is more there than he is here. But now it seems that I have to go. It's a different feeling altogether.

"Of course, this time the plan is to be able to come back and forth with our physical bodies, not as Leif and Eric and Suzanne do, being ghost-like in this dimension. At least I hope that is what happens.

"Suzanne said they have learned how to shift between the two dimensions now and be in your physical body in both places. Not at the same time, of course.

"But that will be better than turning into something like a ghost the way they all do now. Wouldn't it have been nice if they had figured it out before? Then when Leif and Eric were here, we could actually hug them."

"And Tom and Mira could hug their mother too," Grace added.

The two of them had been whispering so that the rest of the diners couldn't hear them, but Mandy heard the last few words and turned her attention to Sarah and Grace.

"Here we are prattling on about the wedding, and there you two are working on something that will change Sarah's life too. Are you scared, Sarah?"

Sarah thought about how to answer and decided that lying about it wasn't what anyone needed, so she replied, "Yes. I am. And excited. And worried. There is nothing I can do about those things except to accept that I feel them and keep going.

"However, I am also hungry, and I can do something about that!" Picking up her Portobello burger, she took a huge bite as everyone laughed and dug into their own food.

Behind the counter, Alex leaned into Pete and asked, "Wedding plans?"

"Wedding plans," Pete answered. "We better get ready. It's going to be a busy month. Sam already called and said that we would be helping with the catering. Makes sense, he won't want to be working his wedding."

Looking around the crowded diner, he added, "And now it is a busy lunch, and it's just you and me until Barbara is done eating."

As Pete turned to watch Alex work as fast as he could, Pete asked, "Have you found anyone else who is at least half as good as you yet, Alex? We could use the help."

"Not yet, but I'm working on it," he said as he flipped two burgers and turned the fries. He also had two slices of pizza cooking in the pizza oven. The oven was a great idea but increased their workload. He was going to suggest to Pete to offer pizza only at night. It might improve their dinner business, and give him a break at lunch.

As he worked, Alex glowed, hearing those words of praise. He hadn't planned to be a cook in a Diner, but right now, there was nowhere else he would rather be. The job was okay. It was the people who made it fantastic.

Twenty-Eight

Lloyd dropped his son Jake off at school instead of sending him on the bus. He thought it would give Jake a bit of a head start on the day. It worried Lloyd that Jake didn't appear to be fitting in at school even though they had been in Doveland for over three months. Lloyd knew that sometimes it takes a while to adjust to new schools, but he thought that Jake would be doing better by now.

Instead, he came home more morose every day. Lloyd remembered when his son was a sparkling light. Everyone who knew him wanted to be his friend. Now Jake struggled to manage a fake smile every morning at the breakfast table. Even Jake's favorite pancake breakfast didn't bring a genuine smile anymore.

Lloyd knew he couldn't blame it all on the move and a new school. It's what happened before they moved.

His wife Julianne's decline had been fast. One day someone offered her a pill for a persistent backache, and within months she was hooked. Nothing Lloyd or even Jake tried helped her at all. She went from supporting Lloyd and his ministry to hating him, the house, and in the end, even Jake. Lloyd knew it wasn't personal, but that didn't stop his, or Jake's, pain or despair.

Explaining it to Jake didn't help much either, but it did help them continue to stand together in their sorrow.

Lloyd explained to Jake that it was her addiction driving every part of his mother to feed it. Anything that got in the way of it was something to push away, steal from, and finally hate because it represented a past she no longer wanted. But that wasn't his mother. It was the addiction. When she was free from it, she would act like his mom again.

They both prayed together to have it stop. Lloyd and Jake went to meetings, where they learned what they were supposed to do to help her. They got ideas to use to help them to cope. Nothing worked, and Jake got more and more sullen and withdrawn.

Lloyd had hoped that perhaps he and Jake would draw together during this time, but instead Jake withdrew from everyone. Finally, Lloyd did what he needed to do. They moved and didn't tell Julianne where they were going. Lloyd assured himself that he wasn't abandoning his wife. He was giving his son a chance to heal. When Julianne got better, he would find her, and they would reunite.

He noted mentally that he still said to himself, "when she gets better." He held hope. A flicker of it, but it was still there. However, in the meantime, he had to take care of himself and Jake, and the move to Doveland came at the perfect time.

More perfect than anyone else would know. Lloyd had wanted the Doveland assignment for years. Even before he met Julianne, he wanted to be a minister at the Chapel in Doveland. Yes, he could have just moved there on his own, but then he wouldn't have been the minister that his church chose, and access to the church would have been harder.

Lloyd took it as a sign that all that he wanted was finally coming together. Now he was where he wanted to be. The problem was, Lloyd had less access than he imagined that he would. Did he expect that he would walk in, look through the files, and find what he was looking for? Well, it didn't turn out that way. Instead, he discovered that many of the old records had been stored in the town hall basement and then the basement flooded years before, destroying all the files before 1999.

The day that they found the box in the church wall both thrilled him and terrified him. However, since Hank had immediately taken the box away, there was no way to find out if what Lloyd was looking for was in there. Now it was days later, and still nobody had told him anything.

Which is why after taking Jake to school, Lloyd was going to the Diner. Lloyd knew, like everyone else in Doveland knew, that Hank Blaze almost always ate breakfast at the Diner. He was going to confront Hank and find out what was happening.

Lloyd knew a little of Hank's redemption story. But even what he knew amazed him. How could a man turn from that kind of childhood, and live the life of a gangster working for a psychopath, and turn that around to find the love and honor that he now held?

Hank's family loved him, the town respected him, and he was a key figure in almost anything of importance that happened in town. It gave Lloyd hope that it was possible for him to find that kind of redemption, too. Not as much for him, but for a past that had haunted him and his family.

****

When the bell dinged, Hank looked up and saw Lloyd standing inside the door looking for a seat. He waved his hand and gestured to the empty stool beside him. Lloyd smiled to himself thinking that it was luck that the stool was empty and that Hank had seen him first.

Of course, this ability of Hank's to notice others and reach out to them is probably one of the reasons he is so beloved, Lloyd thought to himself. He knew it was not easy to keep from falling into self-doubt, or guilt, and then block out the needs of others.

Somehow Hank had managed to do this. With all the things he had seen and done, Hank still found the good in life. Lloyd hoped that when all this was over, Hank would be one of his friends. But Lloyd wasn't sure it would work out that way. Being a minister and all, you'd think he would know how to pray about it, but so far that hadn't been that successful.

Hank watched Lloyd paste a smile on his face and make his way over to the counter. He wondered what Lloyd's story was because something was happening that was creating a simmering anger beneath the surface. Hank understood that anger. He had grown up with it. Now he was growing out of it, or at least he hoped he was. Maybe Lloyd would too.

The two men exchanged small talk while waiting for their food to arrive. Lloyd ordered the same breakfast as Hank figuring Hank knew what was best. Then once it came, eating took over for a few minutes.

Finally, Lloyd asked what he had come to ask. What was happening with the box?

Hank slapped his forehead. "I'm an idiot. I should have told you. Nothing yet. We opened it. There were two letters, a few pictures, and some kind of property thing. But none of it was readable. Sam sent it off to a friend at the FBI to see if they could pull any more info off it."

Lloyd tried hard not to react. However, he felt like he was going to faint, so he made himself cough which brought himself back to his body.

But Hank who had felt Lloyd's reaction, pulled back and looked at him, not sure if he should say anything or not. He decided to wait and see what Lloyd would say.

He didn't need to wait long. Lloyd asked, "Property thing, like a deed?"

"Probably, but it was so old it wasn't written like a deed we would recognize, and it's almost unreadable, so we have no idea what it's for. Hopefully, there will be enough info to read it soon. Do you have an idea what it is?"

"No. No," Lloyd answered. "It just seems like a rather cool mystery that might mean the world to someone if it could be read."

"Could be important," Hank agreed. To himself, Hank thought, "Ah, got you now. Wonder what's up with that deed. I'll ask Sam to make it a priority, and perhaps we need a background check on our friend Lloyd here."

As Hank got up to get to work, he turned to Lloyd and asked him if he would like to come to one of their family gatherings the next night.

Lloyd said he and Jake would love to come. To himself he wondered why he had been asked to come this time.

Both men had the same thought about it. Keep your friends close and your enemies closer. Neither knew which one the other would be.

Twenty-Nine

The only two people who didn't know why they were having a gathering on Friday night were Valerie and Lex. It was a surprise. For Valerie and Lex, it was just another gathering at Ava and Evan's, something the group often did.

It was easy. A text went out to everyone, and each person answered yes or no. Ava and Evan didn't have to do anything other than prepare the space. The group handled everything else. They brought food, started the grill if they were eating outside, and took everything away at the end.

Hannah thought it was like the festival called Burning Man. Well, not really, but the idea that everything was brought in and taken out again was similar. Of course, at Burning Man there was nothing there before, and nothing there afterward, and at this gathering, the place remained.

But there were similarities. It was always a community, and it was always interesting in some way. They talked about ideas and played together. Hannah was especially excited about this gathering. Johnny was coming home for a visit.

Yes, Hannah knew that he was coming to visit his mother and brother. But for Hannah, her best friend was coming home. Johnny still didn't know they were best friends yet, because he was eighteen, almost nineteen, and she was still just twelve going on thirteen.

At their age, it was a huge gap. Someday it wouldn't be. Besides, Hannah knew she was older than twelve because she remembered her past life. Eight years of it to be exact, because that was when she died back then. So she figured twelve plus eight made her older than Johnny.

However, Hannah was beginning to get the sense that the past life she remembered was only a blip in a longer timeline than that. Much longer. She knew that was true for everyone, but most people couldn't remember. She couldn't remember one before the last one either until recently. Now, a tiny door was opening into her memory about something else.

She thought that perhaps it was because she had taken up a practice of meditation. Most of the adults around her were doing some form of a meditation practice, and she had decided to find out what it was all about on her own.

Now, after almost a year of practice, Hannah was beginning to become aware of what Sarah referred to as here and there.

Hannah wondered if perhaps it was merely a leaking in of the other dimension that Leif and Eric and the Forest Circle had gone to.

If that were true, it would be awesome, she thought. It would give her a leg up on making that trip once it was decided that they could go.

In the meantime, something else had happened that was so cool she hadn't told anyone else about, although she had an idea that Sarah already knew.

Sarah had projected herself over one day when it was happening. Hannah didn't think Sarah knew that she had seen her because she never said anything.

Or perhaps she is waiting for me to tell her, Hannah thought.

I'll ask her tonight and see what she says. In the meantime, I can't wait to show Johnny!

****

Edward, Johnny, and Josh were the first to arrive. Josh barely had time to meet the four Anders before Edward whisked him and Johnny away until Valerie arrived. Of course, Hannah went with them.

Not only did she want to have time to talk to Johnny before the party began, but she also wanted to be the one to show Josh the bunkhouse and the room that was waiting for him.

She practically had to push Josh through the door of the bunkhouse because he couldn't stop looking at the view.

"Wow what an amazing place, Edward. No wonder you and Johnny love it here so much. If the rest of the town is like this, I might have to rename the place heaven."

Hannah started giggling. "I can't wait until you see the whole town, but right now I want to show you your room. Mom gave you the room with the best view."

Hannah grabbed Josh's hand and dragged him back through the bunkhouse to his room and then with a wave of her hand said, "Ta da!"

"Oh my God! Is this for real?"

Edward clapped Josh on the back, and said, "Real, and yes, it is heaven. Before you head back, we'll be sure to stop at some of my favorite places. But for now, all you have to do is hang out here while I help Ava and Evan get set up."

Josh took one look at Hannah's face and realized that she wanted Johnny to herself, so he excused himself and said he was going to take a quick snooze. Would they knock on his door when they were ready to go to the party?

Hannah gave him one of her famous smiles. The one that said, "Thank you for noticing," and she and Johnny headed out back behind the bunkhouse. Hannah said she had something to show him.

"Listen," Hannah said.

"Okay. Listening. I hear lots of different sounds. Bird songs. Trees moving in the wind. What am I supposed to be listening to?"

"Do you hear something that sounds like drumming?"

Johnny listened again until he heard a sound in the distance that did sound like drumming. "What is that?"

"My friend!" Hannah answered.

"You have a friend that drums in the woods? Is she coming to the party?"

Hannah started laughing. "I don't think anyone would want Lady to come to the party. I don't think she would fit in very well. Besides she doesn't like being inside."

Johnny gave Hannah a look that meant she better fess up. "What are you talking about? Lady? Lady who?"

Hannah pointed to a shape moving towards them. Johnny looked to see the flash of a bird flying towards them that could have passed for a miniature dinosaur making a loud cuk-cuk-cuk sound as it flew.

Landing on the suet feeder hanging off the back deck, the bird glanced over at the two of them before pecking away at the suet.

"What in the world is that?" Johnny asked.

"That's Lady. She's a pileated woodpecker, and she started visiting the feeder a few weeks back. She's my friend. Isn't she marvelous?"

Johnny glanced at Hannah's radiant face and thought that only Hannah would believe that a pileated woodpecker was a personal friend. But for all he knew, they did have a relationship. After all, Hannah knew what he was thinking unless he had his mind closed on purpose, so why not a woodpecker?

With Hannah anything was possible. He fully expected to see Lady land on Hannah one day and talk together.

Hannah glanced at her Fitbit and said, "Oh, we better hide you. Your mom will be here any moment. I'll come to get you when it's time."

"Are you physically going to come to get me, or will you just pop in and get me."

Hannah laughed. "Don't know. Be ready either way."

Johnny met Josh as he walked back towards the bunkhouse. "That is an awesome bird," Josh said, "And a charming and interesting young lady too."

"Very," was Johnny's response. Lady glanced his way as if in affirmation, and flew off into the woods.

"Something tells me that there is more going on with your friends than you and Edward have told me about," Josh said.

Johnny could only nod in reply, wondering what Josh would think if he knew the half of it.

Thirty

"You know, Evan," Ava said to her husband as they worked the grill together, "I think that surprise parties are not so much for the person that is surprised, but for everyone else. This group is barely keeping it together waiting to watch Valerie's face when she sees her son."

Evan nodded in agreement. Sparks were practically flying off of everyone in anticipation. Valerie had texted Ava that she was running a little late, and told her to go ahead and start the party without them.

When Ava relayed the message to the group milling around waiting, there was a groan as everyone wondered how long they would have to wait for the surprise payoff.

Hannah had taken a tray of food to the three men in the bunkhouse so they wouldn't get too hungry. Johnny said he couldn't eat a bite he was so excited, but when Johnny saw that Hannah had brought him a burger made just the way he liked it, he dived right in, missing the knowing looks that Josh and Edward exchanged.

Hannah didn't miss them though and gave them both her look that said, "Don't you dare tell him."

Edward answered out loud, "Wouldn't dream of it."

"Wouldn't dream of what?" Johnny asked, his mouth full of burger. Both men laughed again, and Hannah flounced out but not before she gave the two men another one of her stern looks.

"How old did you say Hannah is?" Josh asked.

"Twelve," Edward answered.

"Huh. Seems much older than that to me." Josh answered.

This time it was Edward and Johnny who exchanged the look. Josh shook his head. Yes, there is much more going on here than it seems, he thought to himself.

They had polished off all the food on the tray and were wiping their mouths when Hannah came flying back in.

"She's here!"

The three men followed Hannah around the perimeter of the yard and waited outside the circle of people. Johnny could see his mom and brother standing by the table getting ready to fill their plates. Valerie and Lex looked up when everyone fell silent.

"Surprise!" They all yelled and split apart to reveal Johnny standing there.

Valerie barely got her plate onto the table before launching herself towards Johnny who was already walking towards her. He swung her around a few times, surprising himself how strong he had become and said, "Happy Mother's Day, Mom."

Lex got a hug and a smack on the back, while Valerie tried to contain her tears.

"This is the best surprise ever, you guys," she said looking at her boys and the group gathering around them who looked as happy as she felt.

Edward let the initial euphoria die down a bit before beginning to introduce Josh to everyone.

He tried to do it as well as Ava did when he was the new kid in town. She had said everyone's name twice and told a brief story about them. It helped him get to know each person so much faster, and he wanted to do the same for Josh.

However, it was so much harder than he thought it was going to be and by the time they made it around the room he wasn't so sure he had done a very good job.

"Wow. That's a lot of people. All your friends?" Josh asked.

"All my friends. Except we are missing two people. They'll be here soon. Emily said they had a rehearsal and they would be here as soon as it was over."

"Emily?"

"Yes, Emily and her friend Shawn. Emily teaches dance and Shawn teaches music."

"Huh. I used to know an Emily," Joshua said.

"That would be quite a coincidence if you knew her," Edward replied. "If you are doing okay, I want to go see how Lex is doing. Been a few weeks since I talked to him."

Josh nodded his okay, lost in thought about the Emily he had met eight years before in a class on writing. The same course he was teaching now, but in another school. Technically, he never really met her, because he was the teacher and she was the student. It wouldn't have been proper.

She sat in the front row of the writing class that he was teaching. It was the hardest class he ever taught because he had to force himself not to look her way. She didn't do anything to make it hard for him like some of the other female students he had, who thought that flirting or even more suggestive moves would help their grade.

No, she had just listened and watched. Joshua didn't even know how she did in his class. He had an assistant, and he gave him the papers to grade with students with last names that started with M all the way to Z.

Joshua was sure it couldn't be the same Emily. That was almost eight years ago and in the south. Things like that didn't happen to him.

****

Emily and Shawn decided to go together rather than take separate cars. They were rehearsing in the community room at the Town Hall so they could leave Shawn's car there and Emily would drop him off on her way home.

They were rehearsing in the Town Hall because it was easier for the kids to get there than come out to the art center on the hill.

It was a small group of high school dancers and musicians who had decided to do a piece for the school's talent show coming up the next week. Emily had helped the dancers choreograph the dance, and Shawn had helped the musicians compose the music.

They had decided not to go for a big production. Instead, the dancers and musicians wanted a simple but beautiful piece that would make the audience feel something. Both groups had used a poem by Maya Angelou for inspiration. As part of the performance, the dancers would take turns stepping to the microphone to read a line of the poem.

Emily was delighted with their decision and the work that they were producing. They were weaving four art forms together into one performance because one of the art students had hand painted the costumes they would wear. Next time, Emily hoped one of them would also write the poem. But her students were exceeding her expectations in every way. She couldn't be happier.

She and Shawn were beaming as they walked into the party. The dream of the arts working together was happening. The rehearsal was successful, and they were topping off the evening with all their favorite people.

The party was in full swing as they walked around the house to the back. By then it was dark, and fairy lights and torches lit up the back porch and deck. To get to the food, they had to weave their way through the crowd. Valerie met them halfway and hugged them both, thanking them for coming.

"Did Edward bring Johnny home for the weekend?" Emily asked.

"That he did, and he brought a friend he met in State College with him. One of Johnny's teachers, Joshua, or Josh. He says he likes both names."

"Josh?" Emily asked her heart thumping. *There are lots of men named Josh,* she thought. *Even a few teachers.*

"What does he teach?"

"I think Johnny said he teaches writing."

Emily stumbled a little and fell against Shawn who grabbed her arm and stuck with her as she slowly circled the party until she saw him standing at the edge of the group.

He was watching her as if he was waiting for her to notice.

"It's him," she whispered.

Thirty-One

The rest of the party was a complete blur to Josh. He had
gathered his courage and walked up to Emily as she held onto
Shawn's arm. They shook hands and expressed amazement
that they had met again in such an unexpected way. Emily
introduced him to Shawn, and the three of them stood around
together until it became too awkward, and he had excused
himself and walked away.

He thought that was the end of that, but before Emily and
Shawn left the party, she had come over and given him her
number and asked if he would like to visit her art retreat out
on the hill. They were looking for a writing instructor for the
summer session and perhaps he would be interested?

Josh had barely slept the entire night in anticipation of
seeing Emily, but he hadn't expected his visceral reaction to
seeing her hill and what she was doing there. If she hadn't
asked him to teach there, he would have had to beg. It was as
if something he had always wanted had materialized out of
nothing, and standing in the middle of all that was a woman he
never allowed himself to think about.

They had spent the entire day talking, at the hill, over lunch
at the Diner, and back on the hill where they sat on Emily's

stone for the whole afternoon filling each other in on what they had been doing with their lives the past ten years.

They finished the day back at Ava's house to have dinner with her family, Edward, and Hank. Joshua had overheard Emily talking to Hank on the phone as he returned from the restroom. Since Emily had explained that she thought of Hank as her dad, he knew that he was on probation until he got a go-ahead from Hank.

As nervous as he was to pass inspection, he had already made up his mind that he wouldn't step away unless Emily didn't want him around. Her smiles and light touch on his arm as they talked told him he had a chance, and he wasn't going to let it slip between his fingers.

All in all, it was a magical day. A magical visit. He couldn't wait to spend more time in Doveland, at Emily's Hill, and with Emily. They made plans to talk, supposedly to prepare for his stint as a teacher this summer, but both of them knew it was more than that.

******

Joshua was driving Johnny back to school, but not until after Johnny had breakfast with his mom and brother for Mother's Day.

Edward suggested that the two of them go to Your Second Home for coffee, while Josh waited for Johnny.

When Josh hesitated, Edward turned on the sales pitch. Josh wouldn't know the essence of Doveland until he experienced the coffee shop. You never knew who would be there. It was the perfect place to hang out by yourself, or with a group.

Joshua understood what Edward meant as soon as he walked in the door. It was a dream coffee shop. It smelled of rich coffee and warm, sweet pastries. The walls were lined with bookshelves filled with books to read while you ate, or buy to take home.

Some coffee shops were noisy, the sound bouncing off the walls. This one was quiet. Although there were groups of people scattered through the shop, some at tables, some in booths, and a few reading in cozy chairs, it felt like a warm murmur rather than the echo he had come to expect from many coffee chains.

Seeing Josh's face, Edward said, "This is all Grace's idea and Mandy's execution. Mandy makes some of the pastries here, and Sam and Mira make the rest and bring them fresh in the morning."

Glancing around the room, Edward caught the eye of Hank sitting at a table with Sam and Sarah. As he led the way to their table, Edward said, "This is another reason I love this place. It's rare not to find a friend here, and you never know what conversation you will have."

Grace swung by to fill their coffee cups and pointed to a young girl taking pastry orders. "Let me know how she does. I'd like to sit down and chat with you, but it's so busy I can't do it today. But I do need some feedback on my new help. Enjoy yourself, and Josh, please come back soon. I hear there is a young lady who can't wait to see you again."

Everyone at the table laughed. "Word gets around fast here, Josh. Not only are we all gossips to some degree, but we also have learned that secrets don't serve us well as a community. So when someone in our little group meets the person she has been pining over for years, we are all in," Sarah said.

Seeing Josh's face, Sarah added, "And no. We don't share secrets that need to be kept. But this one. It's not a secret. At least not anymore."

"Speaking of secrets, do we have any news of the box in the church?" Hank asked Sam.

"If I don't hear anything tomorrow, I plan on calling them to speed it up. It's been a week since we found it."

They all looked up to see Tom looking for a table, so they waved him over. Edward scooted over to allow a chair to be brought in between him and Josh.

The new waitress appeared with coffee, asked if they needed any pastries, and after telling her to bring a selection, they turned back to the conversation.

Sarah said, "We were talking about the box in the wall and the fact we still don't know what the papers said, or who the people are in the picture. Of course, it's only been a week. "

Turning to Joshua, Sarah said, "We have a few mysteries this month. Besides the box that Hank found in the wall of the Chapel, we had an elderly man who passed away on the bench out in the town square a few weeks ago. We still don't know who he is even though Dan, the police chief, and Hank and Sam are trying to figure it out."

"That sounds tragic. Somebody must be looking for him. How did he die?"

"It looks like it was old age," Sam said. "But no one likes the fact that the poor man died out there all by himself, and as you said, someone must be looking for him.

Tom helped us out by sketching him both as he looked, and without a beard, because we don't think he had it for long. In fact, we believe he had only been wandering around for the past six months, give or take a month or two. Tom, do you have your sketchbook?"

"Ah, it's in the car. I am going out to Emily's hill to do some work with her for her brochure. But, I do have it on my phone."

As Tom scrolled through his phone searching for the picture, mumbling about finding a better way to arrange his pictures, Joshua felt as if a hand was squeezing his heart. His grandfather had been missing for that long. It wasn't possible, was it?

Tom found the picture and passed it to Joshua, saying "Scroll left to see the one without the beard."

Josh didn't need to. He felt the edges of his eyesight go dark, and Tom and Sarah grab his arm as he fought not to pass out.

"I'm sorry, Josh," Sarah said. "Who is he?"

"My grandfather," Josh answered and then found himself weeping as Sarah pulled him into her arms, and patted him on his back.

All he could think was that he had come to Doveland, and now his life had changed forever. First the joy of finding Emily, and now the sorrow of losing his grandfather.

"What is this place?" he whispered to himself. But it was Sarah who answered.

"I believe it's your home, Josh."

Thirty-Two

Josh was taken upstairs to Grace's apartment and left to recover on the couch with Tom and Sarah sitting beside him while Hank made a few phone calls. The first one was to Dan and the next to Emily.

Josh hadn't asked Hank to call Emily, but everyone could see his glow after spending Saturday with her. Hank had a feeling something was up with the two of them, so he went with his gut instinct. When Emily said she'd be right there, he knew he was right.

Dan and Emily arrived at the same time. Dan had just finished making a big breakfast for his wife and kids for Mother's Day when he got the call. He grabbed a biscuit on the way out the door and kissed his wife on the cheek.

As Dan rushed out the door, she hugged him and told him to go help the poor boy who had just found out his grandfather had died alone on a park bench. It was times like this that Dan reminded himself how lucky he was to have found her.

Emily ran up the stairs ahead of Dan and seeing the look on Sarah's face rushed over to take her place beside Josh. "Oh, Josh, I am so, so, so, sorry."

With Josh being taken care of by Emily, the rest of them met around the dining room table to decide what to do next. Sarah told Dan that Josh was leaving that day so whatever he needed from him probably had to happen now.

"Obviously, the first thing we need to do is to be sure that DG is Josh's grandfather," Dan said. "And if it is his grandfather, Josh will need to decide where and when he wants to bury him.

"And I need to spend time with him before he leaves so we can try and piece together what happened, and how his grandfather ended up here."

After everyone agreed to what Dan said, and promised that they would do everything they could to make it as easy as possible for everyone, Dan placed a call to Craig who agreed to meet them at the morgue.

As Dan walked back into the living room, Josh stood. "I'm okay. I know I need to identify him. Could we get that over with please?"

No one was surprised when Josh and Dan returned less than an hour later with the news that yes, it was his grandfather.

Josh returned to his seat on the couch, while Dan and Sam asked him questions. Hank and Emily sat beside him the whole time for which he was grateful beyond words. Sam and Dan took their time. There was no rush, and there was no crime. Only a grieving grandson.

Josh said that he had no idea why his grandfather left or why he had come to Doveland. However, now that he had been there and experienced how beautiful it was, he wondered if perhaps his grandfather had been to Doveland before too, and was trying to return for some reason.

However, that was just conjecture because his grandfather had never mentioned the town to Josh. Before he went missing, he was in excellent health, showed no signs of dementia, and gave no hint of his plan to leave home.

When asked if his grandfather had any other family they could contact for him, Josh said that as far as he knew, his grandfather had no other living family. He was the only one.

The only thing Josh could tell them was that his grandfather's name was also Joshua. But he was his mother's father, so his name was Joshua Lane. Although Josh had never met her, he knew his grandfather once had a sister and talked about finding her one day. Perhaps he was there because he was looking for his sister?

They all looked at each other. "What?" Josh asked.

It was Emily who asked, "Was his sister's name, Lisa Lane?"

****

The fact that his grandfather had a piece of paper stuck in the lining of his clothes that said Lisa Lane on it sent Josh into such a tailspin, that the group took over making decisions for him.

They got permission to have his grandfather's body stay in the morgue for another week while Josh decided what to do. If he wanted to have his grandfather buried in Doveland, Sarah and Grace would make the arrangements. All Josh would have to do is come back for the funeral if he wanted one.

No one thought that Josh was fit to drive back, so Hank volunteered to drive Josh and Johnny back to school in Josh's car. He would rent a car to get back to Doveland. No big deal. Besides, it would give him a chance to see Edward's new home.

As they were making plans, Hank decided he would stay a few days and check out the town which he had heard so much about, and he would be around to help Josh decide what he wanted to do.

What Hank didn't mention to Josh was that he planned to

do a bit of research about Joshua Sr.

Josh's grandfather must have had some friends that Hank could talk to and places he would go that might yield a clue. When his grandfather went missing, he had been living with Josh. So perhaps they would find some clue about what happened by going through his effects. Although Josh said he had done that already, he might have missed something.

As they waited at the car for Johnny, Emily hugged Hank and thanked him for taking care of Josh. Sarah said she would check on him later.

"You mean you are going to drop in on both of us out of nowhere?"

"That's what I mean," she said, winking at Hank.

"Well, then I have nothing to worry about. You'll be watching over me. I won't be too long. I don't want to leave the crews without me for more than a few days."

Sam said he'd call if he heard anything, and Dan gave Hank a letter explaining what they were looking for in case he needed help from the police in State College.

Johnny had been told what happened and wasn't sure what he should do. After all, Josh was his teacher. But his mom reminded him that he knew how it felt to lose someone you love, especially under disturbing circumstances. If he followed his instincts, it would be the right thing.

"He'll be okay, won't he?" Emily whispered to Sarah as Hank drove the three of them around the square and out of town.

"In the end, it will all be okay, but there are more puzzle pieces to find first," Sarah answered.

"The first question to be answered," Sam added, "is where is Lisa Lane and why was it so important to find her now?"

Thirty-Three

The news that the man who had died on the bench was the professor's grandfather reached Lloyd after the Sunday service. Before the service, he had been too busy preparing what he was going to say to have heard the rumors that spread like wildfire.

It turned out that one of the members of his congregation had been sitting a table away from Hank's table when Josh saw Tom's sketches of the dead man.

By the time the service was over everyone but Lloyd knew what had happened. As soon as he stepped off the platform, a bevy of women surrounded him. They couldn't wait to ask him if he had heard the news, and when Lloyd answered that he had no idea what they were talking about, they were overjoyed. They got to be the ones that told him!

Lloyd listened to the story trying to look interested. He wondered why it was supposed to matter to him. It really didn't. He felt sorry for the young man, but what could he do about it? It was over and done with.

However, when another woman joined them bursting with an additional tidbit of information that Josh's grandfather had a sister named Lisa Lane, Lloyd had to control the impulse to shriek in dismay. Instead, he smiled benignly and replied that it was wonderful that they now knew why the old man had that scrap of paper in his coat. He had never heard about the piece of paper. If he had, it would have changed everything.

"Thank you for telling me," Lloyd said as politely as he could to the cluster of women who surrounded him. The women ran the gamut from a little younger than him and almost old enough to be his grandmother.

The older ones wanted to make sure he was well fed and happy. The younger ones either liked to flirt as a pastime, or were looking for a plaything, or perhaps a husband.

What those women didn't realize was that he was still married. Somewhere he had a wife, and he still loved her. He and his son held out hope that someday she would return to them. There was no way he was going to squander the small chance that they would be reunited by playing around.

In a way, Lloyd felt that he was the antithesis of Josh's grandfather. Josh's grandfather went searching for his sister. Lloyd was not searching. He was staying still, hoping to be found.

****

After what seemed like years, but was probably only a few minutes, the last of Lloyd's congregation filed out of the church, and the remaining few who liked to stand by the church's gardens to milk every last drop of gossip had left to have lunch at the Diner to gather more news.

Lloyd closed the Chapel door, turned to lean against it, and took in the room. The arched stained-glass windows that ran down the sides glowed with the late morning sun. The wooden pews were even more beautiful than when first installed so long ago. They spoke of the value of simplicity and service.

He loved this chapel. He had loved it the minute he had seen a picture of it when he was only nine years old. He had been visiting his grandmother's house while his mother wanted to get away by herself. Even as a boy, Lloyd realized that he cramped her mother's style when she wanted to drink herself silly.

On one visit, to entertain him, his grandmother brought out old photo albums and stacked them in the living room for him to go through.

Every morning he would come downstairs wondering what treasures he would see in those old albums. He loved to look through them and then try to identify the people that he saw. Usually, his grandmother would have carefully written the names of the people in the picture on the back, so he would take them out, turn them over to find out if he was right.

One morning he took out a picture and found another one tucked behind it. Lloyd felt as if he had truly found a treasure. He had found a picture that someone wanted to keep but didn't want anyone else to see.

A little tingle of excitement in his belly made him think maybe he shouldn't be looking at it. He knew he should put it back, but he was mesmerized by what he saw and couldn't stop staring at it.

Now, twenty-eight years later, Lloyd knew that he had been looking at a picture of the Chapel in Doveland, but of course, he didn't know that then. It was just beautiful to him.

The picture was taken looking at the Chapel from right where he was now. It was the same view. But in the picture, there had been three people standing at the front of the church.

He couldn't see their faces, but he knew what was happening. They were getting married. The lady had a veil on, and she and the man were holding hands looking at each other. Another man stood behind them. It still amazed Lloyd that he now stood on that platform every Sunday.

When his grandmother came into the room and saw Lloyd holding the picture, she snatched it out of his hand and ran out of the room. Lloyd couldn't decide if he should be mad at her for grabbing the picture or go after her to find out why she had.

He made up his mind when he heard her softly crying in the other room. He tiptoed in and found her curled up at the end of the couch clutching the picture, her head buried in her arms.

"I'm sorry, Nana," he had said, which only made her cry harder. But Lloyd was patient, and he was curious. What had he found? Who were those people? Before his grandmother had pulled the picture out of his hands, he had seen a small inscription at the bottom. The only thing he could read was 1941.

After a few minutes, his grandmother sat up, took the ever-present tissue out of her pocket, blew her nose and dried her eyes.

"Not your fault, Lloyd. I haven't seen this picture for years, and it brought back memories?"

"Bad memories or good ones?"

"Both. Someday when you are all grown up you will know what it's like to be sad about something that is also wonderful.

"I think I have buried these memories long ago, but then I discover they have not gone away. They are simply waiting in the corner for me to notice them again."

"Who are those people?" Lloyd had asked.

"These two people are your grandparents."

"You mean that is you and Poppa?"

"Not Poppa."

His grandmother had slapped her hands on her legs and stood up all business again.

"That's enough for now, Lloyd," she had said. "Perhaps I will tell you more later when you are older. But don't tell anyone about this picture. It's going to be our secret. Just you and me."

She turned to leave the room then came back, sat on the couch and held both of his hands as she said, "Lloyd, if I never have a chance to tell you about this, I want you to know that there is a box where you will find all the answers."

"Where's the box?"

"Find this church, Lloyd," she said pointing at the picture, "and you will find the box."

They never spoke of the picture again. However, when she died, Lloyd's grandmother had left a note on a book in her bedroom and said it was for Lloyd. His mother had handed it to him without looking inside. Much later, Lloyd had opened the book and found the picture, and because he had promised, he never told his mother or anyone else about it.

In fact, like his grandmother, he had forgotten about it until one day while going through boxes in the attic after his mother died, he had found the book and the picture.

It wasn't until her funeral that Lloyd found out his grandmother's name. He had always called her Nana, not thinking that she had any other name. But at her funeral, he had overheard her friends say how much they would miss Lisa.

Leaning against the Chapel door, he thought how much he missed her now. His grandmother, Lisa, married in this chapel, and who left a box in the wall meant for him.

Now he wondered if the box was also meant for Joshua, and perhaps he should care about the old man on the bench now.

Thirty-Four

The news spread quickly through the rest of Doveland that the old man who died on the bench had been identified. His name was Joshua Lane. He was in his eighties. He had lived with his grandson Joshua Baines in State College, Pennsylvania.

Josh was one of Johnny's teachers at Penn State, and he would be teaching writing at Emily's hill during the summer session. No one was sure how they felt about that. They would have to wait and see.

Back in State College, Josh spent Sunday evening reviewing what had happened. He knew people would be talking. Could he have done it any differently?

His grandfather had gone missing only six months ago. One day he was there, the next he wasn't. Joshua Sr. had told his grandson he was going to lunch with the group of men that he went to lunch with at least three times a week, but he had never shown up.

That evening when Josh had called his grandfather's friends to find out why he wasn't home, they told him that his grandfather had never shown up for lunch and everyone feared the worst. Josh called everyone who knew his grandfather and immediately went to the police. The police issued an informal watch for him. No one wanted an old man wandering around town and freezing to death.

By the next day, Josh's worry had turned to panic, and an official hunt for his grandfather was put into action. Day after day Josh would check in with friends and the police. After a few weeks of nothing happening, Josh became terrified every time the phone rang. He would think it was someone telling him his grandfather had frozen to death, perhaps in the woods.

At the same time, he prayed that his grandfather had ended up with someone that Josh didn't know, and the phone call would be his grandfather calling to tell him where he was. That phone call never happened.

Instead of a phone call, Josh found out in person. While sitting in a warm coffee shop, in a town hours away, he was casually shown a picture of a man who had died alone on a park bench. Josh didn't think that the shock of it would wear off, and he wasn't sure the grief would ever go away.

Monday morning, having managed to sleep a few hours, Josh was able to think things through more clearly. Still in shock, still grieving, he was also filled with gratitude for Hank driving him home and then helping him arrange his life for the next few weeks.

It was Hank that suggested Josh get a substitute for his classes for the rest of this summer session. It was Hank who made sure he ate a little dinner, and it was Hank who sat with him as he stared at the wall not knowing what to do.

He found himself reviewing what had happened in a few short days. It was overwhelming. First, he had found the woman he had tucked away as a fantasy. Someone Josh thought he would never see again. Even if he did, she probably didn't have any feelings for him. Then he discovered that Emily had done the same thing about him.

For a brief moment, they shared a time without anything coming between them where they could envision a future together. Then, within a few hours, grief and guilt descended, and Emily could not be first in his mind.

All Josh could think about was how he had failed. What if he had searched harder? Perhaps he would have found a clue to why his grandfather had left, and where he was going. If he had done all that, maybe he could have saved him.

Josh felt guilty wondering what he had done, that his grandfather didn't trust him enough to ask him to help to find his sister.

Josh would have put everything aside and searched with him if he had been asked. How had he failed as a grandson? Why didn't his grandfather ask him?

The whys kept hammering at him until he wanted to cover his ears and scream at it all to stop.

Mid-morning Hank and Johnny arrived at Josh's home, and together they began a search through his grandfather's things to see if they could find something that might answer some questions. While they were searching, Hank asked Johnny if he would mind sharing with Josh what happened with his father.

Josh listened to Johnny tell the story of how he discovered that his father was not the man he thought he knew.

After his father died, they discovered that he had helped Dr. Joe, the town's doctor who turned out to be a serial killer, bury eight women. Four at Emily's hill and four in the lake. It had happened when his dad was still a teenager.

Then his father lived a life as if he hadn't been part of such a horrible thing. Johnny told Josh that the discovery shook him to his core. Made him question if he would end up like his father. Now he was coming to terms with the fact that he had a choice of who he would become.

Johnny shared that it was Edward who brought the proof of who Dr. Joe was and what he had done. He did that even though Dr. Joe was his father. Halfway through the story, Josh stopped everything he was doing and leaned up against the bed to listen.

"So Edward knew his father killed people?"

Johnny and Hank nodded, yes.

"And yet, he managed to let that go, and be happy?"

"He learned to live with it, just as I have learned to live with it. And my mother learned to live with finding out who her husband was, and then discovering that Dr. Joe was her father too."

Josh looked to Hank for confirmation.

"I think you are the teacher here, Johnny," Josh said. "I'm not going to help anyone by beating myself up over not knowing enough to support my grandfather and letting my grief take over. I could do something with this, right?

"Whether I find out why Grandfather left or not, I could do something, so others don't have this same experience. And maybe I will also be able to find out why he was searching for a sister I never met. I thought she was dead. Is she? Why did he go to Doveland to find her?"

Johnny gave Josh a quick hug, and Hank smiled at him while wondering what Josh would say if he knew about him and his father. But now was not the time to tell him.

"Hey, Hank," Johnny said from deep inside Josh's grandfather's closet, "didn't you and Ava find stuff out about her mother and Hannah from a bank deposit box?"

"That we did. And before that, when the Stone Circle first met, they also found stuff in a bank deposit box."

"Well, I think this story might be continuing. The one about bank deposit boxes I mean. Isn't this a bank deposit box key?"

Johnny asked holding up a key he found inside a shoe in the closet.

"I see a trip to his bank this afternoon," Josh said.

"And I see food in the immediate future," Hank said. "Let's make sure there is nothing else here, and then I'll take the two of you out for pizza before we go to the bank."

Suzanne smiled as Johnny found the key. She was still choosing to be invisible, although Hank had glanced in her direction a minute before and she wondered if he had seen her. The fact that he didn't react could mean he knew she didn't want to be seen. Either way, she was grateful that things were moving forward.

In the Forest Dimension things were heating up, and the Stone Circle needed to be completed soon. However, there were still pieces that had to fall into place first.

She had no control over how long it took. All she and her Forest Circle could do was hold the line the best that they could, and pray that it all happened fast enough.

Thirty-Five

Grace wondered how many people were in her coffee shop to have coffee and how many of them were there to gossip. There were little knots of people all twittering about the old man on the bench. Grace resented it, and she could feel herself getting more and more irritable over it. How could they gossip about something so devastating for the people involved?

For Grace, knowing the name of the old man made her feel worse. Now that she had met his grandson, and saw his pain, she berated herself even more for not taking care of his grandfather.

She made a promise to herself to do everything she could to make it up to Josh. That meant that although Grace didn't like what the gossipers were saying she was planning to listen in on every conversation that she could just in case it helped her piece together something that would help. She was going to live up to her reputation as a busy-body.

So when she heard Reverend Lloyd's name mentioned, she grabbed a coffee pot and made her way over to listen in on the conversation between the women at the table.

"So what was that reaction anyway?"

"I know, he looked as if he was going to have a heart attack when we told him about Lisa Lane."

That was enough information for Grace. Something was going on with Lloyd Webster. She liked him, but he always seemed a bit on the outside of things, like his son. Hannah had taken his boy under her wing, which might mean that Hannah knew more.

Grace reminded herself that it was highly probable that Hannah knew more, not just because she was friends with Lloyd's son but because of her ability to see what others couldn't see.

Since Leif and Eric had made themselves scarce the last few weeks she couldn't ask them to check with Hannah. She would have to do it herself. She'd made up her mind. She'd go over to see Hannah this afternoon. Get her two new helpers in and let them take over for a while. So far they were doing well. She'd give them another test and see how they did. Barbara could check on the coffee shop for her to make sure they didn't do anything drastic.

Her mind made up, Grace felt better. It gave her a purpose, and she was desperately in need of a purpose.

****

Hannah found Sarah waiting for her when she stepped off the bus from school. That was so unusual that Hannah had a moment's panic wondering what was wrong.

But Sarah told her that her mom and Evan wanted to go for a bike ride with Ben. So she had agreed to be there for Hannah when she stepped off the bus.

But Hannah wasn't fooled.

"Whose idea was it for Mom and Evan to go on a bike ride, today?" Hannah asked.

"Theirs, of course," Sarah answered, but the twinkle in her eye gave her away.

"Okay then. What is it you want to talk about? But can we have cookies while we talk?

"Thought you'd never ask," Sarah said as they raided Ava's cookie stash together.

All of Ava's friends were never without fresh goodies. Sam and Mandy always distributed the leftovers after a catering job. Some went to their friends before they gave the rest to the services in town who watched over those who didn't have enough at the moment.

Mandy's experiment with sugar-free cookies and pastries was going well, and there was a container full of them in the freezer. Within a few minutes, Sarah and Hannah had compiled a delicious plate of cookies which they took out to the table on the deck.

After they had each eaten a cookie, Hannah said, "Okay. What's this about anyway?"

"Well," Sarah said, "I thought we could talk over a few things together. Perhaps move the three mysteries forward and get closer to being able to begin our dimension traveling."

"Three mysteries? Oh, why Josh's grandfather was here in Doveland, why was the box buried in the wall, and who is the person who is going to complete the Stone Circle?"

When Sarah nodded, Hannah asked, "Are these three separate mysteries? Do we have to solve one to solve the other?"

"I don't know, Hannah. What do you think?"

Before Hannah had a chance to answer, a beep announced the arrival of someone coming up the driveway.

They both looked up at the monitor hanging in the corner of the kitchen to see Grace's car pulling up to the front of the house.

"Probably looking for answers," Hannah said as she ran out to hug Grace. A few minutes later, the three of them were settled in the sun out on the back deck.

Only one couple was staying at the Bed and Breakfast and they were gone for the day, so the three of them had the place to themselves.

Sarah repeated the question to Grace that she had asked Hannah. Grace added one of her own. "What does Lloyd Webster have to do with Joshua Lane?"

"Well, if we are going to go that far, do the Stanton brothers have something to do with this too?" Hannah said.

"What makes you say that?" Grace asked.

"Well, we are waiting for the final person to complete the Stone Circle and we know that person is a man."

"So we have four new men in town. Lloyd, Josh, Elliot, and Eli. Does something connect all of them?" Grace asked.

The beeper announced another car was coming up the driveway. This time it was Mira. She was barely out of her car before she yelled, "I found out something about the church!"

Before they had time to ask her what she meant, Sarah got a text from Sam. He said his friend had made out the name of the person to whom the letters had been addressed. They were to a Lisa, a Lisa Stanton.

Sam was heading over to Ava's so they could talk over what to do next. And they needed to contact Hank about the Stanton brothers.

Hannah looked at the three women and said, "Well that sort of answers the question. It is all connected."

Thirty-Six

Suzanne sat with her back against her favorite tree. She could feel the bark on her back in spite of the tunic that she wore over her leggings. Above her, the forest canopy rustled as birds hopped from branch to branch.

A light wind was blowing from the south. As the leaves swayed and twirled, Suzanne could see patches of the pale blue sky filled with wispy white clouds.

Beside her, a squirrel was busy burying nuts to be used later that year when the weather turned colder. In front of Suzanne, a field filled with spring wildflowers moved with the wind. Every shift of the wind brought changing shapes and colors with each gentle breeze.

If she didn't know better, she would have thought that she was still in the Earth Realm where Hannah lived. But she wasn't.

Suzanne had just returned from traveling to Doveland and sitting beside a tree was the best way she knew to restore herself.

Dimension traveling was hard on her, and now that she was the only one making the trips, it had become harder. More stress and less recovery time. She needed to rest until her energy returned and her body adjusted to the fact she was on a version of earth.

She often rested in the clearing before returning home to where the rest of the Forest Circle lived. She never traveled directly to and from their home. It would have put her friends and family in danger. Besides, she loved this clearing.

It was in this space that she felt the closest to the power of the natural elements. The trees that surrounded her looked almost the same as the trees in the dimension where Doveland existed. Everything was very similar—the air, the sky, the sun were all like the earth she had just visited, and yet it wasn't.

One thing was similar though. There was a massive dividing line between those that lived to gain power and control over others and those that saw community and cooperation as a need for everyone. And that divide was expanding faster than anyone thought possible.

Sometimes it felt to Suzanne that nothing she and her friends did could ever change that. There would always be those who chose greed and power as their driving force. It was an aberration of the male flight and fight response that had helped humans survive for millenia.

However, in spite of the fear that what she did was useless, Suzanne knew that a new millennium was knocking at the door. A time that would change the flight or fight response to the female version of tend and befriend.

Those in power didn't like this change. And in the realm where the Forest Circle lived, it was the same as it was in the Earth Realm.

The increased resistance to the change by those in charge was what was causing the need for members of the Stone Circle to join them. But they had to wait until they could teach Hannah and a few of her friends how to travel between dimensions and have bodies in each place.

Ava would never let Hannah go if she thought that she

couldn't return.

Suzanne, Leif, and Eric were working on that problem. Eric, in particular, was trying to make it work. He wanted to return to Doveland in his body. Healed. Ready to resume his life with Grace.

His desire to return was not the only reason they were spending time on this problem. But it helped fuel the urgency.

But the work that they were doing had to be in secret. Suzanne and her friends didn't want the ruler of this realm to know what they were doing. When the Forest Circle had first appeared in his kingdom, he had not been pleased. But he had ignored them thinking that they had no power. Suzanne thought that it was good that he had never bothered to read the prophecies. Otherwise, the Forest Circle would have caught his eye long before this.

However, now that he had decided to expand his domain, he was taking a closer look at the work that they did. It made the Forest Circle even more cautious. When he discovered their real purpose, everything would change.

To avoid detection, they rarely used their abilities that would draw attention to them. Anyone sensitive to an energy shift might find them. Because of this danger, Suzanne was the only one making trips to the Earth Realm, and even when she dimension traveled she did it as invisibly as possible.

The Forest Circle had done their best to hide the clearing where Suzanne rested by keeping a constant energy shield around it. On the other side of the passageway were the woods outside of Ava and Evan's home.

They had moved it from its original location on the mountains of Sandpoint, Idaho when everyone in the Stone Circle had moved to Doveland, Pennsylvania. In some ways, it made it more dangerous for the Stone Circle, having it so close to them. But it was necessary. When the time came, speed would be of the essence.

Suzanne was waiting for Leif and Eric. They would be walking to get there instead of using the ability to jump to where they wanted to be. Jumping took energy, and it drew attention. Besides, like Suzanne, Leif and Eric loved the walk. Everything about it energized them. They all knew that walking among the fields and forests fed them and they took the opportunity to be amongst the trees as often as possible.

And it was because the natural world fed their abilities that the current ruler wanted to destroy everything natural. It didn't matter to him that in the end no one would be able to live in this realm. He wasn't interested in the future. He was only interested in his lifetime, and the power he had within it.

Suzanne felt Leif and Eric moving towards her, and she rose to greet them. They had a few things to do before the Stone Circle completed their circle.

Thirty-Seven

Emily could barely contain herself. The finished van was more than she ever expected. Seeing the *Emily's Hill* logo and the name *Melvin's Bus* on it made her so happy she was hopping up and down when Elliot's phone rang.

Before Hank could say anything, Elliot said he would call him right back and hung up on him. There was no way that Elliot was going to waste the good feelings that Emily was pouring over the two of them by diverting their attention to a phone call which probably meant Hank had another job for them.

Thirty minutes later, having inspected every inch of the van and given it her seal of approval, Emily said she had a class to teach, and Elliot remembered the phone call.

"Do you suppose he has another job for us?" Eli asked.

"Probably. Let's go to town and celebrate at the Diner first," Elliot said.

When Eli made a face at him, Elliot yielded. Elliot hated to disappoint his brother, and Eli was one for keeping the rules and making sure people were happy.

So, instead of heading to town, Elliot called Hank back. This time it was Hank who was abrupt.

He said, "Bring your brother and come to Ava's right now," and then hung up on him.

Elliot laughed. He deserved that. Because of course, Eli was right. They owed Hank a faster response. He had given them work and treated them, and the rest of his crew, with respect and fairness.

However, the request to go to Ava's was surprising. Both brothers knew that there were often parties at Ava's house, but it was not something they had ever been invited to. Besides, it was the middle of the day.

They decided that it must be about doing some work at Ava's. Although Elliot had joked about another job, they both knew that more work would be good. They had finished the Chapel a few days before and were waiting for their next assignment.

Neither brother had minded the break. It gave them time to finish Emily's van. They had thought that Hank would add them to the crew finishing up the buildings on Emily's Hill, but a construction gig at Ava's would be great too.

Although they had never been there, they had heard how beautiful it was and that only selected people ever worked there. If that was what was happening, Eli and Elliot were both pleased and a bit terrified.

They had heard strange stories about Ava and her friends. Especially the daughter Hannah. Nothing bad. But stories about how they had stopped Dr. Joe from blowing up the center of town and killing his son, using their paranormal powers.

They had once heard a bunch of guys talking about Ava and Evan. They suggested that the Anders should name their place Paragnosis. Someone else said that now that all those new people had moved to Doveland, they could call the whole place Paragnosis.

The nervous laughter that followed freaked Elliot enough that he looked the word up. It meant, "knowledge that can't be attained by normal means." It was that idea that they were going to the hub of the paragnosis in town that frightened them just a bit. And pleased them.

The Stanton brothers knew about the phenomenon of paragnosis. Their mother had a bit of it. She always knew things she shouldn't have been able to know. Things beyond the basic mother skill of eyes-in-the-back-of-her-head. When they were boys, sometimes they thought they saw their mother watching them when they were out even when they knew for sure that she was at home.

One time they had asked her about it, and she had smiled and asked them if they thought it was possible. Then she laughed it off and said it was just her wishing to be with them more than she was, but they never quite bought that.

Even now, long after her death, they still thought that sometimes they saw her. But both of them put it down to wishful thinking.

Before she died, she had promised them that she would watch over them. She had also whispered that she wished she had told them about their father, but perhaps they would find out on their own. After she passed away, the brothers agreed that they had no desire to find out anything about their father, and they still felt that way. It was the two of them, and they didn't need anyone else.

As they pulled up to Ava and Evan's house, they were surprised to see a number of cars already there, and that Sam was pulling up behind them. "Doesn't look like it's about a job," Elliot said.

****

After hanging up on Elliot, Hank called Sam and let him know the brothers were on their way. They didn't know that he wasn't going to be there too, so it was up to Sam to fill them in.

Sam had already called Ava and Evan and suggested that they come back to the house. They were going to hear about what happened anyway. Might as well be in on it.

They also texted Edward and asked him to join them. He was working away at something in his room in the bunkhouse but was happy to take a break.

While they waited, Sam paced back and forth across the back deck, muttering to himself. Finally, Mira yelled at him to stop it and sit down and talk.

"For heaven's sake, Sam. It's not a big deal. That box has been in the wall now for maybe seventy years. There isn't any rush. No one is getting ready to die, they already have."

"Or have they?" Sam said.

"Now, you are just being paranoid," Mira answered. "It's weirding me out. All we are doing is solving an old mystery that is probably more of a love story than anything else."

The two of them glared at each other, so Sarah stepped in to break up the tension.

"Okay, while we wait for the Stanton brothers to get here, let's review what we know so far."

When no one answered her, she added, "Sam, you do it. Might keep your brain from exploding."

"We don't know that much. A few weeks ago the back wall in the Chapel started to crumble…"

"Wait, wait," Grace said. "That's not where it began. It began at the end of April when the old man died on the bench in the town square."

"You're right," conceded Sam. "Even though we didn't know it at the time, his arrival was the first event. Then the wall."

Grace interrupted again, "No, Lloyd called and told you the wall crumbled. I think we have to put in all the details. Okay, now go on."

Chastened, Sam started again, "Then Hank and the Stanton brothers went to the Chapel, and later Hank pulled the box out of the wall."

Getting a nod of approval from Grace, he continued. "Hank brought the box here. We opened it, but couldn't read anything, so I gave it to a friend who thought they could pull some of the words and images off of the papers."

"Now, I am going to jump in," Sarah said. "During this time Edward went to State College, met Josh, and then last week he invited Josh to come back with Johnny.

"Yesterday, Josh saw a picture of Grace's old man on the bench and identified him as his grandfather on his mother's side. Josh told us that his grandfather, Joshua Sr., might have been looking for his sister. And if his sister's name was Lisa Lane that would explain the piece of paper he was carrying."

"And today," Mira, talking over Sarah, said, "I found out that the same back wall of the chapel had to be opened and repaired in 1945 which means that could be when someone hid the box.

"And Sam's friend called and said the letters were addressed to a Lisa Stanton, and that's why we have the Stanton brothers coming over. It's possible that they are related to this Lisa because Lisa Lane might have married someone with the last name of Stanton."

"Which would make it possible that the Stanton brothers are her grandchildren, and Josh is a cousin," Hannah piped in.

"Well, let's see what we find out now," Sarah said, watching the monitor as the Stanton brothers pulled in right ahead of Ava and Evan.

Thirty-Eight

The first time Hank called the Stanton brothers it was on the way to lunch. When Elliot called back, they were finishing up a pizza that was almost as good as Pete's at the Diner. Almost.

Hank had hung up on Elliot not only because Elliot had hung up on him, but because he was having trouble keeping his frustration under control.

When Sam had called and told them that the letter was addressed to Lisa Stanton, Hank wanted to rent a car and drive over to Ava's and be part of the questioning of the Stanton brothers. But he couldn't. He was hours away.

He had to remind himself that he was part of the discovery too by going to the bank. He kept the news about the letter to himself though. He didn't want to bogart Josh's anticipation of what they might find in the safe deposit box. The news could wait.

The whole "going to the bank to look at a safe deposit box" trip reminded him of the time he went with Ava to open a safe deposit box. At the time they didn't know each other.

Well, he knew who Ava was because he was the one who had orchestrated what had been happening to her.

However, Ava thought Hank was a kind stranger who had

helped her escape the men who had kidnapped her. He wasn't. He was the bad guy working for Dr. Joe's protégé, Grant Hinkey.

Grant had arranged the plan to distract the Stone Circle in Doveland by anonymously threatening Ava with her past until she ran away to save the ones she loved. Grant knew that all her friends would put everything aside to look for her. While they were distracted, he was free to put the pieces into place that would blow up Ava and Evan's wedding.

Grant wanted to destroy everyone at the wedding because he believed that their powers would undermine his crime business.

However, it all backfired on Grant and changed Hank's life forever.

Ava had run into his arms as planned. Together they had disguised themselves to get into the bank to open her mother's safe deposit box. Ava was looking for her daughter, Hannah, because she was afraid that someone was trying to hurt her.

Although she had given up Hannah for adoption when she was a baby, Ava believed that her mother had put the information about who had adopted her in the safe deposit box.

However, it was the moment Ava opened the safe deposit box and pulled out the stuffed rabbit that had belonged to her mother Abbie, that Hank's world turned upside down. Abbie was his long-lost sister.

From that moment on Hank's life was transformed. He stopped thinking of himself as an evil man. He began to see himself as a man seeking redemption by doing all the good that he could do in the world. He became the most fierce protector of Ava and her friends. And that circle kept on growing.

Pete became part of the circle because he was the truck driver Hank had hired to pick up the hitch-hiking Ava and take her to California. Mandy and Eric had been keeping Hannah safe.

Leif, Sarah, and Grace had come to Doveland to help find Ava and stayed. That brought Tom and Mira and Craig.

All because Grant had set in motion a plan that was meant to destroy the Stone Circle and their friends. Instead, it had strengthened and enlarged the circle.

Emily had arrived in Doveland searching for her long lost Aunt Jean. Emily eventually found her aunt buried in the hill Emily had purchased to build her dream of an art retreat.

That discovery unearthed the evil that Dr. Joe had been practicing under the ruse of a good man. But that too had backfired. Joe's son Edward had returned home to bring proof of his father's guilt. As a result of his act of courage, Edward had found Valerie, his half-sister.

Now that circle had expanded to include Josh and his grandfather. It was the Karass idea that Sarah was always talking about. People find each other through lifetimes. They come together, again and again, to learn and grow and take care of each other.

All these thoughts were racing through Hank's head as Josh parked the car and the three of them headed into the bank. Would what they found there be as life-changing as what he and Ava found in her safe deposit box?

Hank hadn't been there when Sarah and what would become the Stone Circle opened the first safe deposit box. The contents of that box provided the information that brought the Stone Circle together in the first place. It had been the beginning of something more beautiful and more significant than any of them could have imagined.

Hank hoped that what was in this safe deposit box would change Josh's life the same way. Perhaps the contents would help heal him of his belief that he had failed his grandfather.

And then there was the news that Lisa Lane could be Lisa

Stanton. If that was true, it was possible that Josh would also find a family he hadn't known existed.

As the three of them followed the woman from the bank into the safe deposit box room, Josh turned to look at Hank as if to ask him if it was going to be alright.

"We're right here," Hank said clapping Josh on the back. The four of them filed in, Hank and Johnny standing back to make room.

Once the box was resting on the table, and they were alone, Josh took a deep breath and lifted the lid.

Lying on top was a letter. Scrawled in his grandfather's spider writing were the words, "To my grandson, Josh.

Opening it, he read, "Dear Josh, One day you will come looking for me, and you'll turn to this box, either because I am dead or because I am missing."

That was as far as Josh got before he felt the edges of the room turning dark. Hank grabbed a chair and lowered Josh in.

"He did it on purpose," Josh said. "He left on purpose."

"And there was nothing you could have done to stop him," Hank said.

Thirty-Nine

It was not going well. Hannah wondered what Sam was thinking. Why was he behaving so unlike himself? She thought that Sam was acting like a bully to the Stanton brothers. Did he think that they were hiding information on purpose?

Maybe. Because as soon as Sam started asking questions, they had resisted and reacted by closing down entirely and not talking. Elliot and Eli sat at the dining room table with their arms folded and with closed down faces.

When Sam threatened to call Dan and have the police step in, Sarah and Hannah glanced at each other, and Sarah nodded at Hannah to take over. Hannah smiled at Sarah, grateful that at least one person saw her as more than a twelve-year-old girl.

For Sarah's part, she wanted to be sure that Hannah was stepping into her role as a leader and peacemaker. Here in her parent's home, surrounded by friends, was a safe place to try out her authority.

Hannah stood and walked to the front of the table and stood there until everyone turned to look at her. And then she waited some more.

She knew that Sarah was supporting her in quieting the onslaught of emotions that had taken over the table.

When the dark cloud had lifted, she spoke. "Sam, I know you don't mean to be implying that Elliot and Eli are in on some secret hidden in the wall of the Chapel. How could they be? They weren't even born yet when someone hid the box.

"Mira found out that the wall was repaired in 1945 which is probably when the box was hidden. Who here is old enough to have been there?"

Hannah waited until the obvious sunk in and then added, "Maybe you thought that someone told them about what's in the box. But if that were true, wouldn't they have been more interested?

"I believe, Sam, you are frustrated because you want to do right by Joshua Sr. We all understand that, and I know that you certainly didn't mean to take it out on anyone at the table."

"Good lord," Sam sighed. "I don't know what I was thinking. You're right. I want to solve this mystery and do the right thing for that old man."

Turning to the brothers, he said, "I'm sorry. Can we start over?"

"Well, since neither of us actually knows why Hank told us to be here, you could start by filling us in before you start yelling at us. In fact, maybe Hannah here could do it. She seems to have it all together."

Hannah beamed at Elliot. He didn't realize it, but he had just become part of her inner circle. He and his brother, Eli.

"Okay, here's the thing," she said. "Someone wrote the letters to a Lisa Stanton. Your last name is Stanton. We were wondering if it's possible you are related."

"Wait," Eli said. "Just because our last name is Stanton and the letters are addressed to a Lisa Stanton you think we might be related? There are other Stantons in the world. What would make you think we would be the ones related to that lady?"

"Well," Hannah said. "The thing is, in our little group we have discovered that there are no coincidences. We got to know you at the same time that Joshua Sr. came to town, which makes us think that all of this is related. We already know that Joshua Sr. had a slip of paper with him that said, Lisa Lane."

"So you think that Lisa Lane could be Lisa Stanton and that we are related to her?" Elliot said. "That would be the weirdest thing ever."

"Yes, that's what we think," Hannah said. "And once you get to know us you'll discover that it isn't weird at all. Well, at least not in the context of other things."

"I'm afraid to ask what other things," Elliot said, "So I think we'll let it go for now. But if you're right, we could be related to Josh. Come on, that would be weird."

"Not weird," Eli said. "Probably the coolest thing ever. It's been just the two of us since our mother died. If Josh is a relative, I, for one, would be dang happy about it."

"Agreed!" Elliot said, smiling at his brother. "How can we help to find out if we are the ones you are looking for?"

Hannah sat down and gestured to Sam, "You take over now, Sam."

Sam nodded at Hannah and asked the brothers what they knew about their family.

Elliot told the story. All they knew about their father was that he had abandoned them somehow. No, they had no idea who their father was or what happened to him. They had no idea if he was dead or alive.

Their mother's name was Mary. She married someone named Tom Stanton. Their mom had never told them what happened to their dad. The only reason they knew his name was because it was on their birth certificates. Sure, they could get a copy of it for Sam. Perhaps he could find the dead-beat. No, they didn't have a hometown. They had moved around a lot and didn't have any place they thought of as home.

"Well, now we do," Eli broke in. "Doveland. The first time I came here I loved it. It felt as if I had been here before even though I know that I haven't."

Sarah reached over and patted his hand. "Yes, this is your home, and we are lucky to have you here. The fact that it feels that way to you is another clue that makes us think you are related to Lisa Stanton somehow."

"And the fact that Josh's grandfather came here looking for his sister makes you think that Lisa and Joshua Lane were also from Doveland at some point?" Eli asked.

"I do," Sarah answered.

Forty

Hannah and Sarah had arrived right after Josh read the letter. Well, they didn't really arrive. They appeared. Josh had his head in his hands at the time, so when Hank and Johnny nodded hello to them, he didn't see it.

Hannah told Hank and Johnny that she and Sarah were sitting at the dining room table at Ava's and had the thought that perhaps they better come to see what was going on at the bank. Yes, the Stanton brothers were there. They had just found out about Lisa Stanton. Nothing had been determined yet. The only real news was that the Chapel wall was repaired in 1945. They thought that was when someone put the box inside of the wall.

When Josh looked up and didn't say anything about Sarah and Hannah being in the room, Hank and Johnny decided not to tell him. He had enough traumas going on. They didn't need to add the news that Hannah and Sarah teleported themselves from time to time.

Josh put the letter aside and looked inside the box again. Another envelope labeled emergency money was on top. Inside it was a small stack of one hundred dollar bills. Josh barely looked at it because under it he found an envelope labeled, "birth certificates," and another envelope that said, "marriages," and then one labeled, "deed," and finally his grandfather's will.

He had no idea what to open first, so he just stared at them. Everyone waited. In the silence Josh realized something. He didn't want to open any of them. At least not right then. Instead, he turned to Hank and Johnny and said, "I want to go home."

"Okay," Hank said. "Let's take these to your place, and open them there."

"No, I don't mean my place. I want to go back to Doveland. I don't want to look at these right now. I need time. And more people."

Hank and Johnny looked at Sarah who nodded, yes, and then she and Hannah disappeared.

****

Hank didn't need to rent a car to return to Doveland after all. They left for Doveland right after the visit to the bank. Hank drove Josh's car.

First, they dropped Johnny off at his dorm. Johnny wanted to go back to Doveland with them, but he knew he had a summer session to finish. Hank promised him that they would let him know what they found.

Before he got out of the car, Johnny leaned forward and told Josh that he was glad that Josh thought of Doveland as home. Josh responded with the best smile he had at the moment and said thank you.

They briefly stopped off at Josh's and then at Edward's to pick up their suitcases. On the way out of town, Josh called his dean and confirmed that he would be taking the rest of the term off to bury his grandfather and recover from his death.

There was no reason to tell him anything else. Yes, they would have a funeral. But the need to go back to Doveland was about more than that. What they found in the safe deposit box had shaken Josh up so much he knew he wouldn't be able to teach anyone anything.

Even though they didn't know what was in the envelopes yet, the letter changed everything for Josh. For Josh, it meant that his grandfather went away on purpose without explaining why. Not because he had been confused as Josh had once hoped, but because his grandfather thought he could find his sister without any help. Maybe he felt he had something to hide. If that were true, the envelopes would probably answer that question.

The fact that his grandfather became homeless suggested that along the way, he did become confused. Otherwise, the man Josh knew would never have ended up that way. He would have called for help at some point. Instead, he had chosen to keep his mission secret up until the very end.

Josh didn't know if he was angrier or sadder. He was angry because someone must have taken advantage of his grandfather along the way. Someone must have stolen his wallet and left him without anything. Sad because if his grandfather had asked, he would have dropped everything and gone with him. Together they could have talked over whatever secret his grandfather and his parents had kept from him.

Instead, he was left to sort out everything on his own. What would the information in the box mean to him and his life? Would it change everything he knew about himself?

Even if everything didn't change, Josh knew that what he had thought his future would look like had disappeared. Vanished within a few days' time.

Finding Emily again, and discovering she felt the same way about him, had already begun to alter what he thought he was going to do with the rest of his life. Now, he was afraid that the contents of the box would take that possibility away.

It was just one of the reasons why he wanted everyone to be with him when he looked at what was in the envelopes. The most important thing was having Emily with him when they read everything. That way there wouldn't be any secrets between them.

The letter wasn't long. Josh's grandfather apologized for not letting Josh know before about what he would find. His reasoning was he wanted to find out more by himself before telling Josh about the family history.

Those words confused Josh. Family history? What family history? He had grown up like most people. The fact his parents died when he was a teenager was tragic, but he had his grandparents to watch over him. Yes, he missed having his parents. And he had always secretly wished that he had more relatives, a brother or sister, maybe even a few cousins.

But his work had been enough. And he had his grandfather, who he thought he knew well.

In the bank, Hank and Johnny had waited for Josh to recover from reading the letter and then reminded him that he did know his grandfather. Josh knew that his grandfather loved him. He had memories of the times they shared. Perhaps, Hank had suggested, Joshua Sr. hadn't thought that finding his sister was that important until after his wife died.

After seeing all those labeled envelopes in the box, Josh thought that Hank's conjecture might be right. Maybe his grandfather had wanted to keep his life simple, but towards the end realized that perhaps it would be better to know everything. Maybe he missed his sister, and that was the only reason he went to find her. Josh wondered if his grandfather found her before he died.

Josh wondered a lot of things. And the answers to some of them lay at his feet. He could have put the bag with the documents in his luggage or even in the trunk, but he didn't want to let it out of his sight.

It helped him remember that what was happening was not a dream. It helped him remember what he planned to do. The first step in that process was to stop running and hiding from what he didn't know. And instead of doing it alone as he usually did, this time he would do it with friends.

Forty-One

When Sarah and Hannah reported back what happened at the bank, everyone agreed to wait for Hank and Josh to arrive before continuing. After all, they were less than two hours away.

"How do you know what happened at the bank?" Eli asked.

"And what do you propose that we do while we wait?" Elliot added.

Everyone at the table looked at each other, wondering how they were going to explain how they knew, when Eli looked at Elliot and said, "Maybe someone here does what mom used to be able to do?"

Elliot gave Eli a look that could have cracked a plate in half. "Come on," Eli responded. "We've heard rumors about these people. Maybe some of them are true. And even if they aren't, I don't think we have to worry about them freaking out over anything."

"What did your mother used to do," almost everyone at the table asked at the same time.

"I rest my case," Eli said looking at his brother.

"Before we start comparing stories, why not take this meeting somewhere more comfortable," Ava said. "Perhaps outside if it's warm enough or in the living room? And why not order food that Hank can pick up on his way to the house. That way no one has to break off what promises to be an interesting discussion to make dinner."

"Are you going to use the phone to order, or do you have another way," Eli asked, laughing.

"I think we'll use the phone this time," Ava replied smiling at the young man.

It was decided to order from Pete, and instead of Hank picking up the food, he and Barbara would bring it with them. Alex said he could handle the Diner. One of the new help they hired was working out, and between the two of them, it would be okay.

Pete knew everyone's favorite meal, so no one had to decide anything. He said he would also bring food for everyone because he knew that they would be there once they knew what was happening.

That statement prompted a flurry of calls and texts. Pete was right. It was a night for everyone to be there.

When Emily heard that Josh was on his way back, she said she would be there. She had one more class to teach, and she could turn the next one over to one of her assistant teachers. She had been training some of the older teenage girls to take over the class from time to time.

Craig had a few appointments to finish but would be there by the time Hank and Josh arrived. Valerie and Lex would come with Pete and Barbara because Lex said he wanted to help Pete get the meals ready. Tom and Mandy would walk over in an hour after finishing up a project.

While they waited, Sarah asked Eli if he wanted to tell them what their mother used to do. Instead of answering, he asked her if she could be two places at once. She smiled at him and said, "Yes."

When the brothers didn't say anything, she said, "Oh, you want me to prove it? Or see what I mean?" Seeing them nod, she said, "Eli, why don't you go out with Evan and Edward into the bunkhouse. Maybe Ben could go with you. He's getting restless. Elliot, you stay here with me, and we'll see what happens."

As Eli prepared to leave with Evan and Edward, she added, "Did you see your mother do this?"

Once again, the brothers looked at each other and reluctantly nodded.

"Okay. Go on. I'll be with you in a minute, Eli."

A few minutes later Sarah turned to Elliot and said, "Your brother would like you to come out and see the bunkhouse."

With a huff of what appeared to be impatience, but Sarah knew to be fear, Elliot left to see if his brother had really said that. Once he was gone, Sarah turned to everyone else at the table and said, "Evan, Edward, and Ben are going to take the brothers on a walk down the bike path. It might help to calm them both down. We have thrown a lot of strange things at them. It's a lot to take in."

Ava smiled at Sarah. She knew the walk was also for Ben who at two needed to burn off some energy. For him, it would be a run down the bike path. It was one of his favorite places. He and Hannah often went wandering down the path together exploring the wildlife that grew beside it. Hank and his team had done a fantastic job of constructing it, and now people were walking or biking on it every day.

"Sam," Sarah continued, "Josh's safe deposit box had an envelope in it labeled, "deed." The fact that there was a deed in the box found in the wall makes me wonder if it is like the one we discovered in the box at the Chapel. Copies perhaps? I don't know why that would be true, but once again, it seems too much of a coincidence that there are two deeds in this mix.

"Would it be possible to have your friend send us every word she had interpreted off of the one she has? Then perhaps we could match it to the one in the safe deposit box."

When Sam stepped out of the room to make the call, Sarah turned to Ava, Mira, and Hannah and said, "I think we have some work to do before everyone returns."

They all knew what she meant. They needed to prepare the space, not physically, but spiritually. The four of them followed Ava into her newly constructed quiet room. She and Evan had decided to use only the bunkhouse for the Bed and Breakfast, so they transformed one of the house's bedrooms into a meditation space for either of them to use when they needed some private, quiet time.

Because they had also added a half-bath and a small sauna into the space, the sitting part of the room was small. It was just the right size for the four of them to sit quietly together.

Sarah and Hannah chose a mat so they could sit on the floor in front of the window that looked out onto a private garden. Ava and Mira each took a chair. The chairs were wide enough so that they could bring their legs up if they wanted to, or stretch them out by tilting the chair back and letting the leg rest pop up.

It wasn't how they sat that mattered. What mattered was that they calmed their thinking. Let their personalities float free and listen in the quiet space for the voice within.

It didn't even matter if they fell asleep, as long as they listened.

Sarah saw the forest that she used to see when she worked in downtown Los Angeles, long before she had met Leif. It was the forest that used to frighten her until she followed its call and found the friends they named the Forest Circle.

The forest still called her. She used to think the forest that called her was the one that she and Leif found in Sandpoint. Now she knew it was a different one. It was the forest where Leif and Eric had gone, the one where the Forest Circle now lived. She knew she would get there sooner or later because she was no longer afraid of it.

As she returned to the room, a question followed her. "Where are the stones?"

When Sarah opened her eyes, she discovered that she was the only one left in the room. Everyone else had left to greet the people arriving at the house. Hank and Josh were almost there. It was time to find out what was in the envelopes that Josh was bringing. After that, she could answer the question about the stones.

Forty-Two

Josh's suitcase was waiting for him in the room he had just left a few days before. Ava told him he was staying there at least until after his grandfather's funeral. After that, they would discuss it. As exhausted as he was, Josh couldn't help feeling better having someone else take charge of his life, if only for a few days. It brought back memories of his mother and his grandmother. They were both strong women who ran their houses with a combination of efficiency and kindness.

Josh hoped that he had inherited some of that combination, but he knew that Emily had them. Perhaps that is what attracted him to her in the first place. She reminded him of his mother and grandmother.

Emily had been waiting for him in the parking lot when they drove up. As soon as he stumbled out of the car, she was there supporting him with a smile and her arm around his waist. For a brief moment, he forgot any other reason why he had come back to Doveland. Emily was enough. But when he saw Hank pick up the bag with the envelopes, he remembered.

The rest of the evening was an onslaught of information and questions. Not many answers. Mostly questions.

After the meeting, Hank had stayed over in the bunkhouse

with him. Edward was there too, returning to the room he kept at the bunkhouse until he could force himself to either go live in his father's house or buy a new one.

Josh suspected that Hank had stayed over to make sure he didn't freak out during the night with only Edward to watch over him. Although if what Josh had heard of Edward's past was half true, he was perfectly capable of handling any kind of freak out from anyone.

In spite of Hank's own exhaustion, he stayed up with Josh as the two of them paced the floor while Josh tried to make sense of what they had found.

Edward stayed up with them too, although for the most part he watched and listened. He had spent his whole life hiding from his father, and now Josh was trying to unravel a mystery about his grandfather. Edward didn't know what the magic potion of Doveland was that there were so many people drawn to it who had to find themselves. He hoped that what Josh and the Stanton brothers found would please them.

After everyone had arrived and they had dinner, they gathered around the dining room table to deal with the envelopes. They decided to look at the birth certificates first. They were divided up into separate envelopes inside the larger one.

The first envelope held the ones for Josh's family. He found his birth certificate, plus birth certificates for his mother and father, and his grandfather and grandmother.

There was only one thing in them he hadn't thought about before: his mother's maiden name. He knew his father's name was George Baines and his mother was his grandfather's daughter, so of course, her maiden name had been Lane. Lisa Ann Lane. He realized that his grandfather had named his daughter in memory of his sister.

After opening that set of certificates, he had thought, *oh no big deal, no real mystery here.*

It was the second set that made things more complicated. The first thing they found was a note addressed to his grandfather. It was short and to the point.

"For safe keeping. Thank you, Joshua. Love, Lisa"

Lisa Lane's birth certificate was the first one they pulled out. It proved that she was his grandfather's older sister. No surprise there. But what was a surprise, or at least confirmed what they had suspected, was that both Lisa and Joshua Sr. were born in Doveland.

Lisa was born in 1923 and Joshua in 1931. *No wonder this had felt like home,* Josh thought as he stared at their birth certificates. *And no wonder this is where his grandfather had come to find his sister.*

Joshua was surprised to find out that his grandfather was older than he thought he was. He was eighty-eight and traveling the country by himself. *You cagey old man, you,* Joshua thought to himself. *Lying to me about your age all these years. And why didn't you ask me to come with you?*

But there were three more certificates inside the envelope. On all three the mother was listed as Lisa Lane and the father as Tom Stanton. Three children. A set of twins, and a younger daughter named Diana. The twins were Kathleen and Tom Stanton.

They had stopped after that and talked to the Stanton brothers. What was their father's name again? The chances that they were part of the Stanton family had increased.

Eli asked, "If we are the grandsons of the original Tom Stanton, and sons of the next Tom Stanton, wouldn't that make us cousins with you, Josh?"

"I see a slight resemblance," Mandy said.

"Me too," Lex piped in. "This is so cool. You found a relative you didn't even know you had. Kinda like mom finding Edward."

Edward and Valerie smiled at each other. "I've got to say, I agree. If you guys just found out that you are related, that is such a gift," Edward said.

"We have to check it out before we jump to conclusions, though," Sam said. "Looks like a few more DNA tests are in order. It's time to call in favors again."

"Hey, mom," Lex said. "Didn't you say your mother's name was Diana?"

"Yes, but it's a fairly common name. I don't think it means anything. Besides her maiden name wasn't Stanton, or at least I don't think it was. I'll check. It wasn't something we talked about. Now that I think about it, I don't know why.

"Could we leave it alone for now? It's enough coincidence that these men might be related, there is no reason to make it more mysterious and confusing than it already is."

Everyone agreed, even though it was evident that Lex was hoping for more mysteries to be revealed right at that moment.

They pulled out the deed next. Or at least what looked like a document for a piece of land owned by Tom and Lisa Stanton. Since there wasn't an address listed on the deed, no one knew where the property was, or if it was the same as the deed they had found before.

"Perhaps they were going to build a house on their land?" Hannah piped in.

"Could be," Sam answered. "And it could be a copy of the one in the box from the church. Some of the words are the same. But we are going to need more help figuring out where this is, and even if it is still valuable."

"I'll take it to my archivist friend tomorrow," Valerie said.

"She should at least be able to tell me where it is. Not sure how we are going to find out if it is still good, though, since the town's records were destroyed in that flood. But maybe finding out something small would enable us to figure it out from there."

"Are you saying we might own a piece of property somewhere?" Eli asked.

"Lots of things to find out first before we go there, Eli," Sam said.

"Shall we look at the envelope that says "marriages" next?"

Josh thought back to that moment. If they thought things were weird before, that was when it got extraordinary. The note inside was from his grandfather to him.

"Josh, in case I don't find my sister, perhaps you might be able to find out where her kids are."

Inside they found his grandfather and grandmother's marriage license dated 1950. His parents' marriage license said that they had been married in 1983. He smiled realizing that he had been born a year after his parents' wedding.

They also found Lisa Lane and Tom Stanton's wedding certificate with a date of 1941. Two years later the twins were born, and a year after that they had their third child, Diana. All of it was confirming what they had found so far.

After that, things got a little more complicated.

Forty-Three

Grace wondered if it was possible to keep anything secret in Doveland. Well, she could think of a few things that had been kept secret for over forty years, but these days it all seemed to be out in the open.

The coffee shop was buzzing with gossip. Grace took a moment and imagined herself as the queen of gossip standing in the middle of her kingdom. She had to laugh at herself. When she had the dream of opening the coffee shop, she didn't realize that she was dreaming about a place that would host a group of busy-bodies, just like her.

Well, not entirely like her. Most of the people in her shop seemed to have regular lives. She used to. Now, she was married to a man who lived in another dimension. And she hadn't seen him for weeks. Now that was a cruel kindness. A husband who loves you, but you never see him. Of course not. He lives somewhere else. In another dimension. Not a regular life.

However, Eric used to travel to this dimension to visit her. Now he and Sarah's husband, Leif, were missing in action. Grace wasn't so much worried about it as she was sad.

Leif and Eric had told them that they wouldn't be able to visit for a while. There was trouble in their dimension, and they didn't want to bring attention to the fact that they could travel to this one.

The last time Eric had visited, he had dropped the hint that there was a possibility that he could return to Doveland and stay. In a body. It might mean he could never dimension travel again, but he didn't care.

He wasn't needed as much there as he was in Doveland. If he could return with a healed body, he would do it in a hot minute. Grace tried not to hope too much. But within her heart, she prayed for it with every breath.

Eric and Grace had found each other late in life. Eric had dedicated his life to raising Hank's sister, Abbie, after Hank had left his young sister in the clinic where Eric worked. Somehow teenage Hank had known that Eric would choose to risk everything by moving away and adopting Abbie outside the system.

When Eric moved to Doveland after reuniting Hannah with her mother Ava, he and Grace met. From the very first moment they saw each other, they felt as if they had waited their entire lives to connect. But they knew that they didn't have much time to be together. Eric was terminally ill.

Once he realized he had a chance to leave his human body behind, and move to the Forest Circle's dimension, he made that choice. It meant that he and Grace could continue their time together in this lifetime. It seemed better than dying and having to wait for another lifetime to find each other.

The fact that he could return to a well human body seemed like a faraway pipe dream to Grace, but she kept the hope of it alive. As she listened to the gossip circling the coffee shop, she thought that it was too bad Eric wasn't around to hear the speculation that was spreading through the town. It was interesting stuff. Perhaps it was a good thing that everyone was talking about the letters and what was in Josh's grandfather's safety deposit box. Maybe someone would know something and come forward. In the meantime, it was all conjecture.

Lloyd sat alone in the corner of the coffee shop and listened to the talk swirling around him. He had chosen to come here today because he knew that Your Second Home and the Diner were the best places to find out what was happening in town.

This particular gossip was what Lloyd had come to hear. He needed to know what was happening with the letters in the box, and what Hank and Josh had found in his grandfather's safe deposit box.

Lloyd hoped that someone would come to his table and fill him in with what was happening, but he didn't want to draw attention to himself by asking.

It was Grace that fulfilled his wish.

Lloyd liked Grace. Yes, she was a self-proclaimed busy-body, but she was not a gossip. That might be a subtle distinction, but an important one. Grace had information because she listened and she cared enough to do something about what she heard if it was needed. Lloyd knew that Grace was part of something they called the women's council. Sarah had explained to him that it was a small group of women who supported each other and tried to give wise and supportive counsel to anyone that asked.

He was thinking of asking for support. He surely needed it. But he didn't know them well, so he started by asking Grace what everyone was talking about. Grace took one look at the dark circles under Lloyd's eyes, and his hands twitching on his coffee cup and realized that it was not a casual question.

So she stepped over to her new help and asked her to take over for a minute. She returned to Lloyd's table with a cup of coffee of her own and pulled out a chair and sat down.

"What's going on, Lloyd. Is it your son? I know Hannah has taken him under her protective wing. Is there more that he needs?

"Oh, no," Lloyd said. "Jake is doing well now that Lex and Hannah have befriended him. I probably should do something about thanking them."

Lloyd looked down at his coffee cup and shook his head. "I don't think I have been that good of a father lately. I've been so distracted. I feel pulled off course somehow. I became a minister because I wanted to help people. But I've begun to realize that I have not been doing that because I have been so focused on me."

Grace put both her hands on his, and said, "Can I help?"

Lloyd looked up at Grace and realized that he was about to tell her everything, and he couldn't. Not right now. All he could think about was getting out of there before his whole life spilled out in front of her.

He had no idea whether he was ashamed or angry. Either way, Lloyd's flight response took over. He stood up so quickly the chair almost tipped over. "Sorry, sorry, I just realized I have to go."

Grace watched Lloyd practically run out of the shop. The crowd watched him too. *Great,* thought Grace. *More fuel for the gossip mill.*

Then it dawned on her what was making them so interested in Lloyd's sudden departure. Lloyd Webster. His last name was Webster. Sometimes they were all too close to see.

Grace dialed Sarah's number and asked, "Didn't one of the marriage articles found in Josh's safe deposit box have the name of Webster?"

Forty-Four

Josh had a funeral to plan. Ava said she would help. In fact, everyone said they would help. Just thinking about the group of friends he had found by befriending Johnny brought him to tears. Not usual for him at all. Josh had lived his life straightforward. Do what he needed to do and ignore how he felt about it.

Witness letting Emily drift away out of his life after seeing her in his class and knowing that she was the one. He didn't fight for her or pursue her. Josh did what he thought was right and he pretended that he didn't feel anything.

He couldn't believe that he had found her again. Actually, he could barely understand any of what was happening. It was as if he had fallen into the looking glass and landed in another place altogether. It looked the same as the world he had once known, but everything felt different. The fact that tears were flowing down his cheeks was a testimony to the changes that had come over him, all within a few days. And he knew that the changes had just begun.

Maybe his emotion was a result of where he was walking at the moment. Maybe all the people lying in their graves were rooting for him to find what he was looking for in the cemetery.

Emily had said she would come with him, and he thanked her for the offer, but this was something he had to do by himself. He came to find his great aunt, Lisa Lane. While Sam ran the DNA tests on him and the Stanton brothers, and while they waited for more interpretation of the letters, he wanted to do something himself.

His grandfather had come to Doveland looking for his sister. Now he knew why he had chosen this town. They were born here. His aunt was married here. Doveland was her home. Why wasn't she still in Doveland? Or was she?

And that is why Josh asked where to find the Doveland's cemetery and why he was walking the rows reading every gravestone.

Before driving out to the cemetery, Josh had stopped at the coffee shop for a to-go cup, and to thank Grace for being so kind the night before. As they had read the articles that his grandfather had collected about his sister's children, Grace had held his hand. It was what his grandmother would have done if she had been there.

While waiting for his coffee, Josh noticed Lloyd sitting in the corner by himself. For a moment Josh thought about going to sit with him, but they had barely met, and besides, Josh was on a quest, and he wanted to get on with it.

But Lloyd's sitting quietly by himself reminded Josh of something he often did. *Perhaps I'll get to know Lloyd better later,* Josh thought.

The cemetery was chilly, but coffee was helping to keep him warm. Although Josh knew that later it would warm up, at the moment he was glad he had worn a jacket.

After an hour of having no luck in finding what he was looking for, Josh was even happier he had brought a hot coffee with him. Grace had slipped a breakfast pastry into a bag for him, and he decided it was time to take a break.

Josh had noticed a tree with a bench under it one cemetery row over so he headed over to it. Although he had been looking for an hour at every name on every tombstone, he still had almost as many rows to go through. It was discouraging.

It was an old cemetery. Probably one of the first things the town built after being established in 1840. The oldest stones were hard to read, but there were quite a few deaths in 1840, including too many children under the age of five.

It must have been tough going at first here in Doveland. And now it is such a magical place, Josh thought to himself as he took a sip of his coffee. He stopped mid-sip because he thought he heard giggling, but he hadn't seen anyone here with him. He put his coffee down on the bench and stood up and looked around but still couldn't see anyone.

He decided that hearing something that wasn't there was a combination of an overactive imagination and exhaustion. Add that to the clues he had been getting from the group at Ava's that they knew more than most people did, and could do what other people called magic. It all made for hearing things that weren't there.

But then he heard it again.

This time he didn't stand up to look. He leaned back against the tree and listened. He thought about his grandfather and asked him in his imagination where he would like to be buried. Josh knew his grandmother had been cremated. He and his grandfather had walked to the top of Mt. Nittany to scatter her ashes as she had requested.

He asked his grandfather if he wanted the same thing, or did he want to come back to Doveland. But no one answered him. *Please,* he thought, *I need to know.*

Although his grandfather had left a will, there were no

instructions about his burial in it. In truth, there wasn't much in his will because his grandfather had died without much. Except for that piece of paper about property that looked like an old deed. His grandfather had left Josh his portion of that land.

But since they hadn't yet found out where that land was, or if his grandfather still owned it, Josh didn't put too much thought into it. The funeral was on his mind. He had to make a decision soon. The Chapel had been rented out for a small service. What Josh needed to decide before then was where his grandfather was going.

In the quiet, Josh thought he heard the giggle again, and the words, "Beside me, please."

Josh's coffee sloshed over his hand as he jerked up to see where the voice was coming from. There was a decision to make. Did he hear a voice, or not? And if he did hear a voice, who was it and would he listen to it?

He took a last sip of coffee, finished off the pastry and put both the empty bag and the empty cup into the small backpack he had flung over his shoulder. He hadn't needed a pack. It was a habit. He took it everywhere. When he was teaching, he put his small computer and his notes in it.

What else can I do but listen, he thought. Besides, he wanted to be part of the magic of Doveland. Maybe if he opened himself up to what he couldn't see, he would belong. So he answered, "Okay, great. But I don't know where, or who you are."

Instead of hearing a voice he felt a pull to go past the tree and down a row almost at the end of the cemetery. Once he got there, he waited until he felt another pull that moved him towards the end of the row that ended close to the forest.

As he walked, he looked at the names on the tombstones, hoping against hope, that one of these was his great-aunt Lisa's.

The tears started coming again, and he felt his heart open more and more to the people there, who weren't really in the ground, but who had stayed behind until someone found them, or until it was time for them to go.

When he heard the word, "stop," he wasn't surprised to find that he was standing in front of a tombstone that read, *Lisa Lane Stanton. 1924 - 1992. Sister, Wife, Mother. Loved.*

Josh fell to his knees resting his head on the hard stone and wept. Please tell me he found you here, he begged. A moment later he could have sworn that he felt a hand on each shoulder. A small hand and a hand that felt just like his grandfather's.

He sat back and looked up in the sky hoping that perhaps he could see them. Seeing nothing but feeling everything, he lay back with his backpack under his head staring at the sky smiling at the beauty of life.

He lay there until his phone rang. It was Sarah. "I know you are enjoying your rest there on Lisa's grave, but I think you will want to hear the news."

Josh started to ask, "How do you know where I am," but realized that at this point, it was a stupid question. Of course, she knew where he was.

On the phone, Sarah laughed. "Next time, I won't use the phone. It seems as if you have learned to hear differently. Come back to Grace's. There is someone here I think you will want to get to know."

Forty-Five

Grace, Sarah, Sam, and Lloyd sat at Grace's dining room table and waited for Josh. Sam had brought with him the clippings they had gone through the night before to share with Lloyd even though Sam wasn't sure it was such a good idea. "No one really knows Lloyd Webster," he had said.

But Sarah told him to bring them anyway. If they were going to find out the truth about Lloyd they had to be willing to take the first step with him. When Sam arrived, they took Lloyd upstairs to Grace's apartment above the shop where they could have more privacy.

Sarah always appreciated going to Grace's apartment. Grace loved to redesign her place based on the seasons, so her house was always different, delightful, and often surprising. Since it was spring, Grace had filled the apartment with cuttings of May flowers.

Big bouquets of lilacs sat everywhere, along with small jars filled with the last daffodils of the season. It smelled heavenly. Even Lloyd, tense as a wound up spring, started to relax as he took in the environment that Grace had created.

Grace still had the twinkle lights from her winter decorations strung across the room. As the sun rose higher in the morning sky sending streams of sunlight into the apartment, her twinkle lights started to fade. Sarah admired that detail. Twinkle lights set on a timer based on the light in the room.

The four of them passed through streams of sunlight on the way to Grace's dining room table where Sam spread out the articles in front of him as everyone took their seats.

"What's this all about?" Lloyd asked as they all sat down at the table. He had surprised himself by following them upstairs. It was unlike him to take instruction without questioning it.

He was still trying to figure out what happened. After he had run out of the shop, Grace had gone after him and brought him back. She had patted Lloyd on the arm and told him that she thought they had information he might want to know about.

While they had waited for Sarah and Sam, Grace entertained Lloyd with tales about her life before she moved to Doveland. But once Sarah and Sam arrived, they had hustled him upstairs, and for some reason, he had followed them.

It was Sarah who answered his question. She told him about what they knew so far about the contents of both the box in the church and Josh's grandfather's safe deposit box.

She explained that it never occurred to them that perhaps he was part of the puzzle until this morning when Grace remembered that his last name was Webster. They still weren't sure, and that's what they wanted to discuss.

The more Sarah talked, the more terrified Lloyd became. They knew something, but what did they know? he kept asking himself. He was trying to listen past his fear when Sarah stopped talking.

Sam gathered the papers together instead of showing them to him, and the three of them sat back and waited.

"Not showing you more, Lloyd, until you tell us what you are hiding from us," Sam said.

It was Grace who came to his rescue. "You know, Sam, I don't think he is hiding anything from us. He's hiding something from himself. Besides, what harm can it be to show him what we found? And it may turn out to be a good thing."

So Sam laid it out for him. They knew that Lisa Lane was Josh's great aunt because she was his grandfather's sister. Lisa Lane had married Tom Stanton. They had three children. Each of the three children married and had children.

It was the grandchildren of Tom and Lisa that were the focus of what they wanted to discuss.

"Did you know anything about your grandparents?" Sarah asked him.

Lloyd sighed. It was time to tell. "Not much," he answered, "But enough to think that, yes, I think I am one of the grandchildren you are talking about."

He pulled one of the articles towards him. "It says that Kathleen Stanton married George Webster in 1977. My parents were Kathleen and George."

Lloyd stared at the wedding picture of his parents and felt like crying. No matter where they lived, his mother always had that picture somewhere where she could see it every day.

Sometimes she would smile and trace her finger over her husband's face, other times she would get mad and turn it upside down so she wasn't looking at him anymore. The anger usually happened when there were more bills to pay than money to pay them with.

Her husband, long gone, had spoiled the bright future she had dreamed about the day she had married him.

It was what she would say to Lloyd when she was mad, that had haunted him his whole life.

"It belonged to me, and he stole it. And then that idiot had to go and fight about it. Now both are lost to me forever."

When Lloyd asked who stole what, she never answered. She glared at him, and sometimes mumbled that he looked just like his father. Lloyd never thought that she was giving him a compliment when she said that, so he assumed that the idiot was his father.

Sometimes when his mother drank too much and started talking to herself, Lloyd pieced together stories until he had a vague idea of what caused her to be so angry. But sometimes he wondered if it was his grandmother who had hidden what her mother thought had been stolen from her.

Lloyd looked up at the three people waiting for him to fill in the gaps and decided that it was time to tell everything that he knew. If he and Jake had more family out there for him to meet, it was time to meet them and solve the mystery of his mother's unhappiness. He was lonely and tired of trying to figure everything out on his own to make it right.

"I knew Lisa Lane, or as you said, Lisa Stanton. I didn't realize it until recently though. She was my grandmother, but I knew her as Nana and never thought about her first name. She died when I was eight. It was the hardest year of my young life. She was my rock. The one who took care of me when my mother wanted to go off on her own, which felt like a lot to me.

"Nana must have married again after Tom Stanton. After she died, I learned her full name. It was Lisa Madox."

Lloyd reached into his backpack and pulled out the picture he had encased in plastic. The picture that his grandmother had left for him so that he could find the Chapel and the box.

He had. He found the Chapel. He found the box—or the box had found him—and now he hoped to find out what his mother was talking about and what his Nana had told him was his.

After all the searching, and anger, and loneliness, Lloyd

hoped that it was all worth it.

Forty-Six

During the meeting with Grace, Lloyd, and Sarah, Sam realized that they needed more help, and he knew exactly where to get it. Although they had identified Josh's grandfather, too many pieces were still missing.

This story all began in Doveland, Sam thought, *perhaps the answers to some of my questions can be found in police records.* It was time to talk to Dan, and see what resources he could bring to the table. Besides, Sam didn't know what else to do with himself other than work on this problem.

He and Mira had finished preparing the food for Joshua Lane's funeral. It was going to be held at the chapel, but wouldn't be a religious ceremony. Josh wanted to give his grandfather his time in the limelight. After that, they would bury him by his sister. The plot beside her was empty as if it had been left that way for him. Sam wouldn't be surprised if they eventually discovered that Lisa Lane had set it up that way.

Mandy had arranged to have the small celebration of life at their home, so there wasn't much to do to get ready for it. Mandy always kept their home looking like a showcase. Mira would be helping her brother Tom transport everything for the gathering over to the house later in the day.

Valerie was tracking down the information in the deed. Sarah and Grace were handling the conversation between Josh and Lloyd. Sarah thought it best to keep it relatively private. The two young men probably had some talking to do together.

Discovering a cousin you didn't know you had, could be either good or bad. However, the little he knew of the two of them, Sam thought they would find the good. But it might take some smoothing out of rough patches.

A few friends from his FBI days were handling the other information they needed. He had called in a few favors. One friend was getting whatever she could off the letters. She said she was close to giving him a synopsis of what she had found.

His friend in Pittsburgh who had helped him in the past with Valerie's DNA was running the DNA search on the Stanton brothers and Josh. If it came back the way he suspected, all of them were related. From no relatives to a group of them, all because of a box in the wall and a man who died on a bench.

The mystery that Sam thought he could solve while everyone else was working on the ones they knew about lay hidden within what Lloyd's grandmother had said to him, and what Lloyd had picked up from his mother's drunk ramblings. Something went wrong within Lisa Lane's family. What was it?

Sam had texted ahead to make sure that Dan was in the station and had time for him. "Always have time for you, Sam," was Dan's response.

The station was around the corner from the coffee shop, so it only took a few minutes for Sam to walk over. After turning down a cup of the station's burnt coffee, and spending a few minutes on small talk, Sam got down to business.

"Dan," Sam said, "How possible would it be to get a look at old Doveland police records?"

"How old are we talking?" Dan asked.

"I don't know. Wish I could narrow it down. And I wish that I knew for sure that whatever happened occurred here, but I'm not sure. And to make it even more complicated, I'm not even sure anything at all happened."

Dan started laughing, "It's a joke right? Just trying to see if I am awake or something?"

Sam laughed too. "I know, it's a crazy quest, but the box in the chapel and Josh's grandfather started unraveling something. I keep thinking that there is a piece of information that we are missing, and I think that piece might involve a crime.

"But, you're right. I don't know what crime, or even that there was one. I only have that gut feeling. Putting little things together that don't quite add up. But I don't have the big picture. So, I came to you to see if you have records you could access, that the FBI doesn't."

"Ah. Going with gut," Dan said. "It's often right. But we need something to go on. Tell me what makes you think there was a crime."

As Sam started the story about Joshua Sr. and his sister Lisa Lane, Dan held up his hand. "Wait. I think I have a solution that is better than police records. One that could help us determine if there was even a crime. We need someone that has lived in Doveland their whole life and is the male equivalent of Grace. The town's busybody."

"Do you have someone like that?" Sam asked.

"Sure do," was the reply.

"His memory is still good?" Sam asked.

"His health isn't good. He's in the nursing home in Concourse, but the last time I visited his mind was as sharp as a tack. Especially about things that happened in the past. If it happened in Doveland, he'd know about it. If it didn't happen in Doveland, he still might know about it."

"Who is this guy, and how do you know him?"

"When I took over the police station, the past Chief introduced us. He told me that Leroy was the best source of information I would ever get about Doveland. Leroy and the Chief got to be good friends. The Chief used to discuss cases with Leroy because Leroy would know details about the people involved that no one else knew. The Chief is gone now, but Leroy is still here.

"Leroy is a one of a kind. If we bring your non-mystery, with no starting point to him, he might be able to figure out what you want to know even if you don't and give you an answer. Let me call over and see if he's feeling well enough to have visitors."

A few minutes later Dan hung up with a chuckle. "The nurse said that Leroy said to get my fat ass over there and bring pastries."

Forty-Seven

Dan and Sam ended up bringing enough pastries for the entire staff because Sam and Mira had made too many for an event they had just catered.

Grace came down from upstairs to make them a large carafe of coffee, saying if the nursing home's coffee was as bad as the police stations' it would ruin good pastries. Sam asked how Josh and Lloyd were doing. Grace assured them that they were doing well, and Sarah was taking care of the two of them.

On the way to Concourse, Sam called Hank and asked him to meet them at the nursing home. Hank didn't ask any questions about why. If Sam, or any one of his friends or family, needed him, he was always going to help.

Hank was with his crew finishing up at Emily's hill when Sam called. As he packed up his equipment, he put Elliot in charge of the crew for of the rest of the day. In such a short time Elliot had won over the men. He worked hard and was fair, but strict with everyone.

Eli followed Hank out to his truck to ask him if where Hank was going was someplace where he would get more information about who they were. He had overheard Sam's name, and it seemed that more information gathering would be a reason why

Hank would leave a job site so quickly.

At first, Hank answered with a grunt but then thinking back to when he was lost and realizing that was probably what Eli felt like, he stopped and turned to him and said, "Yes, I might have more information for you two after meeting with Sam."

As Hank climbed into the truck, Eli added, "If it is more information about our father, Elliott and I are ready to hear about it."

Sam nodded his understanding and waved at Emily who was sitting on her rock as he headed off to meet Dan and Sam. *At least this time it's not about Grant or Dr. Joe*, he thought.

By the time the mystery was solved, he would realize that he was wrong about that after all.

****

Hank couldn't stop laughing. Being with Leroy was like turning on a water hose. However, instead of water, he spouted colorful stories filled with the characters he had met throughout the years.

Leroy was a character himself. Although probably tall and hefty when he was young, Leroy was now a smaller version of himself. Hank suspected that Leroy had always sported a grizzled appearance, with bushy white eyebrows which had probably never seen a barber's scissors.

A flannel shirt and suspenders completed the look. In his mid-nineties, Leroy still radiated energy and excitement about life. *No wonder people told him everything*, Hank thought.

Because Leroy's father owned a lumber mill when World War II came around, Leroy had been excused from serving in the war.

The country needed lumber, and his father needed Leroy to get the lumber out.

Leroy not only learned how to run the mill when he was just ten years old, but by the time he was a strapping fifteen-year-old he was cutting logs right beside the crew his father hired. By eighteen he was building homes.

Talking to Leroy was like talking to a human tape recorder. Leroy remembered everything as if it happened the day before. He had never erased anything. Every person Leroy ever met still lived inside his head. Leroy could quickly pull out a file in his memory for every story he ever heard.

It was those stories that had Hank, Sam, and Dan laughing. Back in Leroy's day, if the weather was terrible and they couldn't get out into the fields and forests to get their work done, the men would gather at local diners and talk long into the day. They told stories about each other and what they had done themselves.

The stories that started Hank and Dan laughing were about the man who lived in a makeshift house behind Leroy's father's lumber mill. He built it out of scrap lumber. He kept goats in the house, hardly ever washed, spoke louder than a fog horn, and provided hours of amusement to the men who knew him.

Some of the stories Leroy told them centered around the homes he had helped build. During that time, people didn't go to home supply stores to get wood to construct their homes. They went straight to a lumberyard.

So either Leroy had helped build most of the homes in both Concourse and Doveland, or he and his father had provided the lumber for them.

"Did you build Melvin Byler's farmhouse?" Hank asked.

Leroy paused and took a good look at Hank. "So you're the one," he said.

Hank almost choked on his coffee, "I'm the one what?"

"Ah, Melvin came to see me a few times after he met you and then that kid, Jay. He sure loved you both. You made his last few years the best of his life, he said, except for missing his wife, you know."

Hank turned away to hide the tears that had pooled in his eyes at the mention of his friend Melvin. Everyone waited for Hank to say something. He turned back to the group and said, "He changed my life forever."

Leroy nodded. "That was Melvin. Always helping. Depending on what you believe, that's still Melvin. Me, I'm hoping to see the old goat again. Swap stories, share a beer or two if they have them wherever we're going."

The four of them clinked their coffee cups together. "To Melvin. May he help me raise some ruckus when we meet again," Leroy said.

"Okay, fellas. I'm done telling you some good stories, now tell me what you came here to find out. Me and my guys, we seen everything that happened back in the day, and we shared it.

"Still hear things. People come to visit and tell me the gossip, so I might know what you are looking for, but why not fill me in, so as I could get it right the first time."

"Did you help build the Chapel?" Hank asked.

"Knew it," Leroy said, smacking his hand down on the arm of the chair. "Knew that someday I could tell this story to the right people. You all are the right people, aren't you?"

Without waiting for a reply, he nodded to himself, "Of course you are. You passed Melvin's radar. Okay. Yes, I done built that beauty. It was one of my finest pieces of work. Man alive, that place was beautiful. Still is, I wager. We loved working on that place. Me and my dad.

"But that's not all you want to know, is it? You want to know about the box. And yes, I know about the box cause I helped that lovely woman hide it there.

"I even know what's inside. I never read anything, but she told me, just in case. Looks like this is the just-in-case moment she meant."

The three men sat back in the chairs and stared at Leroy. Finally, Dan said, "Okay, sounds like we are in for a good story. Do you want a bigger audience to hear it?"

"You need to ask that? Damn right, I do. I've been carrying this secret for over sixty years, can't wait to tell the appropriate people. You got them, right? Now get me outta this place to tell it. Go tell Nurse Cutie Pants that I have an excuse to leave for a bit."

Dan went to talk to the nurse, silently agreeing with Leroy that yes, she was a cutie pants. Sam called Ava. Time for another gathering of whoever could be there. They were bringing a friend of Melvin's.

Hank called Grace, and she agreed that she and Sarah would bring Lloyd and Josh. Then he called Eliot. "Might as well shut down construction for the day. Tell the guys I'll pay them for a full day's work. You two get over to Ava's and bring Emily."

Thirty minutes later they had Leroy bundled up and buckled into Dan's car. He felt as if every staff member at the nursing home had stopped by to make sure Leroy had whatever he needed for the day.

Dan almost had to promise his firstborn son in order to take Leroy away. He promised and crossed his heart to take good care of Leroy. One nurse even asked for a pinky promise that Hank would bring Leroy back safe and sound before she let him drive away.

Driving to Ava's, Leroy entertained them by pointing out everything he saw as he passed by. His bony finger was continually tapping the window as they drove. Everything had a story behind it, and Leroy was bound and determined to tell them all.

Forty-Eight

Suzanne, Eric, and Leif were not in agreement about what to do. Suzanne wanted to talk to Sarah directly about the urgency of finding the stones. Leif did not agree. Eric backed his friend up. Even though he didn't completely understand what was happening, he knew the danger was increasing.

The longer Eric stayed, the more he realized that he was never meant to be part of what was happening in this realm. For a long time after they arrived in this dimension, Eric had been burdened with guilt about what had happened. He had made Leif bring him here and leave the Earth he had loved. Eric knew that it hadn't been right for him to demand that Leif give up his time with his wife, Sarah, so he and Grace could have more time together.

So, instead of being a support to Leif, Suzanne, and the rest of the Forest Circle, Eric allowed himself to be moody, dragging himself around as if he had a weight around his neck.

Until one day Leif sat him down and told him in no uncertain terms to get over it.

"You are making it hard for everyone with your constant guilty feelings and moodiness," Leif said. "Guilt does not help anyone when you wear it as a badge of honor. We all suffer because you have decided that what you did ruined things. It didn't. But you carrying on about it does.

"Besides, there is nothing to be guilty about. You played a role in what is happening. If you didn't ask me to bring you here, I would never have come. And yet, you know that I have to be here. It was you who made sure that it happened."

It was true. Leif needed to be there. So over time, Eric let the guilt fall away. But in place of guilt, his sadness grew. He was determined not to let his sorrow be a burden to anyone, but he often found himself silently weeping as he walked through the woods. He missed hugging Grace. He missed sitting at their dining room table discussing the day's events. He missed picking up Hannah from school. And as silly as it sounded even to him, he missed sitting in a chair instead of hovering above it when he did get to visit Grace and his old home.

Which was why agreeing with Leif that it wasn't time to talk directly to Sarah, was harder than it seemed. Because once Sarah got everyone to find their stones and bring them together, they were one step closer to completing the Stone Circle.

That completion, along with what the entire Forest Circle had been working on in the utmost secret, might give him the ability to return to his own life. It was possible it wouldn't work. He could get trapped. He could die. No one had done what they were trying to do for him.

He was terrified of the trapped part. Trapped between two realms. Perhaps forever. That was such a horrifying idea he didn't let himself think about it. The dying part was a little easier. He had been going to die anyway before he came to this realm. If he died trying to return in his body to Doveland, it would be as if he had just delayed his death.

Grace would be devastated, which is why no one had informed either Grace or Sarah what they were planning. If it worked, they could celebrate. If it didn't, Eric didn't want Grace to suffer thinking it was her fault he tried to come back. They would explain his death away as an accident, not an attempt to return.

Everything they were doing was in secret. No one could know their plan. There would be only a small window of opportunity to let Eric return to Grace. But first, the stones and the circle's completion would have to happen.

"Wait until this business is sorted out with the two boxes," Leif said. "You know they have to complete this before we can move on."

Seeing Suzanne's worried face, Leif took her hand in his. "It's going to be okay, Suzanne."

Suzanne nodded in agreement and hoped that Leif was right. *No matter what, though,* Suzanne promised herself, *I'll make sure Doveland remains safe. If it becomes necessary, I'll shut down the passageway, and sever the connection forever.*

Leif smiled at her, acknowledging that he had heard her message. He agreed. As painful as it would be, that might be the only choice. The people of Doveland, and really all of the Earth dimension, needed to remain safe.

Leif was glad that Eric couldn't read people's thoughts. This decision would be his and Suzanne's alone. No one could know their contingency plan. It was a burden that the two of them would carry alone.

Forty-Nine

A few people couldn't make it to Ava's. One of them was Valerie. She told Ava that she had a meeting at the school. Being the principal required her to be there. But Valerie told Ava she wasn't worried. She knew that Ava would keep her up to date with what was happening.

What Valerie didn't tell Ava was that in some ways she didn't care. It worried her a bit that she didn't care.

Valerie had hoped that she would have gotten over the traumatic events of the previous year by now, that it would have faded into the background. However, although slightly dulled by the passage of time, the pain and confusion remained. And that same passage of time had also allowed her to see things she hadn't had time to notice while it was happening.

During the day she managed for the most part. But she still woke up having nightmares. That's if she slept at all. The best part of the past year was her relationship with Craig. Thankfully, he was giving her plenty of room to think and heal, while supporting her in whatever way he could. At least the parts that she let him help her with. Some she kept to herself.

But Valerie knew that without Craig, she wasn't sure how well she would be functioning.

To keep from being too overwhelmed by her feelings after the year she had lived through, she had shut her emotions away. She knew that wasn't healthy in the long run, but thinking about all that happened was sometimes too much.

First, her husband Harold collapsed and died apparently for no reason. Then she discovered Harold had done nasty things for the king of nasty, Dr. Joe Hellard. Next, she found out that Joe murdered Harold to keep him quiet about what they had done together.

Those three events would have been enough for anyone to be traumatized. But there was more. Valerie then learned that Dr. Joe had raped her mother. Her mother had run away and married the man Valerie knew as her father. None of which she had known until she asked Sam to run a DNA panel on her. Then she discovered what she had suspected all along. Her dad wasn't her father.

What she hadn't expected in her wildest dreams, or her worst nightmare, was that Joe was her father. Not a dad. Not ever. A sperm donor. A predator. A rapist.

There was good news out of the "year of tragedy" as she had started to call it. She had found a half-brother, Edward. Their connection had grown in the past year. They had similar fears and similar hopes even if they were dealing with it differently. Maybe it was because she had children and couldn't run away.

Edward, on the other hand, had spent the year visiting old friends hoping to bring his past life into his new one. That was the reason he gave as to why he traveled, but Valerie knew it was also a form of running.

And now this. Valerie wasn't sure that she could take any more. In many ways, she wanted the world to stop turning so nothing new would be brought to light. Because, in her gut, Valerie knew that something was lurking in the shadows that would soon be brought out into the open. It was more than what was in the boxes. She tried to silence the feeling, but when they discovered the identity of the man on the bench, the feeling intensified.

Yes, she could have found a way to go to Ava's if it had been an emergency. Yes, part of her wanted to hear the stories that Leroy was going to tell.

But more than that, she was hoping to put off whatever was going to happen. She wanted a few more days. Perhaps then she could face it.

Besides, she told herself, *it could be a good thing. However, given the year of tragedy that I've just lived through, it's probably not.*

****

Hannah watched Valerie tell her mother, Ava, that she couldn't come to the meeting. She saw Valerie sit back in the chair in her office and let out a small sob. Hannah wanted to do something to help her. But even if Valerie would have let her, Hannah was in her classroom and not in Valerie's office.

Besides, this time Valerie couldn't see Hannah watching her, which was a good thing. Valerie's sorrow was private.

Suzanne had shown Hannah how to remain invisible, even to people like Valerie who had learned how to see astral projections. Being invisible had something to do with molecules or particles or something like that and matching the surrounding vibrations. Hannah didn't understand the explanation, but she did understand how to do it.

Hannah had chosen to be invisible because she didn't want Valerie to know that she was checking on her. She wasn't exactly spying on Valerie. She was doing her friend Johnny a favor.

When he had come back to visit for Mother's Day, he and Hannah had taken a walk together into the woods. Johnny was worried about his mother. She looked like she was doing well, but he knew his mother wasn't sleeping, and even when she did, she sometimes woke up from a nightmare.

Johnny tried to talk to his mom about it, but Valerie had said it wasn't his job to take care of her. It was hers to take care of him. Johnny disagreed, but she wouldn't relent, claiming to be over the trauma of the past year.

"Well, I'm not!" Johnny said to her. "How could you be?"

"I have to be," was his mother's answer.

So Johnny did what he thought he had to do. He asked for help. He asked Hannah to check in on his mom, and report to him if there was anything he could do. Johnny had also asked Sarah and Mandy to check on Valerie. He knew Sarah would do it anyway and Valerie would expect her to. And Mandy had her office in the other half of their house, which meant she would see his mom almost every day.

Johnny didn't tell his brother, Lex. Lex didn't need more pressure. He already felt as if he had to be the man of the house, even though Johnny had assured him that wasn't necessary.

Johnny did ask Lex to let Hannah, Sarah, or Mandy know right away if he suspected their mom needed anything. When Johnny explained why he had asked those three women specifically, Lex's response was to ask Johnny if he was aware he had called Hannah a woman.

He hadn't been. But now that he had said it, Johnny wondered why he had begun to think of Hannah that way. After all, she was the same age as his brother.

But then, he heard girls grow up faster, and of course, Hannah was always reminding him, that because she remembered her immediate past life, she was technically eight years older. *And that is what makes her think she is a woman,* Johnny said to himself.

Still, he wondered. When did he start seeing Hannah that way?

Fifty

By the time they got Leroy to Ava's house, he had said he was hungry again. Then he added that it wasn't so much that he was hungry, he just wanted something different to eat. The food at the nursing home was good, but boring.

"What about that Thai place in town?" he asked. "Heard some old biddy saying her daughter took her there and it was pretty dang good in spite of it not being American. Made me want to see what all the fuss is about."

Well, there goes my stereotyping of old lumbermen and their stuck-in-the-past mentality, Hank thought.

While Sam got Leroy situated in a comfortable chair in the living room, Hank and Ava went through the menu Ava kept in the kitchen drawer. Within a few minutes, they had figured out what everyone might like and placed an order. Sarah said she would wait for it and bring it with her.

At first, Hank thought it was going to be a smaller group this time. Besides Valerie not being able to come, Craig had patients, Pete and Barbara had a full Diner, Mandy was in Pittsburgh picking out furniture for her latest design project, and the kids were still in school. But then he realized that they had added the Stanton brothers, Lloyd, Josh and Dan. Plus Leroy. A full house once again.

Sarah arrived thirty minutes later with enough food to feed an army, which was a good thing based on how many people were in Ava and Evan's living room.

"Good thinking ahead, Evan," Hank said. "When you bought this house did you ever think that there would always be so many people coming over all the time?"

Evan looked out on the diverse group laughing together. Leroy had already learned everyone's name. "This is what I dreamed of having. But it's much better than I could ever have imagined," Evan said.

"Even with all the drama attached?" Ava asked.

"Especially with all the drama attached," Evan answered as he hugged his wife.

Hank smiled at the two of them, and at the crowd in the living room. If he had allowed himself to dream when he was younger, he would have dreamed of this too. No matter what happened from here, this was the only place he ever wanted to be.

****

The boxes and bags of food were all picked up, and leftovers stored away for everyone to take home. In spite of the massive amount of food they had eaten, no one was tired. Leroy had kept them all entertained during lunch but didn't show any signs of slowing down.

"Okay, old man," Hank said, "We're ready for you. Here's your audience. Now, tell us the story of the two boxes."

Leroy roared with laughter. Or what might have been a roar in his youth but now sounded like a hee-hee.

"Suppose you all want me to start at the beginning?" Leroy

said. Catching a look at Hank and Sam's faces, he corrected himself, "Okay, not the beginning. How about why Lisa Lane buried the box in the wall?"

"Go, for God's sake," Hank murmured under his breath. Leroy's sharp hearing caught it anyway, and he laughed again.

"Okay, I'm going. So's you all know that Lisa and Tom Stanton married in the Chapel in 1941. I got to be there since they knew me from helping to build her parents' house. She was so pretty. Anyways, I took a picture of it with one of those old big cameras, and after I had it developed, I gave it to Lisa."

Lloyd held up his hand to stop Leroy from talking. He reached into his backpack and took out the picture that had started his search and laid it gently on the table.

"That there's the one! She was a beautiful bride, that one. I kinda had a crush on her. But it was apparent that the two of them were crazy in love. Tom had enlisted to go into the army, and she wanted to be married before he left. Tom wanted to make sure that if something happened to him, she got everything that was his.

"She wouldn't hear of his dying. Said it couldn't happen. And for a time, she was right. A few years after they got married she had twins. I think you know that part. Kathleen and little Tom. Tom Sr. got to spend some time with them off and on. Short leaves, you know.

"The last time Tom visited was in 1944. The war was almost over. They were both real excited. Me and my daddy added an additional room onto their small house once they decided to have more kids. Good thing, cause Lisa had another baby. In 1945, I think? Bout the same time she also got one of those visits. The one with the uniforms and such.

"Poor girl. The women of Doveland took care of her like they did with all the widows. So many of them." Leroy stopped and shook his head at the memory, dashed his hand across his eyes to hide the tears and started again.

"A few months after Tom died, Lisa came to me. She had met some bigwig who wanted to marry her. She didn't think she had a choice. She had three kids to raise. The guy was moving her away, but she said her heart would always stay in Doveland. That's when she gave me the box. Asked me to keep it safe.

"The back wall of the Chapel had to be opened to fix some wiring, so I hid it there and we plastered over it. Told her where it was. She told me it had their love letters, copies of the birth certificates, and something about some property that Tom owned. Gave the same thing to her brother too, just in case.

"She said the property was the only thing of value Tom had. But it wouldn't feed her kids. Within a week she was gone. I never saw her again. Though she returned in the end. She's buried in the Doveland graveyard you know."

Lloyd burst into the conversation, "How? How could she have been? I remember her funeral. It was where we lived, which wasn't Doveland."

Leroy smiled at Lloyd. "No, it wasn't. But your mama finally did the one thing Lisa wanted. She had her buried here a few years later. Wasn't easy to do, but I am guessing Lisa haunted her until Kathleen did the right thing.

"Lisa had bought a grave site for herself and her brother before she left Doveland. That's how I know. That's the way Lisa wanted it to be. She knew someday people would come looking for her. And that property. And she was right wasn't she?"

Fifty-One

Lloyd wasn't sure he could keep his despair inside anymore. The more impatient he felt, the more he worried he became that he had chosen the wrong profession. A minister should have better control over his emotions than he appeared to have.

He kept telling himself that not everyone knew what he knew. It seemed that he was the only one who had been searching the whole time. Lloyd knew his Nana had married again. That man had been cold and distant, and he hadn't been sorry when he died. When he learned that his real grandfather was someone else, he had wished that he had met him. But then even his grandfather's children didn't get to know him. Who was he to complain?

Leroy was a fantastic storyteller. Lloyd had to give him that. Everyone was utterly immersed in the listening. But when Leroy got to the deed, Lloyd had to speak up.

"Okay. I've heard about this bloody property since I was a kid. Or at least my mother kept saying something belonged to her, and someone had stolen it from her. So I am assuming she was referring to a deed. Being drunk most of the time didn't help her ability to tell me the truth about things. So now that you have brought it up, can we get to it?"

The whole table turned to look at him. "What? Haven't you heard a pastor lose his temper before?"

"Well, I have," Leroy said. "If you've been around as long as I have you've heard most everything. But before we get on with the deed, can I get you all straight in my head. Lloyd, you are Kathleen's son? Dang, I can see that. I hadn't seen her since she and her brother were about two years old, but she was a spitfire, that one. Doesn't sound as if life treated her that well though, and it rubbed off on you, Lloyd?"

Lloyd dropped his head to the table and mumbled, "Guess so."

Leroy turned to Eli and Elliot. "So you are Tom's sons? He was the quiet one of the twins. How did he turn out?"

Eli looked at his brother expecting him to answer, and when he didn't, Eli said, "Don't know. Never knew him. Don't know what happened to him. Didn't even know who he was until we moved here. Don't know any of these things that Lloyd knows."

Leroy just nodded and turned to Josh. "And you. You must be her brother's grandson. He left Doveland when he was a teenager. Lisa sure loved him. Probably her new husband kept her from her family. He seemed the controlling type.

"But what about Diana? Are any of you here one of her children?"

Sarah answered Leroy. "We don't know who that might be. Maybe she didn't have any children? In any case, we have a big part of the family here, and now everyone wants to know about that property.

"Hold on," Hank said so softly they weren't sure he had said anything.

His face looking ten years older than it had moments before, Hank asked, "Your father was George Webster?"

When Lloyd nodded yes, Hank 's heart sank. "I was hoping

I would never have to deal with Grant or Joe again. But here they are again. Didn't put it together until just now, and then it clicked. Your father died didn't he?"

Lloyd nodded. "He did. A few years after Nana died. I was eleven. 1995. All I ever heard was he got into a bar fight with some guy and got himself killed. Supposedly the other guy got away."

Hank turned to Eli. "And you were born in 1995? And you never knew your father, Tom Stanton?"

When they nodded their assent, Hank said, "Damn," and buried his head in his hands. Everyone waited, afraid to say anything. "I guess I'm never going to get away from the horror that was Grant and Joe."

Turning to Eli and Elliot, Hank said, "Your father didn't desert you. He died. In that bar. But it wasn't a fight. It was an execution.

"I was there, working for Grant, and now we know that Grant was working for Joe, but I didn't know that at the time. Tom and George were meeting with Grant. I don't know how he got them there. But Grant was there to make a deal with them. He said he had a buyer for the land. Both men said they didn't know what he was talking about.

"It got heated, and when it was evident that neither man did know what he was talking about, or at least they were not going to tell even if they did, Grant pulled out a gun. Nobody in the bar was going to mess with Grant. He owned the men in that place. Every one of us.

"When I tried to talk Grant out of pointing the gun at the two men, Grant pointed it at me and told me to get out. What could I do? It was just one more day in Grant's reign of terror. I didn't think he was actually going to shoot them. But someone did.

"I assume it was him, because afterward he told me that they were of no use to him, but he didn't trust them to keep their mouths shut."

No one spoke. "I'm sorry," Hank said.

Neither the Stanton brothers nor Lloyd had ever heard of Grant or Joe, and none of them had heard the truth about how their fathers died. So to them Hank's, "I'm sorry" was more than useless. He had been there. Hank had been part of what had happened. He could have stopped it.

The three men stood up and walked out of the room, Lloyd pushing his chair over as he left, letting it crash to the floor. Hank watched them go and then got up and walked outside to the bunkhouse.

Sarah turned to Leroy who looked as stunned as everyone else. "Thank you for this. It had to come out. Secrets eat away at lives."

"Didn't know it would be like that. But you know, it was probably over that property."

"Then it's time to find out about that don't you think?" Sam said. "Tell us what you know, Leroy. Let's get it all out in the open."

Fifty-Two

"Are you all still there?" Valerie asked Ava over the phone.

"Yes. We've had a bit of an upset, so we had to take a break."

"Well, I'm probably bringing more upset, so might as well get it all over at one time then. I'll be there as soon as school lets out. I assume Lloyd is still with you, so I'll bring Jake with Lex and Hannah."

Ava relayed the information to the people still at the table and asked Leroy if he would like a place to rest for a bit before Valerie arrived. After settling him in one of the extra bedrooms, Ava stopped for a few minutes in her meditation space to calm herself.

She understood why the men had been upset and that they needed time to process what they had heard, but if there was more to come, she hoped they would be ready.

Sarah and Sam had gone after them to make sure they were okay. Josh had remained at the table talking to Grace who was treating him as if she was his grandmother. He looked as if he was loving every minute of it.

Ava knew it was up to her to talk to Hank, but she wasn't sure if she was wise enough to say the right thing.

He had been working so hard the last few years to make up

for his years as a henchman to Grant.

Not that Hank has anything to make up for, Ava thought. Hank had done what he felt he had to do, to survive and keep his sister alive. Once Hank discovered that Grant had misled him, he became the most stalwart supporter for good she had ever known. She was proud that he was her uncle.

"Just tell him that," Suzanne said.

Ava was so delighted to see her friend Suzanne that she tried to hug her, forgetting that it wasn't possible. Suzanne looked solid, but in this earth dimension, she wasn't.

Before Suzanne had left with the Forest Circle to go to the other dimension, Suzanne had been her best friend. Suzanne took Ava under her wing when Ava's mother had died, and been her staunch supporter in all that had happened since then.

"You're back?"

"I've been around but not visible so as not to draw attention to my dimension traveling. This time I thought it was wise to let you see me to give you that extra encouragement.

"You are all coming to the end of the mystery and the closing of the Stone Circle. Just a few more threads need to be unraveled so that things can be put right.

"I wanted to remind you that all things do work together for good, for those that love good, like you and your friends. And if it isn't good, it isn't reality or the end. Just keep working through it. You will all find the blessings. You're almost there.

"Now, tell Hank how much you love him, and what he means to you. Oh, and find your stone."

"Wait, find my stone?" Ava called after her, but Suzanne was gone.

****

Leroy was still napping when Valerie pulled up to the house with the three children in tow. Jake was out of the car as soon as it stopped, heading for his father who he could see standing back in the field by the forest.

Hannah and Lex followed Valerie inside. They were anxious to find out what was going on and they wanted to make sure that they were in the middle of the action.

Valerie was so tense on the ride over, she hadn't said a word. Not like her at all. Plus she kept touching an envelope that was sitting on the front seat as if she wanted to assure herself that it was still there.

Although Hannah had been peeking in and out at the meeting while she was in school, she kept missing things because the teacher insisted on asking her questions. Luckily she was getting better at being in two places at once.

But when she missed a question the teacher asked because she was listening to Hank describing the shooting of George Webster and Tom Stanton, it was Lex who saved her. He had popped up and answered the question drawing attention away from Hannah.

On the way to Valerie's office, Hannah filled Lex in with what she had heard. Both of them were worried about what was going to happen now that the three men knew how their fathers had died. Hannah hoped that they would quickly see the better picture. Having been around for all the horrible things that Grant and Joe had done, including losing her past dad Jay twice because of them, she knew that sometimes it was hard to remain calm and rational.

However, Hannah knew that hate wouldn't get her anywhere. But if she were ever going to want to throw darts at someone, it would be Grant and Joe. Hannah knew they were getting what Eric called their "comeuppance" somewhere.

She hoped she never ran across them again because she wasn't sure she would be able to keep herself from doing more than throwing darts at them.

She didn't feel the same way about Harold, Lex's father. In some ways, Harold had been deceived the same way as Hank.

The difference between the two of them was Hank had accepted what he had done and was doing everything he could to make up for it, whereas Harold kept on running from it.

"Although he did say he was sorry to my mom before he died," Lex said.

"What? How did you know what I was thinking?"

"Don't know. Lately, I hear people talking in their heads. Not all the time. Just sometimes."

Hannah shook her head. It appeared that paranormal powers were contagious. Probably because they aren't paranormal, she thought. They were normal. Only people didn't believe it, so they didn't practice or expect to have them.

When Valerie's car pulled up, Sarah was still speaking to the Stanton brothers. They were more distressed that they had not known their father, had thought he had deserted them and hated him for it their whole life, than they were angry with Hank.

Everything they knew about Hank told them that if he could have done something, he would have. Besides, how would he have known that he would meet the sons of the two men in the bar with Grant? So when they got back to the house, they pulled Hank aside and said they understood.

"I don't, really," Hank said. "But thank you."

"I'm sorry too, Hank," Lloyd said. "If there are people to be upset with, it's not you."

"You're right about that," Valerie said. "And when I show you what I have found out, you are going to be even more upset with Grant and Joe."

Hank groaned. "Will we ever be rid of them?"

"It might be a long time before we uncover all the evil that they did. But it doesn't mean that it worked," Sarah said. "We're all still here. We have added more people to our community. I'd say Grant and Joe's powers were useless.

Turning to Valerie, Sarah said, "Okay, show us what you have."

Nobody heard Leroy come into the room until he was standing right beside Valerie.

Looking up at her, Leroy whispered, "Lisa? You look just like Lisa!"

Sam hung up his phone and said, "You're right, Leroy. She probably does look like Lisa, her grandmother. My friend just told me Valerie's DNA matches the ones we ran on Eli and Elliot. Valerie is your cousin. Her mother was Diana."

"No!" Valerie said, as she fainted.

Fifty-Three

"Are we ever going to find out about that thing they are calling a deed?" Evan groused as he made more coffee for all the people in his living room. He didn't like that he felt so irritated. It seemed as if everything was conspiring to keep them from that final piece of evidence.

"It was important enough to kill at least two men over, so what is it anyway? And why is it taking so long to find out?"

Ava crossed the kitchen into Evan's arms. They loved hosting parties and meetings, but it seemed as if this thing that started when Josh's grandfather died on the bench in the village green would never be over.

"It hasn't actually been that long," Ava answered. "It just sometimes feels that way."

"That's because there are so many layers to this mystery," Mira said, leaning on the refrigerator watching the two of them hugging. She added, "Besides, because of this, we now have another person that will keep us all entertained."

Evan laughed. "Leroy! Yes, it's pretty hard not to enjoy having him around. Once this is all over, we'll have to include him in our events."

Mira agreed, "Yes, Melvin will be happy that we found

Leroy. Or Leroy found us. Or however that works. But Valerie says she has information to share so maybe we should go listen."

Valerie had quickly recovered from her fainting spell. As she had slumped sideways, Edward had been right beside her and kept her from falling. Within a few seconds, Valerie had opened her eyes, looked around, hugged Edward and then turned to her new family and hugged each one in turn. By the time she reached Lloyd, tears were running down her face.

"First I found a brother, and now I have all of you. My family has grown. Handsome men surround me. All of you and my two sons. I don't know what I have been moping around about. Life has brought me so many riches.

"Speaking of riches, that's what I have in this envelope. I don't have all the details yet, but I have enough to share. After you gave me the task to find out what that piece of paper called a deed was, I called a friend in the library system who loves old documents.

"She knew exactly what it was as soon as she saw it. But it took some time because she wanted to make sure that she was reading it correctly.

"We were right in thinking that it is about owning a piece of land, so to us, it's a deed. But back when it was drawn up, it was a land contract without much information. Everyone knew the area and the people, so details weren't needed, which is what made this one hard to figure out.

"Josh's grandfather's copy is easier to read than the one we found in Lisa's box."

Valerie paused and looked around the group as she held the papers she had pulled out of the envelope. "I'm glad you're here too, Dan. If this is real, and there is no reason to think that it's not, this will change everything and will have some serious ramifications. Or could. Not only for the decedents of Lisa and

Joshua Lane but also for the entire town of Doveland.

"And once I tell you what it is, you'll see why Dr. Joe sent Grant out to find it. It's interesting that Joe didn't try to get to Kathleen and Diana though. Or perhaps he did.

"I think that my mother, Diana, ended up in the commune where Joe found her because her mother had told her about Doveland. When Joe raped her, he probably didn't know who she was, or he would have tried to find her when she left.

"Why he didn't find Kathleen, I don't know. But from what I heard from you, Lloyd, it sounds as if she thought that someone stole it. Maybe she believed that. Maybe she didn't. Her ravings could have been her way of protecting you."

"Well, that's an entirely new way to look at my mother," Lloyd said. "First I have to see my father differently, now I need to look at what my mother was doing. Perhaps she knew what happened to my father and her fear started her drinking. Whatever happened is different than anything I could have imagined."

"We can conjecture about this until the cows come home, but for heaven's sake, please tell us what that dang piece of paper says," Evan said.

While they were talking, Leroy had slipped the document off the table and was staring at it.

"Should have asked me about this when you found it, young lady. Course you didn't know me then, so I guess that's why. But I'm here now. And I know what this is. Lisa told me. It's why she hid it away for her children.

"I guess I should have brought it out into the open when all the trouble started, but I didn't know where any of her relatives were. Besides, that Joe fella scared the crap outta me. I tried to stay away from him. Me and Melvin. We didn't trust him.

"But going gainst the grain of the town wasn't easy, so we

held our peace. But now here it is. Time to tell.

"This here piece of paper proves that Tom Stanton's great-grandfather owned almost all the property that Doveland is built on." A long moment of silence fell over the group, and then everyone started talking at once.

Hank held up his hand, and said, "One question at a time, please. In fact, let's have Sarah ask the questions. If she misses one, we'll fill in."

Sarah smiled at Hank, took a deep breath and started. "I have a feeling that one question will answer the next. However, the question that begs to be asked is how an entire town gets built on property owned by one man, and no one ever knew."

"Well," Leroy said. "What I understand is that Tom's great-grandfather died right after he purchased the property in 1839, which was about the time the town was founded.

"Maybe the few buildings that had been put up were not on his property. Or maybe he gave them permission. Who knows?

"Anyways, Lisa's husband, Tom Stanton told her that he thought the deed had been lost after that, or at least hidden. He found it when he was going through the old farmhouse that his grandfather had lived in.

"He thought he knew what it meant and was going to do something about it. However, he was called up to serve in the army, and he didn't want to start the process when he wasn't there to help.

"Tom thought when he returned he would do something about it, but he didn't have a chance to. Lisa didn't think she could deal with it, so she left it to her children, hoping one of them would know what to do."

"Which is most likely when Joe came into the picture," Sam said. "He had been buying property all over Doveland for years. Somehow he must have discovered that people were selling property they didn't own. Maybe on purpose, or perhaps they didn't know better.

"But, obviously Joe did. He needed the original document to destroy it. Otherwise, all that he owned would be in question."

"I guess that leaves just one more question. What do we do now?" Lloyd asked.

"Well, if this document is real, and nothing has changed since it was written, it looks as if the five of you own most of Doveland," Dan said.

Turning to Valerie, he asked her if what Leroy had told them jived with what she had learned. When she nodded yes, Dan added, "Then this is the equivalent of a hurricane, tornado, and earthquake hitting the town all at the same time, so I am going to ask all of you to keep this quiet until it is confirmed and you decide what you are going to do.

"When this comes to light it is going to destroy everything the town has built. Families will be devastated. No one will own anything they have spent their entire life building."

Dan stood to go, stopped and turned to the five people who held his future in their hands, and said, "Personally, I've never heard more terrifying news. I hope you all will take this seriously. Our lives are in your hands."

Fifty-Four

"Well, I don't think we should call ourselves the fantastic five, do you?" Valerie said, "Even though the four of you are definitely handsome enough to be called fantastic or even fabulous."

"You're pretty fantastic and fabulous too, Cuz," Josh said.

"Agreed!" all four men shouted and clinked their beer glasses together.

After Valerie's revelation, the meeting broke up at Ava's. No one knew what to say. It was up to the five cousins to decide what to do, and no one felt qualified to advise them.

Ava said all the kids could stay over at the house, so the five of them could meet together. She thought Jake would fit into some of the clothes that Lex always had there, which meant Lloyd didn't have to go home to get anything for him. She would put them all on the bus in the morning. There was nothing to worry about.

Hank got permission from the nursing home to let Leroy stay over in the bunkhouse with him and Josh because Leroy wanted to go to the funeral with them the next day. Hank promised to return Leroy right afterward. Once again, Hank had to cross his heart and hope to die that he would take good care of Leroy.

As all Ava's guests filed out one by one, somber and worried, Sarah stood by the door and hugged every one of them.

Dan was so upset he was shaking. A simple piece of paper could destroy the town that he loved. As Sarah hugged him, she whispered in his ear that it would be alright.

Dan backed up and looked into her eyes, and felt better. He didn't understand what these people did, but it always turned out for the best for everyone, so he would have to trust that it would be true this time too.

Edward hugged his new half-cousins one by one, as they left. He understood that the piece of paper his grandfather had saved could be disastrous. But at the moment, he felt overwhelmingly grateful that he had found more family.

An hour later, anyone watching the five cousins in the tavern drinking beer together, wouldn't have guessed that they were there not only to get to know each other, but to decide the fate of the town.

"There is a strange justice in this, isn't there?" Valerie said. "Joe wanted to make sure he owned all his property, and here I am, his descendant, owning a piece of it without having to kill anyone for it."

"I can't believe our fathers died over this," Eli said. "Do you think that they didn't know where it was, or that they weren't going to tell so we could end up with it?"

"I'd rather have had him," Elliot answered. "All those years wasted over this piece of paper."

Turning to Valerie, he said, "How hard it must have been for you to find out that man was your father. And your husband working with him. How do you keep yourself from being eaten up by hate. Because right now I feel such rage at a man I never met, I think I could kill him if I met him and he wasn't already dead."

"Sometimes I feel that rage too, Elliot. But it doesn't hurt Joe at all. Just me. Think of Hank. Joe directed Grant, and Grant controlled Hank. Joe ran Hank's whole life. Or what about Edward? He knew what his father was, and had to run away to keep from being killed by his father, who had murdered his mother.

"All of us have been affected by that bastard. Everyone in our group has reason to hate Joe. But would we survive if we harbor hate? He'd win. I am never going to let him take away all the good that has come to my family and me in the past few years.

"In a way, all the evil that Joe did has been returned to us as something good. It's the way we react to what happens to us that makes a difference. Do we join him in hating and controlling, or do we choose a different path?" Valerie asked.

"What about exercising our rights in the town?" Lloyd asked. "We could let everyone stay where they are, but we could charge rent for the property. Like a lease. My son and I have struggled for so long. This would be the end of the struggle."

"It would be the end of a money struggle for the two of you, but aren't there other kinds of struggle? I would think a minister would be thinking about those, too. We would be hated. The only people that would like us would be the wealthy people like us, but only because they would want our favor," Josh said.

"Maybe," Eli said. "But my brother has worked his whole life to support me. All we do is work. We wouldn't have to work anymore."

"You'd still be working, Eli," Josh said. "You'd still be managing properties, and money, and people wanting your money. But instead of people loving you the way that Emily does because of things you have done for her, like Melvin's bus, people would be afraid of you and your power."

Valerie sat back and watched the four men talk it over. The lure of what appeared to be easy wealth was there. Maybe not even easy. It would be hard to get. They'd have to prove the deed was legal. So many legal battles lay ahead. But they would probably win. The five of them could be wealthy. Very wealthy.

While they argued both sides of the issue, Valerie imagined having enough money to send her boys to the best schools, maybe in the world. Provide them with everything they could ever need. She could travel anywhere she wanted to go. It was so tempting to choose wealth as she daydreamed her way into unlimited money.

But in the middle of that daydream, she realized who she would become if she got her money that way. She would be like Joe.

Yes, the wealth was tempting. But Valerie knew that she didn't want to be wealthy at the expense of others. She would support whatever her cousins decided, but nothing would be the same. She and the boys would have to find a new town and leave them to it.

"No," Josh was saying. "I refuse to be like him. I refuse to be like that Joe. If you all vote to go after this property, I will turn my share over to you, but I can't be part of it."

"Nor I," Valerie said.

The three remaining men looked at each other and nodded. They had decided.

Fifty-Five

Josh hadn't meant for his grandfather's funeral to be a public event, but it turned out that way. Everyone in town knew the story of the old man who died on the bench. They weren't proud that it had happened, and coming to his funeral to pay their respects to him seemed like a small thing to do.

The Chapel was packed, even though it was a late afternoon in the middle of the week. Josh had asked Lloyd to preside over the ceremony, and Mandy and Grace had provided all the flowers. They had chosen flowers that were bright and cheerful. Not fancy. Simple spring bouquets. No one wore black at Josh's request. They were there to celebrate a life, not mourn one that was gone.

Josh gave the eulogy. He had been writing it in his head from the moment he had heard that his grandfather had died. He missed his grandfather more than he would ever be able to express, but looking out over the sea of faces in the Chapel, he could only feel gratitude.

Over the years, it had been his grandfather and grandmother who had taught him about how to be a good man, about love and family. His grandfather had brought him here. To this town. To this chapel. Maybe that had been his plan all along.

Josh wasn't sure that he would have listened to an argument from his grandfather to come to Doveland. He was happy where he lived. He had his work and his friends.

It took an act of bravery on his grandfather's part to force him to change. Did his grandfather know about Emily, and that Josh would meet her again? Or was he merely seeking his sister? Josh didn't know for sure, but he thought that the answer was that it was both. Somehow his grandfather had known that Josh would find love and a home in Doveland. Somehow his grandfather had known that his sister would have returned.

After the ceremony, the procession of cars made their way to the cemetery where Joshua Lane was laid to rest beside his sister Lisa. Tucked into his hands was a ceramic jar containing the last remaining ashes of his beloved wife. That jar had been sitting on the mantle in Josh's living room ever since his grandmother died.

Although he and his grandfather had scattered her ashes as she wished, his grandfather had kept some for himself to take with him when he was ready to go. Now his grandfather was with the two women he loved the most. They had come full circle.

Last night at the tavern, Josh had realized that his grandfather had known all along that the land in Doveland belonged partially to him. Why hadn't he done anything about it? Josh thought that it was one more thing that his grandfather was trying to teach him. It was up to Josh to decide what kind of man he wanted to be.

The five cousins had asked the people that had been at Ava's the night before to remain after the coffin was lowered into the grave.

Emily had heard what happened and she stood beside Josh wondering what he had decided. She knew what she wanted him to choose, but she had to let him make his own decision because he would have to live with it.

Everyone knew why they had been asked to stay. It was a moment of truth.

Dan thought he might do something he had never done before. Faint. But Grace, feeling his distress reached out to hold his hand, and that steadied him.

This group will help me no matter what the cousins decide, he realized. I won't be facing this by myself. That in itself meant everything to him.

Valerie stepped forward with a document in her hand. "This is the document found in my grandmother's box in the chapel."

Josh stepped forward with another document in his hand. "And this is the one found in my grandfather's box. As far as we know, there are no more copies. Valerie and I have agreed to give our shares to Lloyd, Eli, and Elliot to do what they want with them."

Lloyd stepped forward with both documents. He handed one to Eli and one to Elliot, and said, "We didn't have to talk long about this. None of us have had it easy in life.

"We three, like many of you, have worked our whole lives to take care of the ones that we love. The idea that we could be wealthy beyond our imagination filled us with happiness for a moment.

"Then we realized that what made us happiest would be lost if we destroyed the community of love and respect found in Doveland. Which did we want most? The answer was clear."

Lloyd took a lighter out of his pocket and flicked it on. "We decided that you are what we want most. We thank all those who came before us who wanted us to have this wealth, but we think that what they wanted most of all was for us to discover where our wealth truly lies."

Eli and Elliot held their documents into the flame, and they all watched as they burned and the ashes dropped into the grave. Tears of gratitude flowed freely.

Dan felt a rush as if he had been lifted up off the earth. The thought came to him that Joe had finally lost. The end was good. It had to be real.

At that moment a wind swept across the graveyard blowing a cloud of dandelion seeds along with it so that it looked as if fairies were dancing on the wind.

In the middle of that cloud stood three figures. Sarah smiled at Joshua Lane looking radiant with two women standing by his side beaming with joy at the gathering.

"You've made them proud," she said to the five cousins.

Fifty-Six

How a month could fly by so quickly Mandy wasn't sure. When she and Mira had said they could set up a wedding in a month's time, Mandy couldn't have known what else had to happen first. But they had managed to move forward until now.

She and Mira had been told in no uncertain terms that the Forest Circle said that the wedding couldn't take place until the Stone Circle had found the last person to complete it. That was a problem.

Everything else about planning the wedding, she and Mira had handled easily. In the middle of wedding planning, they continued to run their businesses. Plus, they had helped plan Josh's grandfather's funeral. They had found out who all Josh's relatives were. They had survived the possibility of Doveland's existence as they knew it would be destroyed.

All that. And still, Mira and Mandy had managed to plan a beautiful wedding.

Mandy thought about how she and Mira had become even closer as they made wedding plans. It was a dream to work with the woman she thought of as her sister.

Between the two of them, they had brainstormed the perfect wedding. They made each other's ideas better because they discussed them. The hardest part had been to make sure they chose things that they could do in a month's time.

The other ideas they had, they kept for future reference. Who knew? Perhaps Josh and Emily would tie the knot one day, and she and Mira would have a folder of great ideas ready for them.

Sam and Tom had completely turned the wedding planning over to the two of them. Mandy thought that was the smartest thing she had ever heard a man do. Why fight over what was going to happen at the wedding? It was mostly for the women anyway. She and Tom had picked some of the music, and Sam and Mira had chosen the rest. They had each written separate vows. But the rest of the wedding was all Mandy and Mira's creation.

So even though less than a month had gone by since their trip to State College and their decision to marry, she and Mira had pulled it off. The food was ready, and so were the flowers and decorations. Ava and Evan's house was prepped and ready for the reception.

It was also going to be a celebration of Ava and Evan's anniversary even though the two of them didn't know that yet.

Except for one thing that was stopping everything from going forward.

There was still the problem of the Stone Circle. Even though Mandy was not a member of that Circle, her soon-to-be husband was, and although Tom tried not to show it, he was tense over it. Everyone was because they all had a big problem. No one knew where their stones were.

The stones had been given to them by Earl Wieland, the leader of the Forest Circle, before he had left. At the time, he had told them all to keep them safe, which was what they thought they had done.

But not one person knew where their stone was, except Leif who had taken his with him when he had gone to the Forest Circle's dimension.

So the first problem was finding their stones. The second problem was who was the last man to complete the circle? And that presented a separate issue. Where was his stone? There had not been an extra one in the bag. Did he have his stone already? What if he lost it the same way the rest of the Stone Circle had lost theirs?

All Mandy could think was, hurry up and find them. The wedding is in two days!

Which was why Mandy was delighted to hear that Sarah had called a meeting of the Stone Circle.

The trouble was that was five hours ago. What could be keeping them?

Fifty-Seven

They were all together at Sarah's home—Sarah, Tom, Mira, Ava, Evan, and Craig. The only person they were missing was Leif. But he didn't need to be there. He had his stone. Once they all found theirs, he would be at the meeting where they completed the Stone Circle, but until then he wasn't needed.

It had been a long time since it had been just them. They reminisced about how they had first met. About how Mira had found Tom. How they were suspicious of Evan at first. How Suzanne had kept Ava safe with the Forest Circle until they all found each other.

They talked about how Leif and Sarah had been put in charge of the Stone Circle. Not that anyone knew what that meant, but looking back they would see how the two of them had guided them, mostly behind the scenes, but they were always there.

Sarah talked about her home in Sandpoint and how much she had loved it. They reminisced over the beauty of the mountain and the ever present forest.

Mira said the movie, or whatever it had been, that Suzanne's father Earl had shown them had changed her entire view of life.

All of them had watched their whole lives pass before them.

They had seen the weave of their lives and how each step, each experience, was necessary. They had observed how everything they had done brought them together. Lessons they learned were always useful, and never destructive. It was then that they had begun to understand the idea of Karass. The meshing of lifetimes, the same loved ones meeting together to learn and move forward. The joy of knowing they would always meet again.

Then the stones were rolled out onto the table and glowed for them. Each stone was different. But the stones had only glowed for a brief moment and then gone dark again.

Earl had asked them to keep them safe, and yet none of them could find them now when they knew that they needed them for the next step in their lives. Sarah was ready to join Leif where he had gone. Hannah wanted to go with her, and knowing Hannah, there was probably nothing they could do to stop her. But they couldn't go until they found the two missing pieces.

So after remembering the past, they settled into the questions that were before them. Where were the stones and who was the remaining member of the circle?

"Perhaps we are going about this in the wrong way," Sarah said. Perhaps we need to find the person first, then the stones. For some reason, the stones are hiding from us. They must want something from us before they become visible again.

"That something could be to trust that they are here, but we can't see them until they are ready to be seen."

"We don't have much time," Mira said. "The wedding is in two days."

"We can do it now," Sarah said. We have to trust that the man is already someone we know. Let's bring them all here and talk to them. We'll also have to trust that who the person is will be obvious in some way."

"Does Suzanne or any of the Forest Circle know who it is?" Craig asked.

"If they do, they aren't telling, so it's up to us," Sarah replied.

"All the men?" Tom said. "There's a lot of men in Doveland."

"No, I think it's just the men that are in our group, and that's still a lot of men. But I think there's a way to do it that won't involve them knowing unless they are the one. We are thinking of physical meetings and physical stones. I think we need to do this differently.

"We've been planning and doing physical things for so long we have lost sight of the "magical, mystical" way to do things. In Spirit. Let's take one man at a time and visit him that way. Somehow we'll know if he's the one. Then we can tell him. Or perhaps he will tell us."

So the list was made—Eli, Elliot, Lloyd, Josh, Dan, Pete, Hank, and Sam. Even Alex and Leroy were on the list. Four hours later it was evident that it wasn't any of them.

"Now what?" Tom asked, feeling exhausted and worried.

"I think we've forgotten someone," Mira said.

Fifty-Eight

"He's used to people showing up out of nowhere," Sarah said. "Hannah visits him all the time. Now that I think about it, that was a pretty big clue right there," Sarah said.

"Right there under our nose. I forgot that he's eighteen now. But we could still be wrong about it," Craig answered.

"Only one way to find out," Mira said. "Let's hope it's him because I'm ready to be married!"

The six members of the Stone Circle held hands and left the room. In his dorm room, Johnny let out a yelp as all six members of the Stone Circle appeared in front of him. He had just finished his final exams for his summer session and wondered if he was hallucinating because he hadn't slept much the last few days.

He shut his eyes to see if they would go away, but when he opened them again, they were still there.

"Good God. What are you all doing here? Is Mom okay? Lex? Where's Hannah? Is she okay?"

"Everything is fine, Johnny," Sarah said. "We just need a few minutes of your time, if that's okay with you."

"Sure… but I don't get it. Why all of you?"

Johnny looked at the people surrounding him and realized

that they were the core group Hannah had told him about. The Stone Circle. The whole Stone Circle had come to visit him. As the enormity of it hit him, he sank onto the bed.

"I see that you know who we are," Sarah said.

"Yes. But what do you want from me? I have to admit having you all here like this is scaring me."

Sarah smiled at him as the six of them arranged themselves to look as if they were sitting in a circle around him. "Sorry, we had to visit you this way. We're running short of time. As you know, there is a wedding in a few days, and we need to settle something before then.

"We've visited all the men in our Doveland Karass, but didn't show ourselves to them. Most of them wouldn't have been able to see us anyway. We did what we needed to do without them knowing.

"However, we knew that you could see us. You're accustomed to what we do, and that makes this so much easier."

"Makes what easier?" Johnny pleaded. "Tell me. Seriously. You're freaking me out."

"We can't. Will you sit with us for a moment in silence? It could be nothing will happen, and then we'll be gone. Or something will, and then we'll know."

Johnny wanted to ask again, "Know what?" but realized he wouldn't get an answer. All six of the members of the Stone Circle had settled in and were now sitting around him with their eyes closed. He closed his eyes too, and they all waited together.

Nothing happened for a few minutes, and Johnny was just about ready to open his eyes when the whole room became flooded with light. His body started tingling, and he felt as if he was floating above the bed.

Startled he opened his eyes to see that the room bathed in a pulsing light. Everyone else had their eyes open too. They all watched in wonder as the light shifted through all the hues of the rainbow and then went out.

In front of each of them was a glowing stone. Including Johnny.

"I guess that answers that question," Sarah laughed. "Welcome to the Stone Circle, Johnny."

****

Johnny had no idea what they were talking about, but he knew that something had just happened that would change the rest of his life. Leif had arrived right after the stones showed up and gave Johnny an air hug.

"Welcome, Johnny. It's a big day," Leif said. "However, it's not something that you can process overnight. In many ways, none of us know precisely what it means to be in this circle, or what we are expected to do. We listen and do what comes next."

"Think of it more like a door opening. You've just walked through the door and time will show us all what it means for you."

"Well, I know what it means for me," Mira said. "The wedding can happen!"

Johnny looked at her puzzled, wondering why it couldn't happen before so she added, "Don't worry, It's not important now that you have been found. Not that you were lost or anything. I mean now that the Stone Circle is complete. We'll see you in a few days!"

As quickly as they came, the members of the circle blinked out, the stones going with them. Sarah remained behind for a moment longer. "I'm happy it was you, Johnny," she said and then she was gone too.

I don't know how they expect me to sleep now, Johnny thought.

For the next few hours, he lay wide awake trying to figure out what it all meant. Was he supposed to do something now? Did his mother know? If she didn't, should he tell her? What would she say?

What about Lex? Did it mean something to him? And then there was Hannah. Did she know? Would she care? Johnny's questions just kept piling up, and not one of them was being answered.

So he asked himself one last question. *Do I feel good about what had happened?* When he realized that the answer was yes, he finally closed his eyes and drifted into a deep sleep where he dreamed about a forest, and heard the words, "maybe you'll be a dimension traveler, too." He was pretty sure that it was Hannah's voice, and he smiled in his sleep.

Fifty-Nine

Everything about the wedding was perfect. No one expected any less. After all, it was Mandy, the design queen, in charge of the decorations, and Mira, the queen of planning, in charge of the event. How could it be any less than perfect?

Once again the Chapel was packed with guests. Each of the brides wore dresses made for them by the same seamstress that had made Ava's dress for her wedding. Mandy's dress was covered with little sequins, and Mira's dress repeated the pattern but with tiny pearls.

Now that Lloyd was part of the family, as Ava had declared, he was asked to oversee the wedding, even though it would be Sarah who would pronounce the two couples husband and wife.

Usually, people cry with happiness at weddings, but at this one, people tended towards laughter. This wedding had no ill feelings attached to it. This time there was no danger. There was only love.

Johnny had returned from school and was sitting beside his mother and brother in the front row with all the other members of his mother's new family. He couldn't believe how many uncles he now had. From not having any good male role models to a church full of them reminded him just how much his life had changed in the past few years.

Just a few years before he had been dressing like a Goth, and doing odd jobs for Grant, not realizing that the path he was on would lead to destruction. Now he was a member of the Stone Circle. And if he heard the voice in his dream correctly, it was possible he was going to learn how to be a dimension traveler.

Hannah said she hoped so. She knew she was, and she wanted him to go with her and Sarah. Somehow the Forest Circle had figured out how to travel without leaving their bodies behind. Which meant, that unlike Leif and Eric, they would be able to return in a physical form each time they came back to this dimension.

This ability would make it possible for them to go because Hannah was sure that her parents and Johnny's mom would not be signing any permission slips to let them travel if they couldn't come back the same as they left.

Not that they knew yet. Sarah had told them that they could save the announcement to their families for after the wedding. No need to have anyone concerned for the future of their children on such a beautiful day.

As the "I dos" rang out, people began to clap. By the time the two couples turned and walked down the aisle, everyone was standing and cheering. Sarah knew that not only were they cheering for the couples, but they were also cheering for the future of their town. They might not have realized that a cloud had been hovering over their heads, but once it was gone, they knew something had changed, and they were going to cheer about it.

Sarah glanced at the back of the church where Grace had been. She was gone now. She would have already left with Emily to make sure that everything at the house was ready. Grace was preparing a surprise for Ava and Evan. What Grace didn't know was there was a surprise being prepared for her too.

It was a good thing, Sarah thought. Grace, for all her cheerfulness and attention to others, had been having a hard time. First Josh's grandfather had died, and Sarah knew that Grace still felt terrible about that. And then, it had been almost six weeks since she had seen her husband. Each day that passed without seeing Eric, Grace's face had gotten sadder and sadder.

Grace thought that no one had noticed. But they had. And that's why this would also be a day that Grace would remember for the rest of her life.

Sarah glanced at her watch. They had only a few hours left. It was time to get over to the reception and lend a hand. On the way down the aisle, following behind the brides and the grooms, Sarah caught Hannah's eye. They winked at each other in solidarity. They would be traveling together soon, but first, they had to take care of Grace.

****

Like all wedding receptions, the guests dribbled in bit by bit after having stopped by their homes to make sure their children were doing fine, or to change shoes, or to grab an umbrella in case of rain.

Everyone knew that the wedding party would be the last to arrive. They had pictures to take. The very last to arrive would be the bride and groom. In this case, the brides and grooms.

Even though it was their wedding, Mira and Sam had catered it. They knew precisely what their circle would want to eat and the table set on the back porch was overflowing with food of all kinds. Everyone from the vegans in the group to the meat and fish eaters would be satisfied.

Of course, they weren't going to serve at their wedding, so

Pete, Barbara, and Alex had taken over that task. Grace and Mandy had provided the coffee and tea service, and Grace was behind the table helping people with their drinks, just as she did every day at Your Second Home.

The wedding cake sat on a separate table in the corner, well out of the way of someone bumping into it. It was massive. Sam had baked it. It was so large Grace wasn't sure how it had even been delivered without toppling over. It was five layers tall, with a flavor for everyone.

Somehow Sam had baked it so that half of the cake was Sam and Mira's choices, and the other half was what Tom and Mandy wanted. Grace thought that it was a work of art. Sam had spent the last week working on it, grateful that there were no mysteries to solve this time to distract him.

Everyone was thankful that there were no mysteries to solve and that this day and this wedding was only about happiness. Grace was delighted for her friends.

She couldn't wait for Ava and Evan to discover that there was a separate table for their cake. It was a beautiful anniversary cake, a miniature of their wedding cake, made to celebrate their third anniversary.

It was apparent that everyone was going to be going home with leftover food, so Sam and Mira had put a box of carry-out containers under the food table so that no food, or cake, would be wasted.

Sarah had given Ava and Evan a last-minute task to complete to keep them away from the party until after everyone else had arrived. It was so unexpected that Ava even grumbled to Evan about it. But she did it anyway. Everyone knew there was always a reason for what Sarah asked them to do.

"They're coming up the driveway," Hank yelled, and everyone scurried to their stations. They had already thrown flower petals on the arriving wedding party. Now it was time for Ava and Evan.

It was a perfect surprise. By the time it was over there was not a dry eye in the house. Three couples united on the same day. The gift of unity was what that day's brides and grooms wanted to give to the couple that always took care of them.

In the corner, by herself, Grace watched, happy for what they were experiencing, and thinking about her wedding just over two years ago. A small one. Not glorious like this one. But so heartfelt. And now in spite of knowing she shouldn't be and should get over it, she was feeling heartbroken.

Then Hank yelled out once again, "It's time." And the crowd parted revealing something Grace never thought she would see again. Eric was walking toward her grinning from ear to ear and holding his arms open.

Grace ran to him and threw herself into his arms, and instead of passing through them, was locked tight in his embrace.

"Yes," Eric whispered in her ear, "I'm back. In the flesh. And I intend to stay that way for many more years."

Grace looked over at her friend Sarah, who smiled at her and nodded. Grace knew what that meant. It was true. He was back. And he was well.

Epilogue

A few weeks after the wedding, Sarah and Emily sat side by side on Emily's rock. They were admiring the view looking down into the valley towards Doveland. It was summer, and the trees' green canopy spread out towards the town.

They knew that if they were looking through binoculars, they would be able to see Dr. Joe's old house. It was now Edward's home. It had taken Edward a year to get to the mental and emotional space where he could claim it and move in. During that year, both the house and Edward's memory of it had been renovated.

Things were very different for Edward, as they were for all the members of the Doveland Karass, and Emily knew that Sarah was sitting on the rock with her for a more significant reason than a friendly visit.

But it was so pleasant sitting there with her watching the birds wheel through the sky, Emily wasn't in any rush to find out why Sarah was there.

Sarah sighed. "I love it here. I didn't think I would. I loved my life with Leif, just the two of us in our house by the river. I remember my first response to Mira's phone call for help was to be slightly irritated.

"I wasn't proud of that response, so I hid it. But I knew that everything was going to change, and I wasn't pleased about that.

"I was right though. Life changed even more than I could have ever imagined. I had to grow more than I thought possible. Our Stone Circle was only the beginning of what is now this community.

"However, now that I love this place, and have found my home here, I know it is time for me to do more."

Sarah took a set of keys out of her pocket and handed them to Emily.

"These are the keys to my house, Emily. Please use the house as if it is your own. I know it's lovely here in the summer, but the winters can be isolating. Come into town and live in my house when it gets like that.

"And when you are teaching in town during the week you can stay at the house if you wish to instead of making the drive back here. I've already set up a bedroom for you, but change it however you wish. Make it your own."

Emily stared at the keys in her hands and started to cry. "You're not going to be gone that long are you?"

"I don't know, Emily. That's the thing about stepping into something so new. But, while I am gone, the house is yours."

Sarah reached over to Emily and lifted her chin so she could see into her eyes. "And, I don't want you to be sad about this, but if I don't come back, the house is to be transferred to you."

When Emily started to protest, Sarah shook her head, "Now, I'm not saying I'm not coming back. Only if I don't. Besides, haven't we learned that we could never lose each other?"

Sarah swept her arm taking in the valley below. "All of us are connected. We'll see each other again. That I can promise.

"All of us will meet again whether in this lifetime or the next. Or even in this dimension or another."

Emily nodded and reached out to hold Sarah's hand and felt the truth of her words. Together they sat on the rock until the sunset, and it was time for Sarah to go.

The last thing Emily heard was Sarah's promise, "We'll meet again. All is well. Be happy."

"I will," Emily answered.

Author's Note

Thank you, dear reader, for coming with me on this journey to Doveland.

I write because I love to, but it's the gift of a reader that brings me the greatest happiness.

I invented the town of Doveland as the place I wanted to live myself, the perfect village. People I want to know live there.

Many of you have told me that you would like to live there, too. For now, we'll have to meet at the imaginary Doveland, but who knows? Perhaps someday we'll meet in a real one.

Paragnosis wraps up the Karass Chronicles series, at least for now. I wanted to leave you all with a feeling that for now, all is well in Doveland. We may return. Who knows?

My next series is a spinoff of the Karass Chronicles. It is a fantasy series set in the Erda dimension where the Forest Circle went to live.

For sure, Hannah will be dimension traveling to this new realm. But who else do you think will go? I hope you join me in my new series, The Return To Erda, to find out.

I think you'll like these new books. They have a little more magic, a wizard or two, a few fantastical creatures, and some of your favorite characters. And of course, stories you will enjoy.

I am always interested in hearing what you most want to read! Contact me. I'd love to hear from you!

Love,

Beca

PS

Sometimes it's fun to add something from the "real world" into a book. In Paragnosis, it was the word "fromelize," from the urban dictionary. What made using this word extra fun was the fact that the word was added to the urban dictionary by our son-in-law, David Bush Jr. His team at work came up with the word to describe what someone in their crew did, and in this book, it is precisely what Elliot does when he first meets Hank's crew. Thanks, Dave, for the word. It was perfect! May it spread far and wide.

PS

To be the first to know when there are new books, please join my mailing list at BecaLewis.com, and/or follow me on my Amazon author page.

Connect with me online:
Twitter: http://twitter.com/becalewis
Facebook: https://www.facebook.com/becalewiswriter
Pinterest: https://www.pinterest.com/theshift/
Instagram: http://instagram.com/becalewis
LinkedIn: https://linkedin.com/in/becalewis

ACKNOWLEDGMENTS

I could never write a book without the help of my friends and my book community. Thank you Jet Tucker, Jamie Lewis, Diana Cormier, and Barbara Budan for taking the time to do the final reader proof. You can't imagine how much I appreciate it.

A huge thank you to Laura Moliter for her fantastic book editing.

Thank you to the fabulous Molly Phipps at wegotyoucoveredbookdesign.com for the beautiful book covers for The Return To Erda series.

Thank you to every other member of my street team who helps me make so many decisions that help the book be the best book possible.

And always, thank you to my beloved husband, Del, for being my daily sounding board, for putting up with all my questions, my constant need to want to make things better, and for being the love of my life, in more than just this one lifetime.

OTHER BOOKS BY BECA

The Karass Chronicles - Paranormal Mystery
Karass
Pragma
Jatismar
Exousia
Stemma
Paragnosis

The Return To Erda Series - Fantasy
Shatterskin
Deadsweep
Abbadon

The Shift Series - Nonfiction
Living in Grace: The Shift to Spiritual Perception
The Daily Shift: Daily Lessons From Love To Money
The 4 Essential Questions: Choosing Spiritually Healthy
Habits
The 28 Day Shift To Wealth: A Daily Prosperity Plan
The Intent Course: Say Yes To What Moves You

Perception Parables: - Fiction - very short stories
Love's Silent Sweet Secret: A Fable About Love
Golden Chains And Silver Cords: A Fable About Letting Go

Advice: - Nonfiction
A Woman's ABC's of Life: Lessons in Love, Life and Career
from Those Who Learned The Hard Way

ABOUT BECA LEWIS

Beca writes books that she hopes will change people's perceptions of themselves and the world, and open possibilities to things and ideas that are waiting to be seen and experienced.

At sixteen, Beca founded her own dance studio. Later, she received a Master's Degree in Dance in Choreography from UCLA and founded the Harbinger Dance Theatre, a multimedia dance company, while continuing to run her dance school.

After graduating—to better support her three children—Beca switched to the sales field, where she worked as an employee and independent contractor to many industries, excelling in each while perfecting and teaching her Shift® system, and writing books.

She joined the financial industry in 1983 and became an Associate Vice President of Investments at a major stock brokerage firm, and was a licensed Certified Financial Planner for more than twenty years.

This diversity, along with a variety of life challenges, helped fuel the desire to share what she's learned by writing and talking with the hope that it will make a difference in other people's lives.

Beca grew up in State College, PA, with the dream of becoming a dancer and then a writer. She carried that dream forward as she fulfilled a childhood wish by moving to Southern

California in 1969. Beca told her family she would never move back to the cold.

After living there for thirty years, she met her husband Delbert Lee Piper Sr., at a retreat in Virginia and everything changed. They decided to find a place they could call their own which sent them off traveling around the United States. For a year or so they lived and worked in a few different places before returning to live in the cold once again near Del's family in a small town in Northeast Ohio, and not far too far from State College.

When not working and teaching together, they love to visit and play with their combined family of eight children and five grandchildren, read, study, do yoga or taiji, feed birds, work in their garden, and design things. Actually, designing things is what Beca loves to do. Del enjoys the end result.

35767058R00159

Made in the USA
Middletown, DE
08 February 2019